OLAVA

OLAVA

a novel by

Anne-Lene Bleken

Munay

2020

Olava

Anne-Lene Bleken

© Munay Publishing, 2020

www.munay.no

Cover: Nina Flatnes Bratbak

Translated by Anne-Lene Bleken

Print-on-demand Amazon

ISBN 978-82-93576-04-4

Foreword

With all my heart, I want to thank all the people who have contributed to this book in different ways. If I were to mention everyone here, it would fill up several chapters.

First of all I want to thank my mum for all your love and care and for every time you've said: "Write it down, Anne-Lene." My three children Helena, Julia and Andreas. Helena for your big and lovely heart. Julia for your power and insight. You Andreas who teaches me so much about love and willpower. I'm the luckiest mum in the world. I want to thank my dad for your courage and great love of nature. Thank you Erlend, Bergljot and Hedvig. I'm lucky to have you as my siblings.

I want to thank the people I've met on my way and from whom I've learnt so much; Hawk, Yvonne, Puma, Pablo, Carl, Susan, Gail, Keya, Chanyn and many more. I want to express my deepest love and gratitude to our elders who have kept their wisdom and passed it on to the next generations.

My warm and heartfelt gratitude goes to my mum, Hedvig, Helena, Julia and Yvonne for reading through the manuscript and for encouraging my writing process. My gratitude goes to Yvonne for being the midwife of the last chapter.

So much gratitude goes to Angela Millikin for proofreading the English version of the book.

Finally, I want to thank everyone who has read the book and received the story with so much warmth, heartfelt love and touching words.

FOR THE NEXT SEVEN GENERATIONS

PART I

1

In the seconds before the storm breaks loose, a timeless silence reigns. The air is tense, poised at the breaking point of breathless anticipation. All life is preparing for the inevitable encounter with the forces of nature. In reverent silence the birds listen to the gloomy sounds of thunder in the distance. The water reflects dark clouds flowing in the sky. The trees tremble gently from the touch of the wind. The flowers bow to the first heavy raindrops. In a small eternity all is quiet. Then the forces of nature awaken from their slumber. The heavens open. The rain hammering against the earth. The lightning cutting cracks in the sky. The thunder showing his true voice. All life seeks protection.

Even as a little girl, Olava loved the magic created by the forces of nature. She could sit hopefully by the window and rejoice at the transformation from silence to storm. With sincerity and wonder she would watch how the sky and the sea melted in shared revolt. Patiently, she would wait for the moment when the lightning lit up the sky. Then she counted the seconds before the next roar of thunder. Sometimes she would pretend that her feet were the creaking roots of a tree and her arms the dancing branches. Other times she would sit silently and listen to the drumming of the rain and the longing howls of the wind. Then she would pretend that the mournful sounds brought stories from the bottom of the sea and the stars in the sky. Stories about shining angels who sang for the dead sailors on the ocean floor and stories about bright stars that winked words of comfort to the grieving at the tip of the breakwater. This was her way of discovering other worlds, enchanted by grief and joy. While the storm raged outside, Olava knew how to delight inside the warm house behind the protective walls.

But today everything was different. Today the storm had broken loose inside the house. Olava was sitting by the large dining table in the kitchen next to her little sister. They were both staring watchfully at the ceiling, their eyes blank and insecure. They sat close, both quiet, not saying one word, Olava 13 years old and Runa 9.

The screams from the room above them were terrifying. They had grown in strength all day and now they penetrated the kitchen with a violent force, right where the girls were sitting. Tormod, their father, was standing by the window staring out. He had been standing like that for a long time now, unmoving, with his broad shoulders bent slightly forward, not saying a word. His eyes rested on the small birdhouse standing lonely and abandoned in the rain. The birds had long ago found shelter elsewhere and only a few breadcrumbs dissolving in the violent storm were left.

Everyone on the farm breathed a sigh of relief when the rain finally came. The air had been heavy and dense for two days, but still there was no one who believed they would get such a storm at this time of the year. It was as if the old Thunder God had opened the floodgates of the heavens.

From the large bedroom upstairs they could hear another scream. This time more terrifying and longer. The sound of someone walking quickly over the floor. It was Ragnhild, their grandmother, together with Karin and Gudrun. They had been in the room for many hours without coming down. Olava could feel the lump in her throat growing larger. She hoped so much that someone would say something. Anything, that everything was okay, that it was normal. But no one said anything. No one had said anything for a long time.

Olava tried to swallow the lump in her throat, but in vain. Next to her, her little sister Runa dried her eyes quickly in her blouse. Olava took her hand under the table and squeezed it gently. Runa gave her a faint smile, though her eyes were wet with tears and she was biting her lip in order not to cry. Olava brought her index finger carefully to her lips and nodded quickly towards the window where their father was standing. Runa nodded bravely. They knew it was best to be quiet.

But when one more scream penetrated the house, they cringed. Runa covered her ears, and Olava stood up, terrified.

"Mother!"

"Sit down." Tormod did not move but remained in the same position with his back to his daughters. His voice did not reveal anything. If their father was frightened or worried, he did not show it. The room was filled with unspoken words. Olava sat down reluctantly but could feel how her throat was choking. The fear of what was happening with their mother felt like a tight grip. Runa covered her face in her hands and cried. Any attempt to try and stop it now was in vain.

Olava looked at her little sister, not sure what to do. She was almost four years older and in a way she felt responsible for her. As the oldest she had to be strong. Olava gathered up all her courage and asked as calmly as she could muster.

"What is happening to mum?"

By the window, their father moved his weight from one foot to the other. For what seemed like an infinitely long time, silence was the only answer they got. But then he bent his head slowly.

"I don't know." Olava closed her eyes and under the table she folded her hands in silent prayer.

The door opened and an elderly woman walked quickly into the kitchen. It was Ragnhild, their grandmother. She was pale and sweat shone on her forehead. She worked fast, took the biggest kettle, filled it with water from the barrel and put it on the stove. She gave the frightened girls a quick glance before she spoke to her son with sober authority.

"Get them out of the house."

Tormod had turned around when his mother entered the kitchen. His light blue eyes were partly hidden under his strong, dark blond hair. He looked pale and tired, but sounded almost relieved when he spoke to his daughters.

"You can sleep in the barn tonight."

Olava took Runa's hand and got up slowly. She looked hesitantly from her father to her grandmother, trying to get eye contact.

"What about mum?" She could hear the tears in her own voice.

"We're doing everything we can." Their grandmother looked around the room as if she were searching for the right words. "It's best if you go out to the barn."

"But?"

"Do as you are told. We will come and get you when the baby is born." Ragnhild turned around to the stove, her head bent. Neither she nor their father said anything. Olava knew what all the unspoken words meant. They meant that something was wrong. Something was very wrong. The unspoken fear spread to every corner in the room.

Olava walked towards the door holding Runa's hand. Her sister was crying. She could feel despair, mixed with a growing anger towards the silence from the grown-ups. When they were in the hallway, she signaled to Runa to be quiet. Then she put her ear against the door to the kitchen. Runa wiped her eyes with the back of her hand and did the same. She held her breath not to cry.

"Anna is losing blood. She hasn't got much strength left." Their grandmother's authoritative voice sounded worried.

"I see. What can we do?" The uncertainty in their father's voice was concealed well.

"We must get the doctor." Olava and Runa froze where they stood by the door.

"I'll send Lukas right away."

With the sound of footsteps, Olava and Runa moved quickly away from the door and began putting on their jackets and shoes. They did not move as the door handle went down and their father came out. He walked straight past without looking at them and out through the front door. A moment later their grandmother came out carrying the kettle with hot water. She closed her eyes when she saw them. Her faint, desperate smile was well-meaning, but neither Runa nor Olava smiled back. Their grandmother continued up the stairs to the second floor.

Olava and Runa followed her with their eyes. They could hear that she opened the door to the large bedroom. Olava felt an unexplainable need to run up the familiar steps and into her mother's room as she had done so many times before. Just to see that everything was okay. It wasn't possible. Today the stairs to the second floor seemed endlessly long.

Just as they were about to go outside, they became aware of a tiny voice. It was a voice that sang and it was coming from upstairs. They stood absolutely still and listened. It sounded so far away and yet so near. Olava tiptoed a few steps up the stairs and Runa followed her quietly. The song became a little clearer and all of a sudden they realized that it was the same goodnight prayer that their mum had taught them. They looked at each other. It was the song they sang every night. They did not move as they listened to the familiar words: "I am little, but I will, child of Jesus always be. He can hear and see me, too, when I pray." But then the song became a cry of pain. Olava took Runa's hand and together they ran as fast as they could out the door and across the courtyard towards the barn whilst their tears mixed with the heavy rain.

The old wooden door creaked quietly as they shut the storm out. The familiar smell of dried hay and straw met them as it had so many times before. The cows were chewing, unconcerned, and the horses greeted them with their good-natured nods. The goats stared lazily at them from within their pens. Normally Olava would feel a silent joy coming here, but today everything was different. Today the silence was almost chilling.

Olava sat down before Runa, who was shaking from cold and exhaustion. She had stopped crying, but her eyes were large and shiny and her face was soaking wet from rain and tears. Olava wiped her cheeks gently with the palm of her hand and the little touch gave them both some kind of comfort.

"Come. Let's go and find our place in the hay." Runa nodded and together they walked past the animal stalls towards the door to the barn. The cows turned their heads slowly in their direction and a couple of horses neighed happily as they walked by.

Inside the barn, they grabbed some old blankets and found their well-known place in the back of the building filled with large piles of hay. Exhausted, they curled up under the blankets so that only their eyes could be seen. Side by side they lay as the rain was hammering on the roof of the old barn and the twilight darkness slowly surrounded them.

The barn was the largest building on the farm. With its bright red paint, it towered proudly over the other houses on the farm. Olava and Runa had spent time there playing from when they were little. Often they could sit for hours in the hay and play with dolls and animals that they made from the straw. When they grew older, they would jump from the upper edge of the attic into the soft hay, always with the same mixed feelings of fear and joy. When the cat got a new litter of kittens, they would check on them several times a day and could hardly wait until they got eyes and fur so that they could play with them. But what almost always happened was that, one day, without warning, the kittens would be gone without a trace. The adults said that they had gotten a new home and it was not until recently that Olava had started to doubt if this was true. The oldest boy at the neighboring farm had told her that he had found many dead kittens behind the boathouse by the sea.

Sometimes they would play treasure hunting or hide and seek. On one occasion Olava managed to hide so well that Runa could not find her. She had put on Lukas' big working boots and was standing behind the working clothes that were hanging on a hook on the wall. She had not uttered a sound and after some time, Runa gave up and went inside.

When Olava was alone in the barn, she would walk slowly among the animals, petting them and talking calmly to them. She imagined that they could understand what she was saying and that she understood them, especially the horses. They would stand quietly and listen and Olava could see in their eyes that they understood. One time she had tried to involve Runa in the game, but she did not understand what it was all about, at least not in the same way as Olava. Therefore she made sure that she was alone with the animals every now and then.

When Olava was together with Karin or Gudrun in the barn, she would help milk the cows. Karin and Gudrun were maids on the farm and Olava had known them all her life. Her mother had often told her the first word she had said as a little girl. It was "Alin" which meant "Karin". Today Karin and Gudrun were in the bedroom with her mother. It gave Olava some consolation to know that they were there.

Karin had taught her how to milk. The first time she tried, the cow had whipped her in her face with its tail, dissatisfied with her poor technique. Karin had shown her what to do and with some practice, Olava learned how to milk smoothly and easily.

On one particular occasion, Olava was allowed to come with her father and Lukas as they helped a calf into the world. Lukas also worked on the farm, and like Karin and Gudrun, he had been with them as long as Olava could remember. The calf was stuck and her father had put one hand inside the cow. He and Lukas had pulled the calf out by its legs. The cow had been standing absolutely still, except for one long-lasting moo sound. The calf had stood up almost immediately and was wavering on its wobbly legs while its mother began to lick it. Olava could still remember her father's proud look as the calf took its first unsteady steps.

Another time she had helped when one of the horses gave birth. Olava was allowed to sit by the horse's head and comfort it while the foal was born. It had come all by itself without anyone having to pull it out by its legs and Olava could remember how proud she had been that she was allowed to help.

"His name will be Odin and he will be your horse, Olava." When it was all over, her father had looked at her approvingly and smiled.

"Oh... thank you..." Olava could hardly believe it. She had got her own horse. For a long time she had only admired the beautiful foal, which was golden brown and had a white spot on its forehead like its mother.

Today Olava wondered why it didn't hurt when the animals had their babies.

After a while Runa lay completely still and Olava thought she was asleep. She moved close to her face to check, but to her surprise, Runa's eyes were wide open and she was staring into the darkness. Olava pulled back quickly and regretted that she had interrupted her.

"Do you think mum will die?" Runa's voice was only a whisper, but the silence was broken. Olava had asked herself the same question, but now that her little sister asked, it all of a sudden became so real. But she refused to consider that thought. It must not happen.

"No... they're getting the doctor." She tried to sound convincing and wished that she could believe it herself. Runa did not ask any more and in a way Olava was grateful. She had not known what to say.

Slowly Runa's breath became deep and regular and soon she was fast asleep. Olava could not sleep. She did not know what was worse; to be out here where her thoughts and imagination lived a life of their own, or inside the house where the reality was the only option. Her muddled thoughts were spinning around in her head.

Mother - Olava remembered the time when her mother had told her the story of the night when she was born. It was a stormy night, so bad that people in their small community still talked about it. Even if it was 13 years ago, they had not yet had a storm like that night since. Three sailors from the community had died. Many trees had been torn up by the roots. Roofs were torn off buildings, especially old barns, boathouses and sheds. But what Olava remembered best, was her mother's warm smile when she told her that in the very moment Olava opened her eyes and saw the light of day for the first time, the storm had disappeared almost as if by a touch of magic. The wind had calmed, the rain had stopped and the sun had broken through the clouds as if nothing had happened. The women who had helped at the birth had pulled the curtains and witnessed in wonder the most beautiful summer morning outside the window.

It didn't happen very often that their mother told stories and usually only if their father had been away from home for a longer period of time. She had told the story about the night Olava was born when he had been out fishing with the fishing cutter for many weeks.

They were magical moments when Runa and Olava listened to their mother telling stories. They would always sit with their eyes wide open, absorbing every word. The words were like magical lights, emanating from their mother's inner life. The lights went in through their ears and further into their mind and body, where they became emotions, moods and images.

Father – On two occasions, Olava had seen him stand by the window as he had done today, unmoving, not uttering a word. The first time was two years ago when their grandfather was dying. He was in the sleeping chamber by the kitchen and was muttering loudly and incoherently in the last days of his life. The words he left for his loved ones were anything but loving and reconciling. Their grandfather fought a merciless battle with death with words as his only weapon. He threw expletives and curses in every direction, like a wriggling flounder at the bottom of the boat, fighting to the very last. Those who dared enter the bedroom regretted it immediately and hurried out with the worst insults hailing after them from the bed. No one answered back to the dying man.

Olava was also sitting next to her little sister in the kitchen when this happened. They tried to catch every word that came from the sleeping chamber. It was the first time they heard such words in their home.

Their grandmother had a very uptight look on her face. She succeeded to maintain her dignity in the face of adversity. Only a couple of times did she lower her shoulders and pull her arms around herself, as though protecting herself. It was only for a moment before she straightened her back and lifted her head again. On two occasions she walked into the room with her dying husband, but the second time he shouted so loudly that she almost backed involuntarily out of the room, as though hit by a strong headwind. Olava and Runa heard words like "hag" and "witch".

The only person who was allowed to be in the bedroom, without becoming a target for their grandfather's verbose farewell, was their mother. She seemed to purvey an unlikely calm about the whole affair and when she came into the kitchen a couple of times, Olava thought she could see a well-hidden, amused expression in her eyes. But she could not be sure.

Finally, the minister came. With other-wordly serenity he walked up to the dying man to pray for his salvation. The minister was a stubborn man who took his calling seriously. Moreover, he was also a firm believer in his own skills as a healer of souls. It was not until their grandfather cursed him to eternal torment in hell, accusing him of being a hypocrite and a greedy Judas that he decided to leave the room. Pale, but in control, he came out to the kitchen and nodded quietly to their father and grandmother. Their grandfather's farewell ceremony was probably a bigger surprise to the minister than to the rest of the family. He only knew him as a godly man who faithfully listened to his preachings every Sunday and put some shillings in the collection box.

After the grandfather's rude insults towards the minister, Olava and Runa were sent outside.

Luckily for the two girls, it was a burning hot summer's day and the window to the sleeping chamber was slightly open. They tiptoed to the back of the house, making sure they were so close to the walls that no one could see them. They hid behind a bountiful raspberry bush right under the window to the chamber so that they could hear every word. Whilst enjoying the sweet raspberries, their ears would prick up every time their grandfather had a new outburst. The discomfort from sitting behind the bush was nothing compared to the mysterious delight they felt from listening to the forbidden words that flowed from the mouth of the dying man.

In the days that followed the death of their grandfather, there was an uncommon silence on the farm. A couple of times, Olava and Runa had played in the barn. One of the hay dolls was the dying grandfather and another was the minister. They had whispered the forbidden words to each other. They knew better than to say them out loud. A few times they pretended that they were shouting the words out loud like their grandfather had and the feeling of doing something that was so forbidden was both exciting and frightening at the same time.

After the funeral, Olava had asked her mother if their grandfather had gone to hell. Her mother had looked a little surprised, but then she had smiled.

"I believe that all humans go to heaven when they die."

As always, Olava listened carefully to her mother's words and felt a certain sense of relief. But there was something she didn't understand.

"But... what happens if Grandfather swears in heaven?"

In a split second her mother had the same

merry twinkle in her eyes that Olava thought she had seen when their grandfather yelled his curses to his defenseless family, but then she said quietly.

"When a person goes to heaven, he will get all the love he never got on earth. Then people won't be angry anymore." Olava did not ask anymore and hid the words in a safe place inside her own heart.

The second time their father had been standing by the window as he did today was the day when the best horse on the farm, a beautiful two-year-old fjord horse, had broken its left front leg in three places and had to be put down. It was lying on the ground by the edge of the forest, its eyes wide open and breathing in short gasps. After one hour by the window, while everyone on the farm held their breath, Tormod took the biggest rifle from the wall and walked out to the horse in the field with heavy steps. Without hesitating he put the rifle on his shoulder and shot the horse in the forehead. When the shot broke the silence, Olava went out to the other horses. There she found comfort.

After the horse was shot, Tormod had given the rifle to Lukas, who had been standing in the background with his hands in his pockets and his head bent. Then Tormod walked away and was gone until late in the night. He never told anyone where he had been and no one asked. When he came back, Lukas and a few of the neighbors had buried the horse. Their father never talked about it again and no one on the farm mentioned it when he might be able to hear them.

That night, Olava had asked her mother if horses also went to heaven when they died and her mother had the same little smile on her face that she so often had when Olava asked her about something.

"Yes, I believe that every living being goes to heaven when it dies." She did not say any more and everything was as it should be.

When her grandfather died, Olava had felt some kind of strange curiosity and indescribable delight in the forbidden words, but she had not been particularly sad. Grandfather was not someone she would miss, even if, as her mother had said, Jesus takes care of all humans equally well.

Olava had cried the day their father had shot the horse. Mostly because she knew how much he loved it. Even if he had never said so, Olava could see it in his face every time he looked at it and she remembered the light atmosphere on the farm the day the horse had arrived.

Today Olava was so frightened that she would lose her mother. She folded her hands and curled up under the blanket, the uncertainty and waiting time filling her head with sad thoughts. She was so infinitely weary, but the storm shook the old woodwork and kept her awake. Finally she lay down carefully close to Runa and after what seemed like hours, she fell into a restless sleep. In her sleep, time and space disappeared.

2

Almost with a sense of wonder and tenderness the earth awakens to a new day. Washed clean from rain and wind. A song of silence welcomes the day. The first morning birds singing and chirping. A few clouds float lazily across the sky. The flowers lift their eyes to the sun. The trees stretch their branches. Only a gentle breeze makes the leaves rustle. The storm is over for now and the earth is born anew.

Olava woke up with a start. She opened her eyes and sat up. For a short, confused moment she did not understand where she was, but then she remembered everything. Her shoulders dropped down in discouragement. They had slept in the barn the whole night. Why hadn't anyone come to get them? Olava listened for sounds from the outside, but there was only silence. Where was everyone? It had to be morning now, the light from outside came through the cracks in the barn. Even the animals were quiet. Had Karin milked the cows? Should she sneak out to the courtyard to see if there was anyone? No, it was no good. What if Runa woke up? Restless thoughts spun around inside Olava's head, and she felt a growing turmoil in her body become a lump in her stomach. She did not want to think about what had happened inside the house while they had slept.

    Olava looked at her sister, who was still asleep

under the blanket. She decided not to wake her. Then she would have to be the older sister again. It was best to sit absolutely still and wait. She pulled her legs up under her and rested the side of her head on her knees. From this position she continued to stare into the air and rocked carefully back and forth. The small movements felt good and slowly her body calmed down a little. But Olava felt a loneliness she had never experienced before. She folded her hands and was surprised to hear her own voice whisper into the air.

"Dear Jesus, I hope you can hear me..." Olava stopped. She had never asked Jesus about anything serious before. When they sang the goodnight prayer song, it was never serious. It was always warm and safe when Olava curled up under the quilt and her mother sat by her bedside. She had never known that it could be any different and she didn't know how to pray to Jesus now that she was so frightened. But it was the only comfort she could find. Olava closed her eyes.

"Dear Jesus, I hope you can hear me because it's very... important. It's my mum..." Runa moved and Olava stopped whispering. Instead she continued to pray inside herself in silence.

"Dear Jesus, my mum says that you take care of all people. Will you please look after my mother..." Runa stretched under the blanket and yawned. Olava prayed fast.

"I promise that I will never ask you about anything else in my whole life if only my mum is ok..." Runa blinked her eyes and then she was awake.

She sat up and rubbed the sleep from her eyes. As she looked around the barn and at the blanket they had slept under, she seemed puzzled and almost happy. But then she remembered what had happened and her eyes got a sad, helpless expression. Olava could hardly bear to see it and turned away. The sleep had been a welcome break from reality, but now they were back to the fear and the unknowing.

"We have to wait here until they come and get us." Olava tried to avoid questions she could not answer and Runa fell silent. Instead she began to play absently with a piece of straw.

"Do you want to play?" Runa asked her. Olava looked at her little sister, puzzled. Runa didn't sound happy, but she looked as if she wanted to play. Olava tried to imagine what it would feel like to play now, but she couldn't do it.

"No, not now. You can play if you want to."

"Ok." Runa nodded her head absently and gathered some pieces of straw that she began to shape into a figure. Olava followed her as she was playing quietly. The pieces of straw became an animal that jumped from place to place. Olava thought maybe it was supposed to be a goat. Runa used the blanket as a cave where the goat should sleep. She had just started making another figure when the door between the animal stalls and the barn opened.

"Hi girls." The familiar voice made Olava's heart beat fast from relief. At the same time she was overwhelmed by fear. Runa got on her feet right away and ran to the door where two big, strong arms caught her. It was Lukas. As always, his deep, calm voice and warm, familiar smile spread a wondrous peace.

"Did the two of you sleep out here last night?" He made it sound all normal. Olava looked at him but didn't dare to ask what had happened. Lukas sat down next to her, still holding Runa in his arms. She had put her head on his shoulders and wrapped her arms firmly around his neck. Lukas put one hand on Olava's shoulder. She could feel the warmth from his big palm.

"You have a baby brother now." Lukas spoke with the same ease as he always used when he talked. Runa removed her arms from his neck and both girls stared seriously at the big, safe man with the smiling eyes and the wild, dark hair.

"What about Mum?" Olava had to know, but she held her breath when Lukas answered.

"She's asleep now." He tilted his head slightly and looked gently at the two girls. "It's been a long night and she's very tired." For a short moment he got a serious look in his eyes and Olava frowned.

"But, is she…" She didn't know what to ask, and Lukas nodded understandingly.

"The doctor came last night and helped the baby come out." He smiled calmly, first at Olava and then at Runa, before he continued. "She is doing fine and will recover completely, but she might have to stay in bed for some time." Olava didn't quite know what that meant, but Lukas was smiling, and she was convinced that he would never do that if things were really bad. Besides, he had said that their mother would recover completely. Olava tasted the words and looked searchingly at Lukas. Her mother was not dead. Slowly the fear and uncertainty were transformed into an indescribable relief. Had Jesus heard her? Olava could hardly believe it. Had he really heard her?

"Can we go inside now?" Runa's face lit up in a hopeful smile, but Lukas shook his head gently.

"Not yet. A little later. Karin will come and get us when your mother is awake." He sat Runa carefully down in the hay and placed himself comfortably between the two girls. "In the meantime, I will stay here with you."

Runa took Lukas' big hand and moved close to him. Olava would've liked to do the same, but something kept her from it. Instead she sat a little by herself and stared into the hay, but then Lukas took her hand into his. It wasn't the first time Olava had experienced that Lukas knew how she felt even when she didn't say anything. Her mother had once said that Lukas could talk to the animals. Maybe this was why he knew how people felt even when they didn't use words. Olava could feel how her own hand almost disappeared in Lukas' big, warm palm.

"Does it always hurt so much to have a baby?" Runa looked gravely at Lukas. Olava didn't know if it was ok to ask about this, but it seemed all natural to Lukas. He looked at them before he answered.

"No…" Both girls waited gravely for him to say more. Lukas scratched his neck a little and paused before he continued. "Sometimes it hurts to have a baby, but it was extra painful for your mum because it took such a long time and because the baby needed help to come out." Olava felt that she was on shaky ground but dared to ask anyway.

"But, how come it doesn't hurt when the animals have their babies?" Lukas nodded thoughtfully.

"It's true, Olava. The animals have their babies without pain." He was quiet and Olava didn't ask more.

"I am never going to have a baby." Runa's decision sounded final, and with large, wet eyes she stared at Lukas almost stubbornly. Lukas regarded her attentively.

"Are you afraid that it will hurt you as much as it hurt your mum?" Runa's eyes filled with tears and she nodded slowly. Lukas nodded, too, but didn't say more for a while.

"I understand that very well... but Runa..." Lukas could sound both serious and friendly at the same time and both girls looked at him anxiously. "Remember that you can always change your mind." Lukas looked directly at Runa, who did not react to his words. "Do you understand?" His voice was gentle but firm. "You can always change your mind." Runa nodded almost imperceptibly and Lukas gave her a warm smile. "That's good." He held his arm around Runa, who couldn't hold back her tears anymore. She cried and Lukas comforted her. But he did not let go of Olava's hand and she lowered her eyes so that he would not see her tears.

They sat like that for some time without saying anything and it was only when Runa had calmed down that Lukas broke the silence.

"I brought some food for you." He took the basket that he had brought and now Olava could feel how hungry she was.

"Gudrun made them. She thought we should celebrate that you have a new baby brother." Lukas winked at the two girls from the corner of his eye and Olava and Runa smiled in surprise when they saw what he had brought. It was waffle cakes, something they normally only got when there was a feast on the farm or during the holidays. Olava loved cakes, both to make them and to taste them, and as long as she could remember, she would stand by the kitchen counter to watch and to help when the adults were baking and preparing for feasts.

While they ate, the atmosphere became lighter, and the last gloomy thoughts disappeared and were replaced by joy and laughter. Everything felt almost good again.

"What is our baby brother really like?" Runa asked with her mouth full of cake and Olava and

Lukas laughed at her. Sometimes Olava wished that she could be spontaneous and funny like her little sister without even being aware of it herself.

"Well…" Lukas paused and pinched Runa's cheek gently.

"I have not seen him yet, but Karin said that he is very cute." Runa smiled with her eyes.

"Is he as cute as you, Lukas?" He lifted his brows and looked at her in a baffled yet loving way. He winked at Olava.

"As cute as me?" His eyes grew large and he spoke with a funny voice. "Certainly, there is no baby as cute as me." He fixed his wild hair theatrically and snuffed. Then he put his thumb in his mouth and lay down in the hay and wiggled in a silly manner using his arms and legs. "I am the cutest, little baby in the world." He rolled around and made sounds like a baby.

Both Olava and Runa laughed and soon all three of them played that they were babies. They crawled around in the hay and cried pretending they were hungry. One moment they were riding on Lukas' back, in the next he grabbed them, one girl under each arm, and spun them around. They squealed with joy and delight. After some time they were all lying in the hay, blessed by liberating laughter. They were still laughing when all of a sudden Karin appeared standing in the doorway.

They immediately stopped playing. Olava searched Karin's face for any signs of bad news, but she only smiled at them, tired and relieved. They ran eagerly towards her.

"Can we go inside now?" Runa was almost jumping on the spot in eager anticipation.

"Yes, you can come inside now, your mum is

awake." Runa and Olava were already on their way out, but Karin stopped them.

"Wait. Not so fast." She sat down in front of the girls. "I want you to be very quiet when you come inside and not make any noise." She looked at Lukas, who confirmed her words with a nod. He came over to the girls.

"Remember what I told you, your mum is in bed and she's very tired." Olava and Runa nodded seriously. While they were playing, they had forgotten that not everything was as it used to be and they walked quietly next to Karin out into the yard. Lukas stayed back with the horses.

Inside the house they were met by a strange silence. There were none of the usual morning sounds, neither from the kitchen nor from upstairs. Olava looked up the stairs to the second floor, but it was quiet. All of a sudden yesterday seemed so unreal.

Karin signaled to them to come with her into the kitchen. Olava was surprised to see the doctor there together with her father and grandmother. They were sitting by the long table. The doctor was a stately man with big, grey whiskers in loving contrast to the cheerful smile at the corners of his mouth. Olava knew who he was. He had been on the farm once before when one of the seasonal farmhands got a large fish bone stuck in his throat.

They had been sitting by the large kitchen table when the unfortunate man suddenly stood up and grabbed his own throat. He tried to say something, but all that came out were some strange, gurgling sounds. He pointed first at his throat and then at the fish on his plate. When he tried to remove the bone himself, he gulped blood and nearly vomited. The fish bone was stuck in the flesh and the man was close to panicking. Lukas reacted immediately. He grabbed the man and while the others ran to get the doctor, Lukas sat opposite him and held his gaze with an intense force. Calm and concentrated they breathed together and every now and then, Lukas muttered soothing words to the terrified man whose eyes were staring mesmerized at his only hope.

When the doctor arrived, the man could hardly breathe and the sweat was running down his face. The doctor managed to pry the bone loose with a pair of pliers. The farmhand was lucky and after a couple of days in bed and a week on a liquid diet, he was on his feet again. Afterwards he didn't know how to thank Lukas and instead he made fun of the whole episode. The others on the farm replied with polite, though somewhat strained, laughter, but Olava had seen how her mother had held Lukas' hands when it was all over.

"Thank you, Lukas." It was all she had said.

Today, their father, grandmother and the doctor were sitting on the long wooden benches by the large kitchen table talking quietly over a cup of coffee. They became quiet when the girls came in. Olava could see both relief and severity in their smiles. She and Runa stood by Karin.

"You have a baby brother now." Olava thought she could see the same proud expression in her father's eyes that she had seen the day when the beautiful fjord horse had come to the farm.

"You can go up to your mother now." Their grandmother got up from the bench to get the coffee pot from the stove. She gave Karin an authoritative glance. "It's best if you go in one at a time." Karin nodded mildly and left the kitchen with the girls.

It was Runa who went into the bedroom first. Olava suggested it herself. When they sang their goodnight prayer song, it was always the second who got most time with their mum, or at least, that was how it felt, and Olava hoped it would be like that today as well.

She waited patiently outside the bedroom with Karin, who smiled and winked encouragingly at her. Olava smiled back. It was almost impossible not to. Karin's radiant smile had an effect on most people. Especially Lukas.

Olava and Runa thought Karin and Lukas should get married and when they teased them about it, Lukas' ears became very red and Karin smiled and said that they should stop being so silly. But Olava had noticed how the two of them looked at each other secretively.

Sometimes when Runa and Olava were in the barn, they played with two straw dolls which they named Karin and Lukas. They were getting married and the ceremony began with a wedding march in which the couple was sitting in a horse-drawn carriage, followed by all the guests. The girls made the horses from pine cones and used little twigs as legs. The carriage was a small piece from a tree stump. Olava and Runa had never been to a wedding like this themselves, but they had heard the adults talk about it. One time they were surprised by Lukas who entered the barn while they were in the middle of the game. He had asked them what was so funny and giggling and flushing, they had told him the names of the dolls and what the game was all about. Lukas had looked at them mischievously, but on his way out, he whistled happily.

The next day he made a small, wooden horse

carriage for them. The carriage had real wheels that could turn around, and he had even painted it in the same red colour as the barn. It wasn't often Lukas had time to make toys for them and the two girls had looked at the beautiful carriage in surprise and wonder. Olava was also convinced what this meant. It had to mean that he was in love with Karin. She tried to explain it to Runa, but she was too little to understand.

Olava thought that she had been waiting in the hall for a long time. She listened carefully for sounds from inside the room, but there were none. She was beginning to feel impatient when, all of a sudden, she could hear an unfamiliar sound. It was a small whimper and in that moment she truly understood that she had a baby brother. The little sound had to come from him.

Runa looked thoughtful when she came out and Olava became uncertain. Were things not good after all? She remained in the doorway for a few seconds and not until Karin put a hand on her back as a sign that it was ok, did she walk into the room to her mother.

Her mother was lying in the bed smiling mildly at her. The cradle with her baby brother was standing in the corner. Olava knew that it was the same cradle that she and Runa had used when they were babies. Gudrun sat on a chair by the cradle and smiled as she looked down into it. Her smile was very different from Karin's. It was safe and friendly, but there was also something heavy about it and the expression in her eyes was almost always sad, even when she smiled. Gudrun never said much, only what was most necessary. She always wore her hair in a tight bun, even on the rare occasions that she joined the others at the dance on Saturday nights.

"Hi, Olava." Her mother smiled and Olava walked slowly over to her bed. Anna took her hand and Olava sat on the edge of the bed.

"Hi Mum." All of a sudden Olava felt overwhelmed by inexplicable sadness. It was the first time she sat by her mother's bed. It used to be the other way around and she thought her mum looked like a little girl as she was lying there. Olava felt an unexplainable loss for something that had once been.

"It's good to see you." Her mother's voice sounded tired but mild. "Did you sleep in the barn last night?"

"Yes..." Olava nodded and her mother stroked her gently on the cheek.

"Were you frightened?" At first Olava shook her head, but then she lowered her head. Tears filled her eyes, but she couldn't cry now, not when her mother was sick.

"You were very brave, you and Runa." Olava was surprised. She had not felt brave, but her mother's words were, as always, good and comforting. She smiled a little and was just about to tell her that they had played that they were babies when there was a little whimper from the cradle. Olava looked over to the corner.

"Do you want to see your little brother?" Olava nodded slightly and walked carefully towards the cradle. Gudrun got up from the chair and lifted the quilt a little so that she could see him better. Olava could not remember when she had ever seen anyone so small before. She kneeled down next to the cradle. The baby boy did not have much hair on his head and his skin was very light. He blinked his eyes and his little hands were dancing in the air. Then he yawned wide and made a grimace that looked a little like a smile. Olava laughed. Then he opened his eyes and Olava thought he looked directly at her. She stroked him gently on his cheek with her index finger. Full of wonder Olava examined his tiny fingers. She became so engrossed in her new baby brother that she did not notice her mother looking at them from the bed.

Anna's eyes rested on the small, touching scene by the cradle. In that moment the pain was gone and the fear of the future was transformed into a dear hope that everything would be good. Runa had been a little reserved about her new brother, but Olava took him to her heart right away.

"Would you like to hold him?" Olava was surprised when her mother asked. She wasn't sure she dared to, but wanted to try.

"Yes, but how do I do it?"

"Let me show you. Just watch what I'm doing." Gudrun put one hand carefully behind little brother's neck and head and the other behind his back and bum. Olava followed her every movement carefully.

"He cannot hold his head up by himself yet." With a calm and steady grip, Gudrun picked him up from the cradle and put him safely on her arm while she still supported his little head with the other. She rocked him gently before she put him down again. When it was Olava's turn, she did everything right the first time. She was overwhelmed by the responsibility she felt while holding him, but the initial insecurity was soon replaced by growing confidence. She walked proudly towards her mother with her little brother in her arms. Their mother smiled at them, but then she became serious.

"Olava?"

"Yes?"

"There is something I want to talk to you about." Olava suddenly realized the severity in her mother's voice.

"What is it, Mum?"

"I probably have to stay in bed for a few days, maybe longer. I don't know." Olava nodded slowly and her mother continued. "I will not be able to take care of little brother before I'm back on my feet."

"Are you very sick, Mum?" Olava had an uneasy feeling in her stomach.

"No… but I'm very tired." Olava could see that her mum was trying hard to stay awake. "I want to ask you something, Olava." The baby gave a little whimper, but Olava continued to look at her mother. "I want to ask you to help me look after him."

"Yes, Mum, I will do that." Olava couldn't know what she had said yes to, but she nodded.

"Thank you, Olava. Karin and Gudrun will help you…" Her mother hesitated and considered her next words carefully. "Grandmother should not."

3

Mild days come and go like smooth pearls on a string. The late summer heat sings for the soul. Light and blue, the sky rests above the land. Little babbling clouds beautifully embroidered in the horizon. Nature shares her abundant gifts. The forest floor dotted with juicy blueberries. The fruit trees stand rich and proud. The berry bushes bend their heads, heavy from the sun-ripened berries. Red flames from the evening sun in the west. Golden tones accompanied by the first autumn colours. Soon a magnificent symphony. It is music from the heart.

Something happened inside Olava when she held her little brother in her arms for the first time and she knew that she would do anything to keep the promise to her mother. She felt a responsibility that filled her with awe and pride and for each day that passed, the bond between her and her little brother grew stronger.

The cradle was moved downstairs to the bedroom next to the kitchen. During the days, there was always someone who could hear him and at night, Karin slept in the alcove in the corner. Olava was aware of every little whimper that came from inside the room. If her little brother began to cry, she was the first to pick him up. She would sit with him as often as she could and if he was uneasy and needed soothing, she would walk up and down the floor with him, while rocking him gently in her arms.

When he was hungry, she would take him upstairs to their mother. The first days, Anna was fast asleep and Olava tiptoed over to the bed and shook her arm gently to wake her up. But as the days went by, she was more often awake when they came in. Usually she would have her hands folded in prayer, looking out of the window. Anna didn't ask for much but she had wished that the curtains were pulled back so that she could look out and the light from the outside could come into the room.

Their mother always smiled lovingly when Olava came in with little brother, but her eyes were drained and Olava could see how she had to make an effort when she sat up in the bed. Her movements were slow and careful and Olava took great care when she placed little brother gently in her arms before she sat down in the chair next to the bed. Sometimes she and her mother would small talk while little brother nursed and Olava enjoyed her calm presence and careful questions. On other occasions, she was quiet and her eyes would rest lovingly on little brother. On such occasions, Olava felt sad that her mother wasn't able to take care of him herself.

Olava grew with the responsibility for her little brother and before many days had passed, the grown-ups trusted her to take care of him. The first uncertainty was quickly replaced by willpower and strength and for each day that went by, she would learn something new. Karin and Gudrun showed her how to wash and change him and how to walk with him and lightly stroke his back to make him burp after a meal.

"This is how we used to walk with you when

you were a little baby." When Olava looked at her little brother, it was almost impossible for her to imagine that she had ever been so little. But she always felt good when Karin told her stories from when she was a baby. In some ways it felt good to know that someone had looked after her when she wasn't able to do it herself.

Olava was full of wonder at her little brother. It was almost as if she had known him always. She got all warm inside when she searched the tiny, beautifully shaped face and the small, round head with the fine, dark blond hair. She was amused at his little hands, the tiny fingers and his gracefully dancing arms and legs. On some occasions, she would look carefully into his dark blue eyes where she thought she could see the same deep, infinite gaze that the horses had. And when their eyes met, the two of them radiated in each other's presence. Not until many years later did Olava understand that it was in those moments that the first unbreakable bonds of love were created.

Karin and Gudrun watched them from the side, full of admiration for the tender care that she showed.

"You are very good at looking after your little brother, Olava." Gudrun said it one day when they were in the kitchen, just the three of them. Olava was holding him in her arms while smiling, delighted. He had taken a firm grip around her index finger and she was amazed at the strength in his little hand. She hadn't noticed Gudrun, who was watching them from the kitchen counter, and was surprised when she spoke. The words made her both proud and happy. There was a certain weight behind Gudrun's words, maybe because they were so few and so rare.

Runa also wanted to help look after little brother, but somehow it was almost always Olava or one of the adults that took over. A few times Runa asked her if she wanted to come and play in the hay like they used to, but Olava preferred not to leave little brother. Still she decided to go with Runa a couple of times, but she couldn't find peace in the game like she used to. Even though Karin and Gudrun had told her she should go and play, her thoughts were constantly circling around little brother.

Runa withdrew more and more and after a while she began to go out to the barn on her own. Olava could see that she was unhappy, but little brother was more important than anything else. As so many times before, it was Karin and Lukas who knew what to do. Karin made sure she involved Runa in tasks she could master and encouraged her and thanked her for being so helpful. Lukas also asked her to come with him and help feed and comb the horses and, little by little, Runa got her good mood back.

Little brother was the center of attention for everyone on the farm and the atmosphere in the kitchen was almost ceremonious when they gathered there to see him for the first time. They were all standing around the little boy to admire and hold him. Tormod looked approvingly at his son while Grandmother held her grandchild proudly in her arms. Her face got a mild expression when she looked at the little human being. Somehow Olava found it a bit sad to see her grandmother's face like that, maybe because it happened so seldom.

Even Lukas gathered up his courage when Karin asked him if he wanted to hold him. With the greatest care, he took the newborn in his arms while everyone was watching.

"Look at his tiny little head in your big hand, Lukas." The rippling laugh from Runa made the others laugh, too. The only person who wasn't laughing was Karin. She became all quiet with a dreamy expression on her face and her head slightly tilted. She looked in wonder at little brother in the arms of Lukas.

"He is safe like in a casting mould." She spoke with a quiet longing in her voice, almost as if she were talking to herself. She had not expected that everyone could hear her, but they did, and everyone's attention was directed towards Karin and Lukas as they looked at each other. For a short, hectic moment their eyes and thoughts met in an intense, mutual attraction, but then they broke the connection. Lukas got crimson red and Karin hurried back to the kitchen counter where she was about to make bread. She got busy kneading the dough while Lukas was standing with little brother in his arms, without the same opportunity to hide.

"Why are you so red?" Runa only made things worse with her innocent question and the cheerful smiles from the others didn't make it any better. Olava felt sorry for Lukas and she was eagerly trying to think of something to say that could make the embarrassing moment disappear. But after a few very long seconds, Lukas took action himself. He placed little brother carefully in Olava's arms and muttered something about the horses needing to be fed. He walked out of the kitchen with long steps.

It was a big help for the grown-ups that Olava looked after little brother. Karin, Gudrun and Grandmother were busier than ever. In addition to the daily cooking, cleaning, dish washing, baking and milking, there were many extra chores from having a baby in the house. They had to get more water, rinse, wash and boil baby clothes, bed linens, cotton nappies, towels and wash cloths. The men's working clothes also needed sewing and repairs. Furthermore, when an animal was slaughtered, it was the women's task to prepare the meat. Also, ripe fruit and berries had to be gathered and made into juices and jams for the winter.

It was almost two weeks since the birth when Anna tried to get out of bed. Karin and Olava supported her the best they could, but when she was standing up straight, her back failed her. She froze on the spot with one hand on her hip and the other on the bed. Merely one small, wrong movement made Anna moan in pain. She had to lie down again.

After a couple of days, the doctor came to examine her. When he came down to the kitchen a little later, he shook his head. It was hard to say how long a time it would take. Probably weeks, maybe even months. Most important was that she got all the rest she needed until her back was strong again. He was convinced that she would heal, but more than that, he couldn't say at the moment.

It was quiet in the kitchen when the doctor had left. No one had expected that Anna would have to stay in bed for a longer period of time. Ragnhild was the first to speak.

"It could have been a lot worse." She looked serious.

"Yes... I guess it will work out." Tormod nodded shortly before he got up from his chair. When he had left the room, Runa went over to Karin.

"Can I go up to Mum?" She dried her eyes with

one palm and Karin gave her a warm smile.

"Yes, of course. I'll go with you." She stood up and took her hand.

"I'll come, too." Olava walked with them out of the kitchen while Gudrun stayed back with little brother and Grandmother began to knit.

When they came into the room, their mother smiled at them and Runa went over to the bed while Karin and Olava were standing behind her.

"When will you get well, Mum?" Runa tried to be brave.

"I don't know, Runa. I will have to stay in bed for some time… It's my back, you see. But I'll be right here and you can come up and see me whenever you want to."

"Okay, Mum." Runa nodded understandingly and Anna's comforting words made them all smile.

"And there is one thing you can be absolutely sure of…" Anna looked at them and smiled mischievously. "I am not going anywhere." Then she laughed, a mild, surrendered laugh and the others couldn't help but laugh, too. Both Olava and Runa knew that when their mother could joke like that, it wasn't so serious after all. When they went down to the kitchen a little later, the atmosphere was lighter and good-natured. Now they had to make the best out of the situation.

From the neighbouring farms, guests came to see little brother and everyone was invited inside for coffee and cookies. Olava was both proud and a little shy from all the attention she got when she showed them her little brother. Still, she could also sense that Grandmother and the other grown-ups on the farm were somehow careful about what they said to some of the guests. The rumours about the dramatic birth had spread and some tried to lead the conversation to Anna who was in bed upstairs. Olava noticed that the adults avoided the subject if someone began to ask. It was correct that Anna was in bed, but everyone was assured that everything was well and that she would soon be back on her feet. No one on the farm said anything that could become a good story in the community. Rumours about other people's trials were for some a dear subject which could make their own tribulations seem a little easier, at least for a little while.

There was one woman who came without any hidden agenda. It was Majbritt from the neighbouring farm. She and Anna had been friends for many years, ever since Majbritt became a widow at the age of 28. Her husband had climbed up on the roof of the barn one late afternoon to fix a small leak when he slipped and fell. For two weeks he was floating between life and death before he passed away one misty morning in late winter. Majbritt was left alone with two little children and a big farm with animals and fields, her heart crushed by the loss of the man who was her wildest lover and best friend.

    Majbritt had become a target for gossip in the community after she had decided to run the farm by herself and politely denied a few suitors who offered her marriage, all with different intentions. Two men proposed to her directly while others left a random comment as if to probe the terrain. Majbritt was always friendly but also direct in her answers. It was better to avoid any misunderstandings in such sensitive matters. Most men understood and let it pass, but there was one man who took the refusal personally. In the name of his hurt pride, he began to spread false rumours about Majbritt.

The challenges of life had not made Majbritt bitter. On the contrary, as the years passed, she had developed a disarming kindness, a personality trait that most people were touched by. No one who got to know Majbritt was able to talk about her behind her back. Still there were only a few who could admit to themselves that they at some point had been riding the wave of false rumours that were circulating in the community.

The adversity became Majbritt's strength. She never defended herself against the rumours and never judged either those who spread them or those who listened to them without asking questions. Moreover she never forgot Anna's support during those times.

Before the accident, Majbritt and Anna were good neighbours who greeted each other politely when they met at the Sunday service in church, the yearly Christmas tree party in the assembly house, and the celebration of May 17 at the school or on other formal occasions. Apart from that, they didn't know each other and it was not until a few days after the funeral that Anna decided to walk over to Majbritt. She couldn't forget the sight of the grieving woman and her children standing by the coffin and at last she gathered up her courage and walked over the field and through the forest to the neighbouring farm.

Majbritt's grief had been transparent during the funeral, her face was both ravaged and mild at the same time and her eyes didn't leave the coffin all through the ceremony. She was standing a little by herself with her two boys close to her while the rest of the funeral procession stayed more in the background. The ceremony ended at the church.

Majbritt had not invited anyone for funeral coffee at her farm, which was the usual custom. Most people understood.

The farm looked completely abandoned when Anna walked over the yard towards the house. She knocked on the door and waited, but there was no sign of life, neither from inside the house nor outside. After a while, she knocked again, this time a little harder, but still no one answered. Anna stood bewildered for a moment and considered whether she should leave when the door slowly opened from inside.

"Yes?" Anna had never seen grief like that before. Majbritt's eyes were lifeless, empty and colourless and she leaned heavily on the door frame, almost as if she had to use all her strength to keep standing up straight.

"I only want to ask you if there is something I... I can do..." Anna hesitated and became painfully aware of her own uncertainty. She looked despairingly at Majbritt, who wasn't answering.

"I only want to know... how you are doing." Anna regretted the words the moment she had spoken them. She could easily see how Majbritt was doing, but her reaction came as a total surprise. For a long time Majbritt just stared at Anna, puzzled, almost like a child that experiences something new and incomprehensible for the first time. Then she cried. She sat down on the stone stairs outside the door and with her face hidden in her hands, she opened up to the hopelessness and despair and cried in bottomless grief for more than an hour. Anna sat down next to her. She didn't move until Majbritt's crying slowly subsided.

"But I have my children." Majbritt was still hiding her face in her hands and her voice could hardly be heard.

"Yes." Anna said as little as possible. It was Majbritt's own words that could comfort her now.

"I have my boys." Majbritt looked at Anna through the veil of tears and there was a little glimpse of hope in her eyes. Anna nodded mildly and put one careful hand on Majbritt's shoulder, almost without touching her. Majbritt cried for another hour, this time in the arms of Anna.

It was the beginning of a long and lasting friendship between the two women. In the beginning, Anna came over as often as she could and helped her with the children and the daily chores. In time they became each other's support and confidants, two women who instinctively understood each other. The friendship became a gift for them both. It was Majbritt who taught Anna that there were men who could be soft as a summer breeze and wild as the western wind and the confidence brought stories of rainy days full of laughter, disagreements followed by gentle reconciliation and of sleepless nights with glowing lovemaking.

"I miss him a little every day." Majbritt spoke with a quiet smile one afternoon while she and Anna talked over a cup of coffee and the children played outside. The words hit Anna more than she wanted to admit. For a short moment she was painfully aware that she would never be able to say the same if she became a widow. The thought crossed her mind, but then she pushed it aside.

On one occasion, Anna forgot the realities of her own marriage, and inspired by one of Majbritt's stories about a swim in the lake under a star-specked summer sky, she asked Tormod if he wanted to go for an evening walk with her.

"Why?" Tormod had looked sullen and sceptical.

"I thought maybe it could be nice." In that very same second she began to doubt if she really meant it herself.

"Do you all of a sudden have time for evening walks?" The hard voice wasn't something new and Anna tried to avoid any further conversation.

"Just forget about it."

"Forget about it? What do you think people would say?" Anna remembered a story about mild reconciliation after disagreement and gathered up her courage.

"Do you know what, Tormod. I don't think I want to go for an evening walk with you anyway. In fact, I would rather not." Tormod had looked really surprised, but the result was a wall of silence that lasted for more than three weeks. It was after that episode that Anna began to laugh quietly at her own marriage. It was pure survival and a way for her to stay sane.

It was six months after the funeral that Anna heard the first rumours about Majbritt. Tormod had quietly accepted Anna's visits as long as they were under the cover of helping a neighbour. Anna never mentioned that as time went by she looked forward to the visits with great joy. The truth was that Majbritt was doing just fine. She had rented out one of her fields to one of the farmers in the community and she had sold some of her animals at a good price and kept the ones she needed. She was also a skilled weaver and earned some money by selling table cloths and bed covers.

Anna had no idea what was going on the day that Tormod suddenly stood in the door to the wash house and said that they should not have anything more to do with Majbritt. She was certain it had to be a mistake and looked blankly at her husband.

"What do you mean?" She put a pile of dirty laundry to the side and looked at Tormod.

"People are talking." He looked a little embarrassed.

"About what?" Anna was completely puzzled.

"People talk about Majbritt. Someone has seen her."

"Seen her?" Anna shook her head.

"She seems to be taking money for it." Tormod coughed a little.

"For what?" Anna had begun to sense something ominous in his meaning.

"She takes money to be with men." Tormod tried to sound natural. Anna could feel how she had to digest his words before she was able to think fairly clearly again.

"Who says these things?" She had to make real effort to try and sound calm.

"Well…" Tormod seemed reluctant. "There are several people who say so."

"Who?" Anna had begun to shake on the inside from repressed anger.

"People talk. Someone has seen her in the city. We will not have anything more to do with her." It sounded like a final decision.

"It's a lie. Every word. It's gossip. It's meanness." Anna felt the coldness in her heart. "As long as I can remember, you have risen above gossip, Tormod." Anna could see that her words hit him. Tormod avoided her eyes and stared stiffly into the wall. He was known in the community as a righteous man, respected for his generosity to those who needed a helping hand in hard times. Gossip was something he avoided, but the only thing he managed to do now, was to stick to his decision.

"We will not have our own name and reputation ruined. We will have nothing more to do with her." He turned around to leave.

"Tormod... do not leave now..." Anna got up, but Tormod was already on his way out the door.

Next Sunday in church, Anna noticed how people sent Majbritt furtive glances and she realized that she was probably one of the last people to have heard about the rumours. Even the minister let his eyes rest on Majbritt for a moment during his sermon about remission of sins. The only person who didn't understand anything of what was going on, was Majbritt herself. After the service, Anna walked over to her and told her quietly what had happened. Majbritt looked bewildered at the others in the church. Their avoiding eyes confirmed Anna's story.

When they got home, Tormod had a rage attack. Accusations hailed down on Anna, who, wise from experience, did not answer her husband as long as he was irrational. The others on the farm held their breath until the storm was over.

But Anna continued to visit Majbritt. It was a battle she chose to fight and for a long time, she walked over to her friend despite the bad remarks and tacit accusations. She also made sure that she always stood next to Majbritt at public events and if a natural occasion presented itself, she always spoke of her with respect and kindness. This was often met with a certain kind of bafflement followed by silence, but slowly the rumours began to disappear and in time it was as if they had never existed. To Anna's relief, Tormod began quietly to accept her visits at Majbritt's.

Olava could remember Majbritt and her children from when she was very little. Many times she and Runa were allowed to go with Anna when she went over to her friend. Olava remembered how her mother would often hum a song as they walked through the forest and how she and Runa would jump and dance next to her, happy to come along. They were almost the same age as Majbritt's two boys and when they were little, they could play together for hours, forgetting everything else around them.

Majbritt came to visit Anna a few days after her back had failed her. Olava was in the kitchen together with Karin and Runa. Little brother had just fallen asleep in her arms when someone knocked on the door. Karin went to open and Runa followed. Olava could almost guess who it was from the light atmosphere in the hallway and when she recognized Majbritt's voice, she smiled a little to herself. There was always a calming peace in the presence of Majbritt. Olava came to think of something her mother had said may years ago one time when they were walking back home after one of their visits.

"I think Majbritt sends little rays of joy out to everyone she meets." It was not until many years later that Olava began to understand what her mother had meant.

When they entered the kitchen, Majbritt stopped for a moment at the sight of Olava with little brother sleeping in her arms. She smiled, touched, before she walked towards the rocking chair where they were sitting.

"He is beautiful." Majbritt bent down so that she could see him better. Olava could see that her eyes were wet.

"Yes..." She looked proudly at her little brother.

"He is almost as cute as Lukas." They turned around, surprised at Runa who was standing next to them with a cheeky glimpse in her eyes. They laughed at the unexpected comment, but quietly so that they didn't wake up little brother.

"Yes, he is." Majbritt caressed Runa's cheek, and then she became serious. She folded her hands in her lap and let her eyes rest on them for a moment before she looked at Olava.

"How is your mum?" Olava could hear in her voice that she was worried.

"She is... fine." Olava didn't quite know what to say and looked at Karin, who took over.

"Anna is feeling better, but she still needs quite a lot of sleep. She really wants to see you." Karin knew well that Majbritt and Anna were friends, but it was not until Anna asked her to send Majbritt up to her room that she realized how close their friendship was.

"Is she awake?"

"Yes, I think so. If not, she wanted us to wake her up."

"Okay, I'll go up to her now." Majbritt caressed little brother gently on his head and smiled warmly at Runa and Olava before she stood up and walked out of the kitchen.

Majbritt stayed in the bedroom for a long time and Olava wondered what they were talking about. When the men came in to eat, they didn't mention anything about Majbritt's visit. It was not something they had agreed on. They only knew it was better that way. The friendship between Anna and

Majbritt was already a sensitive matter and Tormod's mood could be unpredictable. Sometimes it didn't take much before it changed and this was the last thing Anna needed now.

When the meal was over, the men went outside to work and Grandmother went over to her own house. Little brother woke from his midday nap, well rested and hungry. He sucked eagerly on his hand when Olava came into the sleeping chamber. It was the first time she saw him do this and she stopped for a moment just to watch him. She smiled in wonder at the serious look in his eyes as he was sucking with such concentration. When there was no milk, he got impatient and Olava picked him up from the cradle. She tried to distract him by talking, smiling and rocking, but it wasn't long before he began to cry for milk so she went upstairs to her mother with him. Olava would rather not have disturbed her mother and Majbritt and she knocked carefully on the door.

"Come in." It was Majbritt's voice from inside the room.

When Olava came in, she could see that her mother had been crying and she stopped uncertainly by the door.

"You can come, Olava." Her mother waved at her and Olava walked over to the bed. Majbritt looked at her and little brother in admiration.

"It's so good for your mum that she's got you now." Olava smiled shyly. It always felt a bit strange to get praise like that and she wasn't sure what to say.

"I think he is hungry." Anna rolled around to the side and in spite of the awful pain, she managed with cautious movements to sit up. She would usually nurse little brother lying on the side, but if she put pillows behind her back and leaned over to one side, she could just manage to sit up for a very short period of time. Olava placed little brother carefully in her arms.

"I'll come downstairs with him when he has eaten." Majbritt smiled warmly and Olava felt relieved when she left the room. It was hard for her to deal with all the emotions that were in the air.

After a while, Majbritt came downstairs with little brother, who was resting, satisfied and full in her arms.

"He is gorgeous." Majbritt was completely engrossed in the little boy. "It's like holding one of my own." She rocked him quietly in her arms while Runa and Olava stood close and watched. Olava wished that the moment would last, but it wasn't long before Majbritt had to go home. She refused politely when Karin asked her if she would like another cup of coffee and Olava felt an unexplainable loss when she left. What she didn't know, was that she would soon see Majbritt again.

The atmosphere on the farm had been vulnerable when Anna's back failed. The fear of how they should manage the new situation was lurking in everyone's mind, but the uncertainty was soon replaced by faith that everything would be okay. As the days went by, the atmosphere on the farm changed for the better and everyone's mood became significantly lighter. Everything was good until Anna lost her milk.

4

The mild days linger on with rare determination. Only the bright moonlight of Autumn warns of colder times to come. Slowly the sun loses its warming power. Almost imperceptibly, the nights get cooler. The colours start to fade. The leaves leave the nourishing power of the trees. Gently falling to the ground. The cool morning air filling the lungs of Nature. Keeps her awake and sharpens her senses.

Little brother was nearly one month old when Anna lost her milk. Olava was sitting in the chair by the bed observing how he got more and more impatient while nursing. She could see the worry in her mother grow as the days passed. Her normally mild face got a serious look and she stopped making small talk as she used to do when little brother was nursing. Instead she became thoughtful and quiet and Olava began to understand that something was wrong.

"Why is he so uneasy?" She asked her mother one day when he began to cry after only a couple of minutes nursing at the breast. Her mother had a worried frown on her face and looked at little brother for a long time before she answered.

"I don't think I have enough milk for him." Her words were subdued and quiet and intended as much for herself as for her daughter.

"But... is it serious?" Olava looked bewildered

at her mother who was still engrossed in her own thoughts. "Mother?" She asked again, this time louder, and now her mother looked directly at her.

"We'll have to wait and see… Maybe things will be better in a couple of days." Her words gave Olava a small hope that everything would be okay, but she could hear the doubt in her mother's voice and when she turned around in the doorway on the way out, she could see that her mother had closed her eyes and folded her hands in prayer.

Things did not get any better. Little brother just got more and more restless and unwell each day that passed. It was difficult for him to come to rest and after some time, he only wanted to sleep if he were in someone's arms. When he woke up, he would cry for food. Olava continued to take him upstairs to their mother until she had no more milk and had to give up nursing him. She was lying helpless in her bed listening to how little brother was crying downstairs.

The light atmosphere that had been on the farm the past weeks changed again into uncertainty. Little brother's crying turned everything upside down and in the kitchen they tried everything to find a solution. First they gave him cow's milk diluted with water, but the milk gave him stomach cramps that kept him awake most of the time. When he finally fell asleep, it was only for a short while. They took turns walking up and down the floor with him, but not until late evening would he fall asleep, exhausted, and could sleep for a few hours straight.

Sometimes when little brother was inconsolable, Olava went outside. The feeling of helplessness felt like a lump in her throat, ready to burst. Most of all she only wanted to surrender to crying herself, but she had to be strong and hurried back inside to be close to her little brother.

Olava tried in every possible way to comfort him when he cried. Sometimes it helped to hold him over her shoulder and walk with him up and down the floor with firm steps. Other times he calmed down if she held him in her arms with one hand flat under his tummy whilst dancing and rocking him from side to side with big movements. Olava also began to take him outside if the weather was good and often he would relax when he felt a cooling breeze against his face.

Still, little brother continued to cry and after a few days, Lukas was sent to the neighbouring village where a nurse lived on one of the farms. He rowed over the fjord the fastest he could, but when he arrived, the nurse had gone to another farm several days' journey away where the mother had died in childbirth. It was with long strokes and a heavy heart that Lukas rowed back with this news and on the farm they had no other choice but to continue with the cow's milk. Olava heard the grown-ups mention that little brother might get used to the milk and she hoped so dearly that it would happen. But the days went by and little brother didn't get any better. On the contrary, their worries grew as little brother began to throw up the milk.

There was a hectic silence on the farm. During the meals, Olava, Karin or Gudrun went into the guest living room with little brother, but no one could avoid hearing him cry and everyone ate quickly and without talking. Runa became silent and often she would go out to the barn to play by herself. Karin looked more and more tired every day. All those nights with too little sleep left their mark and her natural smile faded with the weariness. Sometimes when their grandmother was over in her own house, Karin went out to the barn to get some rest while Gudrun and Olava looked after little brother. But it came to an abrupt end the day that lunch wasn't ready on time.

When Tormod and the others came in to eat, Olava was walking with little brother in her arms while Gudrun and Grandmother were quickly setting the table. Grandmother had just come in and had looked really uptight when she saw that lunch wasn't ready. She hurried to help, but it was too late. When Tormod came into the kitchen, he stopped for a moment, and then ordered everyone back into the fields. He said that they would not eat until the evening and only if the people in the kitchen were to be trusted. Gudrun assured them that lunch would be ready any minute, but Tormod was already on his way out and the others followed him without any questions.

Grandmother didn't say anything but she looked pale and upset and when they had left, she said that from now on they would first and foremost have to do their duties around the house. In the meantime, little brother would have to lie in his cradle. Her face was tight as she spoke and she crossed her arms to underline that her decision was final.

Both Karin and Gudrun knew it was best to obey Ragnhild when she was in that mood. They remembered all too well the episode with the new servant girl who was sent home without any warning when their grandfather was dying. She had been so unfortunate to say that if the Lord had known that humans were going to use words in that way, it was not certain he would have given them the gift of speech. Afterwards she had shrugged her shoulders and smiled a little, overbearingly.

They did not know what led to Ragnhild's reaction, whether it was the girl's actual words or her little smile, but Grandmother told her to pack and leave the farm immediately. The surprised girl tried to understand what she had done wrong but got no explanation. It didn't make any difference that she cried and apologized. Grandmother had made up her mind. Confused and unhappy, she packed her few belongings and left the farm, unaware that she had, with the best of intentions, awoken Grandmother's own feelings of helplessness by breaking one of the unwritten laws on the farm and touching on a sensitive topic.

Now Grandmother had decided that little brother would have to lie in his cradle in the room next to the kitchen so that they did not neglect their duties around the house. After the episode with the lunch, she sent Karin out to wash clothes and Gudrun to the stalls. Olava was given the task of peeling potatoes while Grandmother found her sewing kit and sat down by the kitchen table to fix some clothes. Olava could feel how unjust it was that Grandmother could make this decision and when little brother began to cry, she gathered up all her courage and walked towards the room.

"Do not go in there now." Grandmother looked firmly at her and Olava stopped in the doorway, uncertain what to do.

"But… he is not supposed to cry like that." She tried to sound determined but knew that she didn't succeed very well. Grandmother stood up with a tight face.

"You can pick him up and feed him when you are done with the potatoes." Her voice was hard and implacable and Olava felt how her courage left her. She sent the cradle with her crying brother inside a guilty look before she reluctantly went back to the kitchen counter.

"He will probably fall asleep soon." Grandmother tried in her own way to find words that could soften her decision, but it was no comfort. Olava didn't answer and was standing with her back to her grandmother while she worked. Her eyes swam with tears and feelings of anger and despair were simmering inside her. She was so torn up by little brother's crying and so angry at Grandmother who was so stubborn, and at herself because she didn't dare to defy her will. She also began to understand what her mother had meant when she said that Grandmother should not look after little brother.

Little brother was crying almost the whole time while Olava was standing by the kitchen counter and even though she worked as fast as she could, the time felt endlessly long. When she was done, she hurried into the room to pick him up. She hid her face, partly because she didn't want Grandmother to see that she had been crying, and partly because it was difficult for her to meet her eyes.

Olava stayed in the sleeping chamber with little brother and closed the door to the kitchen. She held him close whilst walking with him and whispering soothing words to comfort him. When he finally calmed down, she went back into the kitchen and prepared the milk with one hand while holding little brother with the other arm.

Olava worked slowly to stretch time. The milk from the morning milking was in the big pail in the corner by the door and she poured some of it into a kettle that she placed on the stove to heat. Afterwards it had to cool before little brother could have it. A couple of times, she could feel her grandmother's eyes in the back of her neck, but she avoided looking at her. When she sat down to give little brother milk from the tiny spoon, she made sure she sat with her back towards her.

When little brother had slurped some of the milk, Olava went back into the chamber with him to wash and change him. He was calm and content while lying on the changing table and Olava enjoyed the cherished moment. It wasn't often he was so much at ease and she stayed in the room and cared for him as long as she dared. When she came back into the kitchen, her grandmother had finished sewing the clothes and was standing by the kitchen counter where she was about to mix ingredients for bread. She looked over her shoulder at Olava who came with little brother in her arms.

"You may put him in the cradle and go outside and help Gudrun in the stalls." Olava didn't notice that Grandmother tried to sound gentler. Inside she could feel a simmering turmoil. She went back into the room and put little brother in the cradle without objecting, but when he began to cry, she quickly left the room and walked out of the kitchen with firm steps. In the hallway, she felt a sudden urge to slam the door behind her, but she didn't. It was unthinkable to behave in such a way towards her grandmother. Instead she remained standing for a moment staring at the door. Then she made a quick decision and without considering it any further, she walked up the stairs to her mother. She made sure to walk quietly so that Grandmother wouldn't hear her.

When she entered the room, her mother was awake and looked at her questioningly from the bed as if she had expected her to come.

"Olava, what is wrong with little brother?"

Olava could hear little brother's crying from the chamber downstairs and she realized that her mother had heard him the whole time. All of a sudden she felt so sad and she swallowed a lump in her throat before walking up to the bed. Her mother looked worried.

"Why is little brother crying so much?"

Olava searched for the right words.

"He is in his cradle and..." She hesitated and her mother took her hand as a sign that everything was okay.

"Is he in his cradle crying?" Her voice was gentle, but also insisting, and Olava nodded. "But where is Karin and Gudrun?"

Olava shook her head and it was hard for her not to cry.

"They are out... Gudrun is in the stalls and Karin is in the wash house."

"Are they out?" Her mother frowned questioningly, but then she became quiet. After a few thoughtful seconds, where confusion turned into understanding, she looked directly at Olava.

"Is it Grandmother who has decided this?"

It was almost a relief that her mother could guess what had happened and the only thing she had to do was nod.

Anna stayed quietly in her bed for a little while. Her hands folded, as Olava had seen so many times before, crossing her thumbs again and again. Then she took a deep breath and removed the quilt.

"Will you be so kind to help me?" Anna moaned

in pain when she sat up and let her feet fall down from the bed.

"But Mum?" Olava was both worried and surprised. "Don't…"

"Yes…" Anna clenched her teeth and with Olava's help, she managed to get up. She took the first careful step out on the floor but then her back failed and she lost her balance.

"MOTHER!" Olava just managed to grab her around the waist before she fell, and her heart beat fast from the shock. "Mother, you musn't…"

"Yes, I shall." Anna straightened up as much as she could and there was an unknown power in her voice that Olava had never heard before.

"I am going down to little brother… and talk to Grandmother." Her voice was softer now, but there was something unbending in her decision and in some ways Olava was full of admiration. When her mother took another careful step, she supported her as much as she could, and like this, they walked slowly across the floor towards the door.

In the hallway, her mother grabbed hold of the banisters and with Olava's help, she managed to sit down at the top step. She sat quietly for a while to rest before she put her legs on the next step and carefully began to move down the stairs, slowly step by step. Olava walked backwards just before her, ready to grab her if she should need it.

When they got down to the hallway and were standing by the door to the kitchen, they could hear little brother's distressed crying more strongly. Her mother spoke quietly.

"Just you stay here." Olava understood and nodded, but she could feel her heart in her throat as her mother opened the door and took the first careful steps by herself.

"My child is not going to cry like that." There were no accusations in her words, just a sober ascertainment. Anna almost got to the door to the chamber before she fainted.

"Mother!" Olava run towards her. "MOTHER!" Anna didn't answer and Olava looked in despair at her grandmother who was standing frozen to the floor staring in disbelief at her daughter-in-law. Right then Karin came in with two baskets full of clean clothes. At the sight of Anna on the kitchen floor, she dropped them down on the spot and run towards her. She sat down next to her, lifted her head and held it carefully in her hands.

"Get Lukas. He's in the woodshed." Karin spoke with a loud voice and Olava was already on her way out the door. She yelled to Lukas who was standing with the axe above his head, ready to cleave a big tree stump in two. When Olava breathlessly told him what had happened, he planted the axe in the stub, and they run into the kitchen the fastest they could.

In the kitchen Anna was about to wake up. Karin was holding her head in her lap and dipping her face gently with a cold, wet cloth. Olava realized that it must have been Grandmother who had found it and given it to her. She was still standing by the counter looking frightened. Lukas and Karin helped Anna into a chair so that she wouldn't lie on the cold floor. Olava found a blanket which she put over her. Her mother looked pale and tired, but her eyes were clear when she looked at Olava. She had defied her own helplessness to get down to little brother and she wasn't finished yet.

"Olava, will you please get little brother."

Except from the heart-breaking crying from the room, it was completely silent in the kitchen.

Olava knew that she would defy her grandmother by doing what her mother said. The others knew it too and no one looked at each other.

"Olava?" Her mother's gentle, questioning voice removed the last remnants of doubt and Olava nodded.

"Yes, Mum." She hurried into the chamber with the crying baby and her tenderness for the little boy was bigger than ever when she picked him up.

A little later, when little brother had fallen asleep and Grandmother had gone over to her own house, Anna asked for help to get back to bed. Lukas and Karin helped her and when Tormod and the others came in for dinner a little later, no one mentioned a word about the episode. It was better that way.

After that episode, Anna's back slowly began to recover. Every day she got out of bed to walk a little around the room and even if it was with small, careful steps and just for a few minutes at a time, there was progress. Grandmother kept mostly to herself and left the care for little brother to the others. When she occasionally came in to help with the house work, she was quiet and avoided the others. Olava almost felt a little sorry for her, but most of all she was so relieved that little brother wouldn't have to cry so much. With common effort they continued to walk with him when he was upset, but they also made sure that the meals were ready on time so that the daily rhythm wasn't disturbed.

Still, as the days passed, it got more and more obvious that little brother wouldn't adjust to the cow's milk. It was increasingly difficult for him to keep it down and he began to throw it up after he had eaten. Olava could see the worry in the grown-ups' eyes, but everyone was quietly hoping that everything would change for the better.

5

Autumn comes with all its might. Dark clouds lurking on the horizon. The wind rising with rare determination. Days with powerful blasts. The ocean simmering in rebellion. Sending hefty waves towards the shore. Tree crowns bowing in the mighty wind dance. Withered leaves swirling in circles on the ground. The last fruit fall of the trees. One by one. Only a few remain. Defying autumn with stubborn endurance. Until they surrender, too. Flocks of birds in the sky. Together they fly south. Colder times are on the way. Still, under the surface there is life and deeper down the roots get their power from the soul of the earth.

Little brother got slowly thinner and weaker. He began to sleep more than he used to and when he was awake, he was drowsy and passive. Olava made small talk with him like she used to, but when he looked at her, their eye contact was brief and fleeting. He didn't smile and chatter like he used to, either, and when she held her index finger in his little hand, he didn't have the same strength as before.

To begin with, it was almost a relief that they didn't have to walk with him as much as they had done, but as the days passed, Olava began to sense that something was wrong. Karin and Gudrun didn't say much, but Olava could see that they were worried. They checked on him many times when he was asleep and they always asked how much he had been drinking if it was Olava who had fed him.

After a few days, Olava wished that little brother would begin to cry again. At least then he would show signs of life and power and will. One day she got really scared when she overheard Karin and Gudrun talking in the kitchen. She was in the chamber with little brother and had just finished changing him when she became aware of their low voices from the kitchen. The door was partly open and through the crack, she could see that they were standing close by the counter whispering to each other. Something made her stand completely still and listen. She was rocking little brother gently from side to side so that he wouldn't reveal them.

"I am so worried for him." Karin's voice sounded serious. Olava sharpened her ears. Was it little brother they were talking about?

"Yes... he has become so thin." Gudrun shook her head in a distressed manner and the two women were silent for a moment.

"There must be something we can do... anything..." There was something insistently hopeful in the way Karin spoke and Olava could feel how the worry came creeping in on her. It had to be little brother they were talking about.

"But what?" Gudrun sounded desperate.

"I don't know... but if he continues to throw up... he won't make it..." Olava didn't hear the next thing Karin said, but she was certain she had heard right. A few seconds passed before she really understood what the words meant, but then she felt as if the floor began to turn. It could not be true. Make it? Little brother? It was impossible. Again and again she tried to find another explanation to what Karin had said, but no matter how much she wished it to be different, it could not be misunderstood. She felt a sickness rise up within her and she had to lean her back against the wall. She sank quietly to the floor while she held little brother close to her chest. The warmth from the little body filled her with so much love and the fear of losing him overwhelmed her. Olava began to cry, first silently, but then she couldn't hold it back anymore. Karin came into the room and when she understood that Olava had overheard their conversation, she sat down on her knees, carefully, in front of her.

"It will be okay, Olava. We'll find a solution." Olava nodded. She knew that if she tried to say something, she would start to cry even more.

That afternoon they worked together in silence. Olava could sense how Karin and Gudrun were around her looking after her and even though they didn't say much, she knew they kept an eye on her. A few times they tried to smile encouragingly at her.

The same evening at the dinner table, Karin spoke. Olava could not remember that anyone had stood up like that before and everyone looked at her in surprise when she remained standing until everyone was quiet.

"Yes?" Grandmother cleared her throat.

"It is little brother." Karin spoke with a loud and clear voice and it was difficult to see what a challenge it was for her to stand up like that.

"What is wrong with him?" Tormod sent her a quick, sharp look but continued to eat. If he was uncomfortable with the unusual situation, he hid it well.

"He has become thinner and he continues to throw up."

"I see..." Everyone waited for Tormod to finish

chewing, but Karin continued.

"We are worried about him."

"Who are we?" Tormod's sharp question made Karin waver for a moment, but then she continued.

"I am worried about him." She emphasized the first word and hereby she avoided involving others in the conversation against their will. Olava looked at Gudrun who was sitting with her hands in her lap, moving a little restlessly on the bench. First she stared at the table-top, but after a few troublesome moments, she stood up, too.

"I am also worried." Gudrun's unexpected action made the situation even more unusual. "He has become so thin." Her eyes wandered uncertainly around the room and her voice wasn't as clear as Karin's. Everyone sat completely still.

"I see." Tormod stopped eating and crossed his arms. He frowned for a moment before he stood up and walked into the room where little brother was sleeping. Olava saw that Karin sent Gudrun a little smile which the other returned with a careful nod. Apart from that, everyone was quiet. When Tormod came back, Olava noticed a rare glimpse of tenderness in his eyes, but it was gone in the same second that he sat down at the table. When he turned to Lukas, it was impossible to see if he was affected by the situation.

"We will have to make another attempt to find a nurse. Tomorrow I want you to go to the other farms in the area and ask if anyone has heard any news."

"Yes." Lukas nodded seriously.

"That's a deal, then." Tormod got up and without saying more, he walked with heavy steps out of the kitchen to be alone with his thoughts. The others remained silent for a while, but after some time everyone got up from the table to finish their evening chores.

That night Olava couldn't sleep. She was moving and turning restlessly in her bed while her thoughts kept wandering back to the night when little brother was born. She had prayed for her mother's life and had promised that she would never pray for anything else in her life if only she survived. A couple of times she tried to fold her hands to pray for little brother, but her thoughts kept circling around the promise she had given.

The next day, little brother was warm and lethargic. He slept most of the time and even though they tried to wake him up to make him drink, he only managed to swallow a few drops before he went back to sleep. Olava sat by the cradle watching over him most of the day. Her heart felt heavy in her chest and a few times she only wanted to cry, but most of the time she would just sit completely still to look at her little brother in wonder. He was so little and helpless and yet so endlessly strong. Helpless because he was completely dependent upon those who were around him and strong because everyone would do everything they could to help him. The thought filled some of the void that the fear had created.

    Runa came into the room a couple of times but left quickly. Olava was grateful that she didn't stay. She could see her own anxiety in her little sister's face and the silence between them was difficult to handle. Karin and Gudrun came in to check on him many times and even though they tried to conceal their worry for her and Runa's sake, it made Olava feel lonely.

It was Karin who went upstairs to tell Anna that little brother was sick and that they would make another attempt to find a nurse. When she came downstairs again, she went into the room and sat down next to Olava.

"Has he been drinking any more water?" She looked at little brother in the cradle and felt his forehead.

"No, not much." Olava shook her head imperceptibly and they were quiet for a while before Karin spoke again.

"I have talked to your mum. She would like to see him." Now Olava could see that Karin's eyes were wet from tears.

"Does she know that…" Olava didn't know how to ask and Karin understood.

"She knows that little brother is sick and that Lukas has gone to ask for news. She wants you to come up with him."

"Okay…" Olava nodded. In a way it almost felt like a relief to do something else than just sit still and she picked her sleeping brother carefully up from the cradle.

"Thank you, Olava." Karin smiled at her, but it was far from her usual beaming smile that made everyone feel good.

Seeing her mother in bed hurt more than ever before. Her eyes were mild and fragile from grief and when she got little brother in her arms, she held his warm forehead against her cheek while rocking him gently. After a while, she looked at Olava.

"Karin told me that you have been sitting by the cradle all day." Olava looked down, shyly.

"Yes… He has been sleeping most of the time."

She didn't quite know what to say.

"Thank you for looking after him so well." There was a faint smile in her mother's face and her words felt good.

"How about you, Olava. How are you?" Olava lowered her head. It didn't feel right to talk about her now.

"I'm okay…"

"You look tired."

"Yes…" Olava paused. "I didn't sleep very well last night." Her mother's calming presence made Olava relax and for a short moment she considered whether she should tell her about the promise she had made the night that little brother was born.

"Are you worried?" Her mother looked at her questioningly.

"Mmm… it's just that…" Olava stopped in the middle of the sentence and looked at her mother.

"Yes, you can tell me what it is, Olava?" Then Olava told her about how she had prayed to Jesus the night that little brother was born and about what she had promised. Her mother listened carefully to everything she said and when she had finished, she paused for a moment before she spoke.

"Olava… Jesus understands more than we know. He understands how you felt that night when you were so scared and what made you promise what you did. Jesus doesn't count, Olava. He understands that you need to pray now that little brother is so sick." It sounded so simple and right when her mother put it that way and she could feel how her words rang true.

"You can always pray to Jesus when something is hard." Her mother reached out a hand and stroked her cheek tenderly. "Do you understand?"

"Yes…" Olava nodded warily.

"Good." She didn't say more but continued to rock little brother in her arms while Olava quietly considered what she had just said. When she was back in the chamber a little later and little brother was sleeping in the cradle, she folded her hands and prayed for him. This time it felt right.

Lukas came back later that afternoon. They were all gathered around the table and everyone's eyes followed him as he entered the kitchen, took off his hat and greeted everyone with a small nod before he sat down at the edge of one of the long benches.

"I have asked around on all the farms. There is no news…" Lukas hesitated a little before he continued. Still, I was told that there is a gypsy family nearby. It seems that they are on their way to town and stop by all the farms to ask for work. He paused for a while. Rumour says that one of the women has a little child, a little older than little brother, but still a baby. The hope rose inside Olava like a warm wave. Could it be a chance? What if they could help?

"Taters!" Not until now did Olava become aware of her father who was sitting at the end of the table.

"Yes, from what I was told, it is a family with three horse carriages." It seemed as if Lukas took no notice of Tormod's sceptical tone.

"They lie and they steal." Tormod underlined his disgust with a fleeting grimace. Olava looked at Lukas, but he showed no signs of wanting to say more.

"But what about little brother?" Karin got up abruptly and her voice was trembling. "He is getting weaker every day." Everyone was silent and Tormod answered with his eyes glued to the table-top.

"They smell and they have lice. We will find another solution."

"But Dad..." Olava was just about to stand up like Karin had, but something held her back.

"It is out of the question!" Tormod rumbled and Olava remained silent. In the corner of her eye, she could see how Lukas and Karin exchanged glances and nobody said any more, absolutely convinced that only a miracle would make Tormod change his mind now.

"My son is not going to be nursed by outcasts." With those words, the decision was final and a moment of hope crumbled with the stubborn verdict. A few seconds followed where a strange silence spread in the room and mixed with the serious atmosphere around the big kitchen table. Tormod turned to Lukas.

"I want you to pack the carriage tonight and get ready to leave tomorrow morning. You might have to travel far. You can take Storm." It was the strongest horse on the farm.

"Yes." Lukas nodded heavily.

No one said more and after a while, everyone, except for Karin, Gudrun and Olava, left the kitchen. Karin was sitting by the table staring emptily into the air. Then she banged the table with her fist.

"He is so stubborn. It's his son." She was angry but then despair took over. "What are we going to do? What are we going to say to Anna?" Gudrun sat next to her and put a careful hand on her shoulder. Olava was standing on the floor, uncertain what to do. She had not seen Karin like this before and she had never heard her say anything about her father.

"We must have faith that Lukas will find help." Gudrun tried to comfort her, the best she knew how.

"But it might take a long time." Karin shook her head. "What if he doesn't..." She stopped in the middle of the sentence and looked despairingly at Olava.

"Oh, Olava, I'm so sorry..." Olava felt as if her head was about to explode and before anyone had time to say any more, she ran out of the kitchen into the hallway where she grabbed her jacket and out to the yard. She continued to run the fastest she could, first over the field and then further into the woods. Tears filled her eyes as she ran further and further away from the farm and when she was so far away that no one could hear her, she ran in between the trees. She didn't stop until the forest floor was so wooded that she couldn't go any further. Olava turned her eyes to the swaying tree crowns and without thinking, she shouted out as loud as her voice could carry. Again and again she yelled her despair out to the trees that were all standing quietly in silent understanding.

When she couldn't shout any more, she fell down to the forest floor where she began to cry. She was lying like this for a long time until there were no more tears left in her. All of a sudden she became aware of an ant that was eagerly pulling a small twig three times its own size towards the ant hill a few meters away. She observed in amazement how it worked tirelessly and defied all obstacles to reach its goal. While she was lying there, a thought appeared in her head. At first she ignored it, but then it was there again. Could it be a possibility? The more she thought about it, the more impossible it seemed. Still, maybe there was a small chance?

And then, in that very moment, Olava made a decision. She had to try. The thought made her dizzy. Again and again doubt took over. Still, she pushed it away, stubbornly. A plan began to take shape in her mind. She had to try, but she would have to act quickly. She knew that. Otherwise the small chance would be thrown away.

When she got up from the forest floor, she realized that the twilight was falling and she began to run towards Majbritt's farm the fastest she could. If it got dark, they would probably start looking for her and she didn't have much time.

Majbritt smiled at first, surprised at the unexpected visit, but then she saw Olava's tearful face.

"Olava! What has happened?" Olava was trying to catch her breath after the run through the forest.

"It's Mum."

"Your mum? Has something happened to Anna?" Majbritt looked distressed.

"She doesn't have more milk… it… it is little brother… he is sick…" Majbritt looked at her with worried eyes.

"Come inside, Olava, and tell me what has happened." Olava followed her into the kitchen and when they sat down by the table, the words flowed from her mouth.

"Mother doesn't have any more milk… and little brother… he has been crying so much… he gets sick from the cow's milk and his tummy has hurt so much… but now he has almost stopped crying and he is throwing up… He is sick and running a fever… and he sleeps almost the whole day and won't drink."

"My dear girl, what is it that you're telling me…" Majbritt looked at Olava with growing worry and Olava could feel that she was about to cry.

"Karin and Gudrun are so worried… and we cannot find a nurse. Lukas has been asking on every farm, but there is none… and… and we don't know what to do."

"But... is there anything I can do to help?" Majbritt looked at her uncomprehendingly and in that moment, Olava felt that she shouldn't have come. What had she been thinking when she ran over to Majbritt's? There was no way she could ask if they could stay at her farm.

"If there is anything I can do, Olava, then please let me know." Somehow Majbritt could sense that she was hesitating.

"It's just that..." Olava paused for a little while, but then she found the courage. "There is a tater..." She searched her mind for another word. "There is a gypsy family nearby... one of the women has a baby..." Majbritt looked questioningly at Olava and it was obvious that she was trying hard to understand what was on her mind.

"Do you think they can help?"

"Yes... no... maybe..." Olava shook her head. "I don't know... but Dad won't have it... he says that they..." Olava stopped. She couldn't use the same words that her father had used. Instead she continued. "Lukas leaves tomorrow to get help somewhere else... but it's not certain he'll find someone..."

"But Olava... what can I do?" Majbritt looked bewildered.

"I was thinking..." Olava didn't know how to say it. "If Lukas finds the gypsy family... then... then maybe they could live here with you and then little brother could get real baby milk." Majbritt looked at Olava both surprised and worried.

"But your father... he would find out, wouldn't he?"

"He works in the woods or on the fields most of the day... and he might go sea fishing soon. If Lukas stayed here, then maybe he could help you..." Olava could hear how impossible it all sounded, but Majbritt was listening attentively.

"What about Karin and Gudrun?"

"They don't know that I'm here… Karin is mad at my dad…"

"I see…" Majbritt looked serious.

"What about your mum?"

"She is still in bed and there is nothing she can do…" Olava shook her head in despair. "It's just that… if we don't do something, then little brother might not… he might not… he…" Olava's voice broke and she hid her face in her hands and cried.

"Oh no… not that…" Majbritt's eyes grew dark.

"I don't know what to do." Olava looked up, her face was wet with tears. For a short moment Majbritt closed her eyes and when she opened them again, she looked directly at Olava.

"They can stay here with me."

"Really?" Olava could hardly believe it.

"Yes, if they want to… it might work."

"Oh, thank you, thank you so much…" Olava didn't know what to say, but Majbritt shook her head as a sign that it wasn't necessary.

"You are a brave girl, Olava… Now run home and tell Kari, Gudrun and Lukas." There was a certain weight behind her words and Olava nodded sincerely. "One of you can come over tomorrow and let me know what you have planned."

"Yes." They said goodbye quickly and Olava ran back home the fastest she could in the darkness. Halfway through the forest, she almost ran into Karin who had gone out to look for her. She looked both relieved and worried at the same time.

"Olava… Where have you been, we have been so worried." Olava didn't know where to start.

"I have been at Majbritt's. The gypsy family can

stay at her farm... and if Lukas finds them, maybe they want to help us..." Karin stared at her in bewilderment.

"But... I don't understand... what do you mean?" And then Olava told her about her idea. In the darkness, Karin was only a dim figure, but she was listening carefully and when Olava had finished, she was silent for many seconds.

"But Olava... did you plan all this by yourself?" Karin was truly puzzled but also alarmed.

"Yes..." Olava nodded eagerly, but Karin sounded hesitant.

"We... would be running a great risk."

"We must try... what if they can help?" Karin couldn't say no, not now, and after a few moments of silence, she nodded slowly.

"You are right... we must try. But we need to keep it a secret from your dad and grandmother." Olava nodded. "We must tell Runa so that she knows." Olava nodded again. Karin was already planning what they should do and she could feel how her heart was beating fast. What if this could work?

On the way home, along the winding path, covered by darkness, they continued to talk about what they had to do. Only the twilight beings of the woods could hear their lowered voices and the sound of their soft footsteps on the autumn leaves. Back on the farm, Karin went over to Lukas who was preparing the horse carriage while Olava went into the kitchen to Gudrun.

Later that night, when the others had gone to bed, the four of them met in the barn. They had been careful to make sure that no one had seen them and if they heard someone at the door, they would quickly be able to scatter or hide so that no one would get suspicious.

The severity of the situation was heavy in their minds as they went through what they had to do. Yet, at the same time, there was a mysterious strength in their joint decision. The gypsy family was most likely nearby and if they were lucky, Lukas might already find them the next day. If they wanted to help, Olava would be the one to run over to Majbritt's farm with little brother. Only Anna and Runa should know about it. The biggest challenge would probably be Grandmother, but luckily she stayed in her own house much of the time. Majbritt's children were so old now that they could keep a secret. Three horse carriages indicated that the gypsies were many and Karin and Gudrun would most likely have to prepare extra food. Lukas was to stay at Majbritt's farm to help out, but Storm and the carriage had to be hidden away so that no one would find out. Still, first of all, Lukas would have to find the family and ask them if they wanted to help. Before they knew that, there wasn't that much they could do.

Early next morning, Lukas harnessed Storm to the carriage. Karin and Gudrun helped him pack while Olava was standing in the doorway with little brother in her arms. He was a bit more awake than the day before but still warm and she had wrapped him in a blanket so that he wouldn't get cold. There was an atmosphere of excited anticipation in the air and Olava could see how the three of them exchanged quick glances and whispered short messages to each other as they worked. When Lukas was ready to go, Tormod came with a bag of coins for food and shelter on the journey and Grandmother gave him an extra thick woollen blanket for cold days. Lukas nodded kindly in gratitude and got into the carriage. As he hoed Storm, he looked at Olava and smiled and waved goodbye. She waved back and, like the others, she followed him with her eyes until the road turned and they couldn't see him anymore.

The day passed slowly. The sound of someone in the kitchen door made them all simmer with anticipation, but the hours passed and nothing happened. After lunch, Karin walked over to Majbritt to agree on what they should do if Lukas arrived with the family. When she came back, she could tell them that the small farm house was ready for the family to move into. It had been empty for many years and it could house many people if some slept on mattresses.

When the afternoon came, Olava felt how her body had grown restless. A couple of times, she went out to the courtyard and scouted towards the forest to Majbritt's farm in the hope that someone would come, but it was all quiet, and when the evening came, she was just about to give up hope. She could see that Gudrun and Karin felt the same way. The surprise was huge when suddenly there was a knock on the door. Grandmother was still in the kitchen and they looked nervously at each other when she went out to open the door. From the sound of the familiar voice in the hallway, they all three got up at the same time and when Majbritt was standing in the doorway, they knew that the plan had succeeded. Her eyes and an almost imperceptible nod told them so. Olava could hardly believe that Lukas had found the family and that they were now on Majbritt's farm. The excitement made her body shiver and she avoided Grandmother's eyes out of fear that she might see her reaction. But Grandmother didn't take notice of anything and when Majbritt gave Karin a package with one of her woven blankets, there was a perfectly natural explanation to her visit. Majbritt apologized that it had taken so long before it was ready, but Karin thanked her many times and assured her that it was perfectly okay. The story they had come up with worked as it should and Grandmother did not get suspicious.

When Olava was lying in her bed that night, she could almost feel how the blood pumped through her veins. The thought that they were going to defy her father and grandmother so that little brother would get real baby milk was both frightening and uplifting at the same time. In one moment she felt light and hopeful, in the next, nervous and anxious. It meant that she would have to lie. She asked herself whether lying was the same as not telling something to someone, but then she stopped in the middle of her own thoughts and remembered her mother's words. Jesus understands more than we humans believe. Olava felt certain that Jesus would understand what they were about to do now and with that thought in her mind, she fell asleep.

To her own surprise, Olava was calm and determined when she walked through the forest with little brother in her arms the next morning. The cool morning air sharpened her senses and it was as if she experienced everything around her more strongly than she used to, as if she were one with the sounds, colours and every little movement in nature.

Little brother was still warm and had drunk only very little water in the morning. They had gotten up early and as soon as everyone had finished their breakfast and they were alone in the kitchen, they began to prepare for Olava to leave. Karin wrapped little brother in warm clothes; woollen underwear and stockings and his hat and winter suit made of leather. She also found the big sheepskin to wrap him in. Runa observed with interest the calm, but intense activity in the kitchen. When Olava came into the kitchen fully dressed, she began to suspect that something was not as it used to be.

"Where are you going?" Runa asked Olava who looked at Karin and Gudrun. They both nodded. Their plan was to tell Runa as soon as Olava had left, but now Gudrun sat down next to her. She told her in a calm voice what they had planned while Runa listened wide-eyed and in surprise. When Gudrun told her that she must not tell anyone else on the farm, Runa nodded slowly. Karin and Olava also went over to her to underline the seriousness of the situation.

"When Olava has left with little brother, we'll go upstairs and tell your mum." Karin looked at Runa questioningly to make sure she had understood. "Apart from mum, no one must know. Do you understand, Runa?" When she repeated what Gudrun had just said, Runa looked directly at them.

"I have understood." She almost looked a little angry and the resolute look in her eyes told them that she both wanted to and was able to keep it a secret. Olava blinked thankfully to her little sister and the others smiled in relief.

"Do you think maybe you want to help us with something?"

"Yes..." Runa nodded, surprised at Karin's question.

"Well, you see, it's a big family and we need to make sure they have enough food. If you want to come with Olava over to Majbritt's every now and then and bring some eggs, flour and maybe some potatoes and meat, it would be a great help."

"Yes..." Runa looked excited and happy and Karin smiled encouragingly at her.

"Thank you." Karin looked from Runa to Gudrun and Olava and nodded. It was time to go.

Olava walked through the guest living room and out the back door to the garden as they had planned. In this way she wouldn't have to walk across the courtyard where someone could easily see them. Karin and Runa walked them out and before she left, Karin put one hand on her cheek.

"Be careful..." It was as if she wanted to say more, but the words didn't come and there was no time. They said goodbye and with a firm grip around little brother, Olava went outside. She hurried over to the hedge and followed it until she was at the bottom of the garden where she crawled through the hole in the bushes. From there she followed the row with the little trees and hurried across the small field until she was in the forest where she could easily hide between the trees.

She looked over her shoulder, but there was no one to be seen and she continued to walk fast through the woods and made sure to lift her legs high to avoid stumbling over a stone or branch on the path. Little brother was wrapped warmly in the big sheepskin and she held him close to her body so that he wouldn't freeze. He was a little uneasy to begin with, but after a while he fell asleep to the rhythm of Olava's feet hitting the forest floor.

When Olava saw Majbritt's courtyard, she stopped. The feeling of calmness and determination which she had had walking through the forest was all of a sudden replaced by uncertainty. Could it be true what her father said about these people? She could feel how doubt came sneaking in on her, but she pushed it stubbornly away and continued over the courtyard to the main house. There were no signs of life outside, but when she knocked on the door, Majbritt opened almost immediately.

"Oh, there you are. Hurry into the warmth." She looked relieved and inside the hallway, she took little brother so that Olava could take off her shoes and jacket.

"Hi, Olava." Lukas appeared in the doorway to the kitchen with a cup of coffee in his hand. He smiled at her.

"Hi." Even though she knew he was there, she was both happy and surprised to see the familiar face.

"Come, let's go and sit for a while before we go over to the family. I'm excited to hear how things went this morning." When they sat by the table, Olava could feel the pleasant warmth inside the kitchen and together with Lukas' safe presence and the sounds from Majbritt caring for little brother, a certain kind of calmness spread over her. Slowly her body forgot the strain from the trip through the forest.

"How did things go this morning?" Both Lukas and Majbritt looked at her.

"It went well... no one found out... and little brother fell asleep in the forest... We told Runa who has promised to keep it a secret... and Karin will tell Mum today."

"I see... well done, Olava." Lukas nodded approvingly.

"Yes, you are a brave girl." Majbritt looked at her with a mix of wonder and pride and Olava smiled shyly. It felt a bit strange to get approval from both Lukas and Majbritt at the same time.

"Are they… was it difficult to find them?" She was curious to hear more about what had happened after Lukas had left the farm.

"No, they weren't far away from here. I met someone who had seen them and when they heard about little brother, they decided to help right away." Lukas paused before he continued. "One of the women. Her name is Malou. She has a little girl, 8 months old, whom she is still nursing. The girl's name is Emilia and she's so big now that she's begun to eat other foods…" Lukas looked almost solemn when he continued. "Malou wants to give little brother milk." The words needed no reply and the feeling of gratitude made them sit in silence for a long time.

A little later when they knocked on the door to the small farm house, it was opened carefully from the inside and a small, dark brown eye looked at them through the crack in the door.

"Hi, is Mum in?" When the boy recognized Majbritt, he opened the door completely and a smiling face, surrounded by the same dark, wild hair that Lukas had, appeared. He didn't say anything but ran into the house and soon a grown-up woman came to greet them. She smiled warmly when she saw them.

"Come in, come in…" She spoke with a foreign accent, but her natural radiance made Olava feel safe. Behind her, four children were curiously observing what was going on, but soon they ran happily back into the kitchen.

"This is Malou and this is Olava and little brother." It was Majbritt who introduced them to each other and Olava politely put her hand out the way she had learned. But the lush and loving woman simply embraced her and gave her a warm hug as if it was the most natural thing to do.

The house was full of life and joy and Olava felt at home almost immediately. The four children ran around playing and in the kitchen, two women were about to clear up after breakfast. Olava was both surprised and grateful at the welcome they got. The two women were Aishe and Nadya and, together with the children, they gathered around Olava and little brother. Everyone wanted to admire and touch the baby boy. They were talking and laughing and everyone was amused when the youngest boy, two years of age, gave little brother a loving kiss on the cheek. In the corner by the stove, an elderly woman was sitting with a baby on her lap. Olava understood that the little girl had to be Malou's daughter, Emilia. The old woman gave her a friendly smile and deep wrinkles formed a beautiful pattern around her dark eyes and made her face look mild and young. The old woman's name was Raya.

When Malou got little brother in her arms, Raya spoke in a language that Olava didn't understand. Malou went over to her with the little boy while one of the other women took Emilia. Everyone in the kitchen was quietly observing the old woman as she held little brother and began to examine him. Even the children stopped playing and came to watch.

At first, she tried to get eye contact with him by talking to him and making sounds with her tongue. For a short moment, it seemed as if he was looking directly at her, but then his gaze drifted away. She felt his forehead and took his pulse and then she pulled up his sweater and pressed one finger gently on his tummy. Finally she made some signs in the air that Olava had never seen before and when she spoke, there was a quiet solemnity in her voice.

Malou, Aishe and Nadya nodded. It was obvious that they took the old woman's words seriously. Malou turned to Olava, Majbritt and Lukas to translate.

"She says that he must not have much to eat to start with... He is so thin and weak now that his body will not be able to deal with much milk... We must also try to make him drink water mixed with a little sugar and salt... only a little at a time."

Lukas, Majbritt and Olava nodded to show that they had understood.

When little brother had had the first nourishing drops of milk, Malou continued to sit with him in her arms and made small talk with him. Little brother looked almost surprised, and for the first time in many days, his eyes were clear and direct. When he got uneasy, the strong and safe woman began to sing for him, a song in her own language. With deep, soothing sounds, she found a way behind the crying and little brother was calmed.

Olava stayed in the kitchen while Majbritt went over to her own house and Lukas went out to the barn to check on Storm and work with the men. Aishe asked her if she wanted to hold Emilia and Olava was happy to help. She was enchanted by the little girl who was staring at her with big, seeking eyes. She also noticed the youngest boy who was standing in the background observing them. When Aishe took Emilia to feed her porridge, the little boy went hesitantly over to where Olava sat and reached his arms up towards her. Olava was both surprised and touched when she lifted him up and he put his arms around her as if they had known each other always. The other women laughed heartily and the old woman smiled a little to herself.

Olava had agreed with Karin and Gudrun to be

back at the farm in good time before the others came in for lunch and when little brother had had some milk for the third time, it was time to leave. She felt as if she was almost about to burst from contradictory feelings when she trotted through the woods with little brother sleeping in her arms. The fear because he was so sick, the excitement of putting the plan into action, the relief that it seemed to succeed, but most of all a feeling of deep gratitude, like a fragile flower in her chest. Tears filled her eyes as she walked, but she couldn't cry now, there was no time, and she had to concentrate so that they wouldn't get caught.

When she was standing at the bottom of the garden, still hidden behind the hedge, she looked up towards the kitchen window. They had agreed to put a white cloth behind one of the curtains if the coast was clear, and a red if someone was in the kitchen and she had to wait. To her relief, she saw the white cloth and hurried up along the hedge over to the garden door which was open as they had planned. She tiptoed inside, through the guest living room and the door to the chamber next to the kitchen.

There she took off little brother's outer wear and her own before she went into the kitchen.

No one had heard them come and they looked totally surprised when Olava suddenly appeared in the doorway with little brother. She met their worried looks with a big smile and could hardly wait to tell them what she had experienced. As she was telling them about the gypsy family and how they had welcomed them and looked after little brother, she could see the relief in their eyes. She was just about to tell them about Emilia and the little boy when they heard someone in the hallway. Quickly Karin went over to the counter and Gudrun to the stove. Runa continued to set the table and Olava walked towards the room to change little brother. When Grandmother opened the door, everything seemed normal.

After lunch Runa came with Olava. In one hand she carried a bag of potatoes and in the other a basket with eggs that were wrapped in a small cloth. She didn't say much and Olava could sense that she was a little nervous to meet the strangers. But when they arrived, she got the same warm welcome that Olava had got and she quickly felt safe by being there.

They stayed on Majbritt's farm all afternoon. Malou, Aishe and Nadya looked after little brother and Malou gave him as much milk as they dared to give him. A couple of times he cried from stomach cramps, but together with singing, rocking and soothing, they managed to calm him down. Malou and the other two women gathered around Raya, the elderly woman, a couple of times to discuss what they should do. When they talked together, they used their own language. Lukas told Olava and Runa that is was Romanian and that most gypsies around the world knew how to speak that language.

In the course of the afternoon, Olava and Runa went out to the barn where the men were working together with Lukas. To begin with, they were shy and watched them from a distance, but Marko, who was Malou's husband, waved at them to come over. When they did, he showed them a basket which he was about to plait and told them that he used branches from a willow tree because they were strong and supple and could stand to be bent and twisted. He asked if Runa and Olava wanted to try and Olava was surprised to find out how simple it looked when Marko did it, but how difficult it was when she tried it herself.

A young man named Nanosh was about to decorate the hilt of a knife. With careful movements he made little cuts in the wood and slowly a beautiful pattern began to appear. He was concentrating deeply, but when he saw Olava and Runa, he lifted his eyes for a moment and gave them a friendly nod. Olava smiled back at him, a little shy. There was something in the young man's eyes which seemed familiar, but she didn't know quite what it was. The other two men were Stevo and Shandor, and while Stevo was chopping wood, Shandor was about to fix one of the wheels on one of the carriages. Lukas helped him and together they managed to stabilize the carriage so that they could lift off the wheel.

When Olava and Runa came back that afternoon, they hurried up to their mother. A wave of relief crossed Anna's face, but her eyes revealed how worried she had been. By the bed, she embraced both of them and while the two girls told her about the meeting with Malou and the rest of the family, she looked attentively from one daughter to the other. When they were finished, she shook her head involuntarily.

"My two girls... You are so brave..."

"It wasn't dangerous at all, Mum." Runa sounded excited and her innocent joy made her smile.

"Still, I want you to promise me to be careful." Her voice was sincere and Olava and Runa nodded.

"Yes Mum, we will." Olava tried to sound convincing and their mother smiled faintly.

They stayed for a while, but before they went downstairs again, they told their mum one more time about everything that had happened that day. When they waved goodbye by the door, their mother smiled proudly, but Olava could see that her eyes looked tired and weary.

From now on Olava left with little brother every morning as soon as Grandmother had gone over to her own house and their father and the other men had gone out on the fields to work. She made sure to be back before lunch, but as soon as it was over, she ran back again with little brother and was home before dinner. Gudrun and Karin were there to help when they left and when they came back. After a few days, Runa came along almost every day, mostly to help carry extra food for the family, but also because she thought it was fun and exciting. Lukas continued to live on Majbritt's farm where he helped her with practical tasks.

For each day that passed, little brother got a little more milk from Malou and slowly he began to gain weight. In the evenings and when he woke up during the nights, he got water mixed with a little sugar and salt as the old woman had said. In this way they managed to keep him calm most of the time until he got milk in the morning. If he cried too much, he got cow's milk, but only as little as possible.

Karin continued to look after him during the nights so that Olava could sleep undisturbed. The strain from walking through the forest many times every day left its mark and Olava could not remember that she had ever been so tired. The first days, her whole body ached and often she would fall into a deep and dreamless sleep early in the night. As the days passed, it was as if she got strength from somewhere else and it became increasingly easier for her to walk through the forest.

The atmosphere on the farm became lighter and Olava began to think that they would succeed with their plan without being caught. Every time she walked through the woods, the hope got stronger, but one day she was taken by surprise.

"Where have you been?" The familiar voice came from in between the trees. Olava stopped abruptly and could feel how her throat thickened. It was Grandmother. She froze on the spot while her heart beat fast in her chest. Should she run? She might not have seen little brother.

"Where have you been with him?" Olava felt how her heart sank within her. She had seen him. Grandmother had found out. She didn't know what to do but turned around slowly without speaking.

"Where have you been with little brother?" Grandmother walked towards her, a sceptical frown on her face.

"I've been out walking..." Olava's thoughts were working intensely. Could she come up with something that sounded credible?

"I see. Where have you been?" Olava looked at her grandmother. She didn't speak. "Olava?" Grandmother looked bewildered and then Olava decided to tell the truth.

"I've been at Majbritt's farm..."

"I see. With little brother?" Grandmother lifted her brows.

"Yes. There is a woman, a gypsy woman... her name is Malou... and she has a baby, a little girl whose name is Emilia..." Olava could feel how tears were burning in her eyes but forced herself to look Grandmother directly into her eyes. "Malou nurses little brother..." Grandmother continued to stare at her, speechless, and for a short moment, Olava thought she could see insecurity in the old woman's eyes, but then she spoke.

"How many know about this?" Olava lowered her head. It was no use lying now and after a few moments, Grandmother began to understand how it all hung together.

"They are very nice... they are not like Dad says..." Olava wanted to explain, but her grandmother interrupted her and spoke firmly.

"You better hurry back home before he gets cold." Grandmother looked at little brother and Olava turned around and ran the fastest she could directly home and into the kitchen.

"She knows... Grandmother knows." She was gasping for breath and Karin quickly helped her with little brother.

"Oh no." Gudrun put one hand over her mouth.

"What has happened?" Karin had a deep frown between her eyes.

"It is Grandmother. She saw us... she was in the forest." Runa began to cry and Karin sat down next to her to comfort her.

"Did you meet Grandmother in the forest?"

"Yes, she was standing between the trees... I didn't see her." Olava sat down on the bench and felt a strong need to just cry. Karin and Gudrun fell silent and even though their reaction was surprisingly calm, it was obvious that they took the situation seriously. No one said very much and the fear of the consequences lurked in everyone's mind when they began to prepare dinner.

When they were gathered around the table a little later to eat, the atmosphere was electric. Luckily, little brother took some of the attention as he was sitting with Gudrun and was awake and content. It was a long time since they had seen him like this and Tormod smiled at the sight of his son.

"He seems to be better." Olava looked down and felt her cheeks burn.

"Yes, he is better..." Karin had a tight look on her face.

"That's good." Tormod didn't notice the tense atmosphere and continued to eat.

"He has begun to get milk..." Karin looked stubborn as she spoke and Olava held her breath, but then Grandmother coughed.

"Yes. It seems that he has begun to tolerate the cow's milk." Ragnhild's voice was loud and she looked almost as stubborn as Karin.

"What did I say? Then I only hope Lukas will be back soon." Tormod nodded and continued to eat.

Several seconds passed before Olava realized that Grandmother had lied and when she looked at Karin, the surprise was written on her face. Gudrun began to cough so violently that she had to leave the table and Runa was staring gapingly at Grandmother, her mouth shivering and her eyes wet from tears. Olava was convinced that the lie was obvious to everyone around the table, but no one seemed to take any notice. Olava could hardly believe it. Grandmother had lied.

When Olava went to bed that night, she prayed to Jesus while she was cheering on the inside. Grandmother had lied.

6

Quiet waves come rolling in. Rising and falling in a rhythmic flow. The slow pulse of winter resting time. Seeds lie dormant in the ground. A sleepy daylight covers the land. These are the short days before the sun turns. The first snow-flakes whirling in the air. Dancing lightly before softly touching the ground. The night frost shines in the light of a clear winter moon. Leaving magical patterns on branches and leaves. Then the snow starts to fall. Tightly packed for days from a light grey winter sky. The earth resting under silk soft blankets of snow. Bushes and branches abundantly white. The small birds sing of joy. Celebrating winter in the snow covered bushes. Then the veil of fog eases and behind the rib shaped clouds in the east, there is the pulsing of a golden morning sun.

After lunch the next day, Grandmother stayed in the kitchen when the men went out to work. Olava could sense that Karin and Gudrun feared the worst and Runa was staring at the table-top biting her nails. She sent her grandmother quick glances every now and then. The worst thoughts were running through Olava's mind. Would Grandmother tell their father anyway? Was she going to say that little brother could not get milk from Malou? Or that Karin and Gudrun had to leave the farm? And what about Lukas? As soon as they were alone in the kitchen, she took the word before anyone else had a chance to speak.

"It was my idea. It was I who asked Majbritt. Karin and Gudrun didn't know anything about it." Grandmother and the others looked at her in surprise and a few seconds of tense silence followed. Then something happened that they had never experienced before. Grandmother's old eyes filled with tears until they began to run down her cheeks.

"Oh, Olava... is it you?" Grandmother quickly wiped her eyes with the palm of her hand and looked down whilst shaking her head thoughtfully.

"Are you not mad?" Runa stared at her with a doubtful look on her face.

"No, Runa... I am not mad... I am..." Grandmother stopped and coughed to clear her throat. When she continued, she sounded mild and conciliatory. "I am... proud... of you..."

Her reaction came as a surprise to them all and a few moments passed before the first confusion was replaced by relief. But when they realized that Grandmother really meant what she said, Runa laughed and Karin smiled. Gudrun closed her eyes in a moment of silent prayer and Olava held little brother close as if to tell him that everything was okay. Grandmother's eyes rested on her little grandchild and the frown in the old woman's forehead deepened.

"Tormod... he means well..." She stopped in the middle of the sentence and nodded to herself a few times as if quietly confirming what she had just said.

"He is stubborn." Sometimes Olava wished that she had her little sister's courage. Runa had the determined look on her face that they knew so well. Olava on the other hand looked at Grandmother uncertainly to see her reaction, but to her relief, she only nodded and there was a trace of a smile on her face.

"Yes... he is..." Nothing else was said about Tormod's mind-set, neither that day nor any other day.

Olava could feel how the atmosphere in the kitchen changed and when they were just about to get little brother ready to leave, something happened for the second time that morning which they had never experienced before. Grandmother turned to Karin and Gudrun and asked if there was something she could help them with. It sounded completely natural, as if it was something that happened every day. Still, both Karin and Gudrun looked as if they didn't understand the question. A few moments passed where none of them knew what to say.

"I was just thinking that maybe there is something I could assist with?" Grandmother sounded almost a bit uncertain and now Karin smiled and dried her hands in her apron as if to underline that they had plenty to do.

"Yes, oh yes... that would be lovely... Olava will be leaving soon... and we need to make more bread today. If you would like to..." Karin sounded a bit confused and stopped in the middle of the sentence.

"I would love to bake." Grandmother suggested it herself and Karin looked relieved. In spite of it all, it felt too strange to be the one to tell Ragnhild what to do.

A little later when Olava walked through the forest with little brother in her arms, she had a butterfly-like feeling in her stomach. Most of all she wanted to shout out her joy to the birds and the trees, but she knew she had to be careful. Instead she sang quietly and was dancing gently from side to side whilst walking. Little brother's eyes were wide open, enjoying his sister's soft joyful singing and her safe, rocking movements.

It was a great relief to them all to have Grandmother's support. The chances of getting caught were a lot smaller now and it eased their workload that she helped out with the extra chores around the house. She baked bread and cookies and knitted warm sweaters, socks and scarves for Malou and her family.

As the days passed, Olava could sense that Grandmother seemed more happy and relaxed than she used to. She had more life in her eyes and it struck Olava that she seemed milder than before. She was totally surprised one day when she came into the kitchen and found her sitting with little brother in her arms. Grandmother was prattling and babbling childishly with him and the old woman even laughed when little brother smiled at her. She was so enchanted by the little boy that she didn't notice Olava, but when she realized that they were no longer alone in the kitchen, she stopped laughing as if caught in the act of forbidden joy. In that moment, Olava wished that she had not disturbed them.

Little brother got better with each day that passed. Slowly but surely he began to gain weight and his cheeks got chubbier. His face got brighter and his eye contact was much better. Soon he also began to sleep longer. When for the first time in a long time he fell into a deep and calm sleep which lasted for several hours, Olava was almost worried that something was wrong.

He fell asleep on the way through the forest after the morning trip to Malou and Majbritt and continued to sleep when they came home. As the hours passed, they began to wait for him to wake up and Olava went into the room several times to check on him. She was standing quietly by the cradle and not until she was certain that his little chest was rising and falling or he moved a little in his sleep, did she leave the room. When little brother finally woke, he was lying in his cradle talking softly and eagerly moving his little arms and legs. The sight of him like that sent a warm wave through Olava and she tiptoed to the doorway and waved to the others to come, so that they could all see him. For a long time they were all standing around the little boy in the cradle, quietly, so that they did not to disturb the precious moment.

The days passed and after some weeks, little brother was again bursting with good health. No one could describe it, but there was a new atmosphere among the women on the farm. As little brother got better every day, there was a feeling of community among them. On the one hand, it was the strength of working together, and on the other, the infinite vulnerability of knowing how fragile life could be.

Anna could hardly take her eyes off her little son who was so much better. In the beginning, when Olava told her little stories from the day, she would sit quietly with her eyes resting on little brother. Olava knew she was listening anyway because every now and then she would ask more about some of the things Olava told her.

When she heard the story about how Grandmother had discovered them in the forest and then lied to their father by the dinner table, she stared shockingly at her, but then she couldn't help but laugh. It was so good to hear her mother laugh like that and many years later, Olava realized that her mother had one of life's gifts of grace. She could laugh despite harsh odds and sacrifice.

One night at the dinner table, Tormod told them that he was planning to go out with the fishing cutter, but that he would wait until Lukas came back.

"I cannot understand where he is." It was the first time Tormod mentioned Lukas' absence and the others sharpened their awareness. "Lukas has probably not found a nurse yet." Grandmother sounded convincing with her neutral voice.

"Yes, but then he should turn around and come home. He is much needed in the work on the farm." There was a trace of irritation in Tormod's voice and Grandmother sent him a sharp look.

"He has probably gone far since little brother was so sick." Grandmother sounded sharper than she had meant to and for a short moment, Tormod lifted his brows and looked at his mother in surprise.

"Well, I guess it wasn't that bad. He seems to be able to digest the cow's milk without any problems now." Tormod waved it away and Grandmother took a deep breath but kept quiet. Karin got up quickly to get more potatoes.

"We could have lost him." Grandmother whispered and only Olava, who was sitting next to her, could hear her.

"What did you say, mother?" Tormod raised his voice.

"Lukas is probably on his way home." Grandmother's voice was again neutral and Tormod nodded.

"Still, maybe we should send for him." He mumbled mostly to himself, but the others heard him and they knew that it was time for Lukas to come home.

"Give him a few days and then we'll see." Grandmother spoke with authority and Tormod seemed to accept her suggestion.

Two days later, Lukas came back with Storm harnessed to the carriage. He was driving into the courtyard and tried to look like someone who was exhausted after a long journey, but it was obvious that Lukas found it difficult to lie to Tormod. He chose to say as little as possible and, fortunately, Tormod did not ask about the details from his trip.

It was a relief a few days later when Tormod left with the fishing cutter. Now Olava and Runa could stay with Malou and the others without running home for lunch and one of the grown-ups could come along and help carry food or other things for the family. Runa had done a great job, but there was a limit to how much she could carry.

Olava and Runa had a wonderful time at Majbritt's farm and as the days passed, they began to feel as if they were a natural part of the big family. The women spent most of their time in the kitchen and when they had time, they would often crotchet pot holders and tablecloths or embroider cushion covers and small pictures to put in frames.

The men spent most of their time in the barn doing different kinds of craftsmanship. In addition to baskets plaited from willow, they made wooden frames for the women's embroideries, trays and plates of various sizes, kitchen tools such as pot spoons, spatulas and butter knives. It was all made of wood. Most of all Olava and Runa enjoyed watching the young wood carver Nanosh when he worked. Olava thought it looked so easy when he with smooth quick movements transformed the wood with fine cuts and beautiful patterns. Lukas had told them that he was very good at his work and sometimes Olava thought that he had magical hands. After some time, the family had a stock full of different things which they had made and Majbritt explained to Olava that they were going to sell it when they left the farm to travel on the country road. There was something very sad about her words, because even though Olava knew that the time would come when the family would leave, she felt a deep sorrow at the thought that they would have to say goodbye.

Even though Majbritt looked tired sometimes, it was obvious that she got along with the family very well. She was grateful for the repairs they made on the farm and one day Marko gave her a big and beautiful plaited basket. He had made it especially for her and Olava could tell how surprised and happy she was at the unexpected gift. Majbritt's boys got along with the family, too, and they spent much time with the men in the barn, eager to watch and learn some of their craftsman skills.

Tormod came back from the sea just before Christmas and, as always, his mood was lighter after the time on the water. On the farm, they were busy preparing for the feast and for little brother's christening, which was on the fourth day of Christmas. They had decided upon the date a long time ago, but for some reason, not yet on his name. It had been a long tradition in the family to name the newborns after their grandparents. Therefore, everyone assumed that little brother would be named Leif after his grandfather. When Olava looked at her little brother, she didn't think that the name suited him well. Instead, there was another name that kept popping up in her mind, but she hadn't told anyone yet.

Olava was upstairs with her mother and little brother when Tormod came back. He hadn't visited Anna many times during her time in bed, but now he went upstairs to say hello. They were taken by surprise when all of a sudden he was standing in the doorway and came over to the bed. He smiled at the sight of little brother who was lying relaxed and contented in the arms of Anna.

"He seems to be doing really well." Tormod bent down to take a closer look at his son who looked at him with inquiring eyes.

"Yes, he is doing very well." Anna nodded reassuringly.

"Is everything else okay around here?"

"Yes, everything is fine... Did you have a good trip?"

"Yes. Not that much fish, but it was a good trip."

It wasn't very often that Olava heard her parents talk together like this and even though they didn't use many words, she enjoyed it.

"Will you get out of bed before Christmas?" Tormod scratched the back of his head a little absently as he asked and Anna looked a little surprised, but then she centred herself.

"Yes, I'm counting on that. The christening will be soon, too." Olava could hear how tired her mother's voice sounded. When none of them said anymore, she decided to ask about the name.

"Have you decided what his name shall be?"

"We haven't quite decided yet." Anna smiled.

"Yes... well no. We don't know quite yet."

When her father hesitated, Olava took the courage to ask.

"What about Eystein?"

"Eystein. I see." Tormod looked searchingly at his son as if to see if the name suited him.

"It goes with his eyes. They are dark and deep like the horses." Olava was a little surprised that she dared to say it out loud and her mother smiled at her.

"It's a beautiful name." Olava looked at her father to see his reaction.

"Yes, it's a fine name." Tormod seemed pleased and nodded in agreement and with those words, it was decided that little brother's name would be Eystein.

Everyone on the farm wondered what had made Tormod break an old tradition so seemingly easily. Maybe it was his good mood after a fishing trip that did the trick. Maybe it was because Anna was weak and in bed. Maybe it was because of the minister, who would perform the ceremony, because although it would never be mentioned in words, he had seen a side of Grandfather which he most likely had not forgotten. Another possibility was that somehow deep down, Tormod was pleased that his son wouldn't be named after his own father. No one knew and they could only guess.

When Anna got out of bed a couple of days before Christmas, she was still weak. Olava noticed how she would stop in the middle of a chore sometimes and whilst holding on to the table, would sit down with one hand carefully resting on her back. It was never long before she got up and continued with her work, but there was something fragile about her movements, as if she was afraid to break.

Olava had always been excited about Christmas as long as she could remember, but this year was different. The holidays disturbed the daily working rhythm and even though Lukas tried to keep Tormod out of the house with tasks that needed two men and Grandmother asked him for help in her own house, the chances that he would find out were much bigger.

They had to be extra careful and even though Olava ran over to Malou as soon as they thought it was safe, she wasn't gone for long and they couldn't go every day. They had to give little brother cow's milk again and he reacted by getting restless and uneasy.

Once again the atmosphere got tense and the situation did not improve when they were very close to getting caught the day before the christening. Olava had just left with little brother when Tormod unexpectedly came into the kitchen and walked determinedly towards the door to the chamber. Karin, who was about to cut vegetables by the counter, reacted instinctively when she saw where he was going. Without hesitating, she cut herself in the finger and yelled out so loud that Tormod stopped. The blood spurted from the wound and he resolutely grabbed her hand and held it high whilst shouting to Gudrun to find a clean cloth. In that moment Anna entered the kitchen and with the help from Gudrun's eyes and imperceptible nods towards the chamber, she realized what had happened. When the blood stopped running, she asked Tormod carefully if there was anything he needed from the room. She had guessed correctly. He needed the big leather bag which they used for the sledge in the winter and which was stored in the big basket at the end of the guest bed. Storm and Odin were to be harnessed to the sledge which they would use the next day to go to church. Anna and Gudrun quickly found the bag and their relief was great when Tormod left the kitchen.

After that episode, they were extra careful and it was not until the christening was over and the New Year was approaching, that things went back to normal.

7

A beaming winter sun welcomes the New Year. Defying the biting cold. Trees and bushes dressed up in frost. Immersed in a dazzling fireworks display of rime and hoar. The sun and the snow sing together. Thousands of diamonds glittering in the snow. Crystal clear as far as the eye can see. Fairy-tale white clouds rising in the horizon. Showing their well-shaped muscles towards a clear blue sky. There are tracks in the snow. The animals find their own path through the woods.

Shortly after New Year, Anna got sick again. It wasn't her back that failed her this time, but she had been dizzy and unwell for some days and, eventually, she went back to bed. It was Karin who persuaded her and she was also the one who told the others at the breakfast table. Olava noticed that her father seemed silent and irritated. There was something impatient about the way he ate and when he had finished eating, he got up abruptly and walked noisily out of the kitchen. The others remained seated for a while and the silence around the table spoke more than a thousand words. Olava had a funny feeling that something was wrong and when she looked out of the kitchen window to see where her father was going, she couldn't see him anywhere.

When they were finished, she went out to the hallway. Her father's jacket was still hanging on the peg on the wall and his working boots were standing on the mat by the door. From the bottom of the stairway, she could see that the door to her mother's room was slightly open and she could hear low voices. With her heart in her throat, she tiptoed up the stairs, avoiding the spots she knew creaked. When she was up, she placed herself with her back close to the wall so that they couldn't see her. From inside the room, she could hear her father's low, angry voice.

"All you do is just lie in bed looking like a sick, old woman." Olava froze when she heard the harsh words.

"Tormod, please…" Her heart beat hard when she heard the vulnerability in her mother's voice.

"You have been lying in bed for months now. How do you think I feel? How do you think the rest of us feel when we have to do all the work?" The anger in her father's voice grew with the accusations.

"I am sorry you feel that way." Her mother sounded almost calm now.

"How do you think this is for me… the fact that you just lie here day after day?"

"I don't know, Tormod."

"No, I bet you don't. You don't know a thing, do you?"

"Yes, there is something I know for sure." Olava felt completely helpless as she was standing there and at the same time, she was puzzled to hear how calm her mother sounded.

"You know nothing. All you think about is yourself."

"I know one thing, Tormod, and that is that you are an ugly man." Her mother's words were frozen, but her father continued.

"It's pathetic to see you like this."

"I'm sorry you feel that way."

"You leave all the work to the rest of us and do nothing." More than anything, Olava wanted to shout out that it wasn't true, but she felt paralysed as she was standing there.

"You are an ugly man, Tormod." Again this unnatural calmness in her mother's voice.

"Do you even think about your son? Do you?" This accusation hit Anna where it hurt the most and she left it unanswered. The silence that followed was cold and dark and before Olava knew it, her father was on his way out of the room. She just managed to take a few steps down the stairs and turn around before he was standing before her. She hoped it looked as if she was on her way up.

"What are you doing here. Are you eavesdropping?" He looked furious and Olava pulled back a few steps, instinctively.

"No…" She shook her head.

"What are you doing here?"

"Leave her alone." Her mother's voice sounded angry and clenched from inside the room and Olava feared a terrible scene.

"I only want to ask Mum if she would like some breakfast." Olava tried to sound calm, but she was trembling on the inside at lying so directly to her father. Fortunately, he seemed to believe her and hurried down the stairs.

Olava was standing a little uncertain outside the room before she went in. When she got to the bed, her mother was lying completely still, just staring emptily into the air.

"Hi, Mum."

"Hi, Olava." Her mother smiled at her but it was a smile without joy.

"I only wanted to ask you if you would like

something to eat?"

"No, thank you. I'm not hungry."

"But... would you like something to drink?"

"No, my dear, I would rather just sleep now."

"Okay." Olava wished that she could come up with something nice to say to her mother, but she couldn't think of anything. Instead, she smiled and slightly nodded before she went out of the room. She was both sad and confused and, in the middle of the staircase, she stopped to ponder what she had just experienced.

The episode between her parents continued to rummage through her mind the rest of the morning. She could not remember that she had ever heard them talk to each other like that before. Her father's angry words and unreasonable accusations and her mother's calm answers. No one else knew anything about it and Olava felt that she couldn't tell anyone. It occurred to her that it might not be the first time her mother experienced her father being like that. To Olava's great surprise, her father was in an unusually cheerful mood a little later when they ate lunch. He was smiling and talking and the good atmosphere spread to the others. Olava felt even more confused than before. She could hardly believe that the episode from earlier that morning had happened. It could not have been as bad as she thought it was. Maybe there was something wrong with her? She began to doubt herself. All of a sudden, everything seemed so unreal.

Two days later, Anna got out of bed. She was pale and quiet and had a troubled look in her eyes. When Tormod was in the kitchen, Olava noticed that she avoided his eyes. He, on the contrary, would often look at her mother, especially if she showed any signs of weakness. Still, his good moods continued and together with the others, he seemed happy and relaxed.

Olava, on the other hand, found it difficult to get the ugly episode out of her mind and like her mother, she did not take part in the cheerful atmosphere.

Olava was relieved when the hunting season began a couple of weeks later. Her father and Lukas had gone hunting in winter as long as she could remember and often they would leave early in the morning and not be back until late evening. When they were not out hunting, they would work in the woods, chopping down trees for firewood. This meant that Tormod was out of the house most of the time and they could go back to the old routine.

Little brother continued to grow and thrive. He could easily hold his head by himself now and with bright and eager eyes, he observed everything and everyone around him with real wonder, often followed by a beaming smile. His stomach got better and in addition to the milk from Malou, he began to eat small portions of baby food, gruel and porridge. If he was crying, it was mostly because he missed nursing at Malou's breast and the loss was mutual. Malou's face lit up in a big smile every time she held little brother in her arms and she always spent a long time nursing and caring for him.

"Little Oystein..." The first time she saw him after the christening, Malou lifted him into the air and said his name with her strange accent.

"It is Eystein." Runa had giggled a little and emphasized the first syllable when she repeated his name.

"Yes, exactly, Oystein." All of them laughed when Malou said his name in exactly the same way as the first time.

The winter days turned into weeks and the forest began to show the first signs of spring. Slowly the snow began to melt and everywhere there was the sound of drops falling from the trees. Olava enjoyed the warmth from the first spring sun on her cheeks as she walked through the forest and on Majbritt's farm, the children were running around and playing outside. Still, as the days passed, Olava could sense that behind Malou's usual warm smile, she was also sad, especially when she looked at little brother. Even though Olava tried to push the thought away, she knew that the day when they would leave was coming closer.

It was Majbritt who told them one morning. They were walking over the courtyard towards the small farm house when she appeared in her doorway and waved at them to come inside. She had a warm shawl around her shoulders. It was always nice and warm inside Majbritt's house, but today Olava noticed that she seemed sad. When they were sitting around the table in the homely kitchen, Majbritt took little brother on her lap and began to take off some of his outer wear.

"Did he sleep well last night?"

"Yes..." Olava nodded. "He woke up once but went back to sleep almost immediately." Little brother was the natural center of conversation, both at Majbritt's and back on the farm. Every morning Karin told them how the night had been.

"That was good." Majbritt smiled thoughtfully, her eyes resting on little brother.

"Did he eat anything for breakfast this morning?"

"Yes, he ate a small portion of porridge, not that much, but some. He has begun to want to hold the spoon for himself." This was something new and Olava smiled when she told it to Majbritt.

"Yes, and sometimes he's got porridge all over his face." Runa laughed and so did Majbritt and Olava. Majbritt looked at little brother.

"What is it that I hear? Have you begun to eat all by yourself?" Eystein responded with a beaming smile.

"Are we going over to Malou soon?" Runa was getting impatient.

"Wait... there is something I want to tell you." Majbritt sounded serious.

"What is it?" Runa looked surprisingly at Majbritt, but Olava guessed what was coming. She tried to prepare herself for the news. Majbritt looked at them for a few seconds before she continued.

"They will be leaving soon." Olava nodded slowly and swallowed a lump.

"Who is leaving?" Runa looked confused.

"Malou and the others. They will be leaving in a few days." Majbritt tried to smile encouragingly at Runa.

"But, where are they going?"

"Nowhere in particular. They travel from place to place." Majbritt tried to explain, but Runa still looked puzzled.

"But, do they not have a house?"

"No, not the way we have. They live in their wagons."

"But, can't they just build a house? Lukas can help them." Olava and Majbritt smiled. It sounded so simple when Runa put it that way.

"You see, Runa... they don't have any land."

"Can't they just get some land?"

"Land is something you buy and they think that land should be for everyone and not just for people who have money." Majbritt lowered her head for a moment.

"Why can't they just get some money?" Olava shook her head, imperceptibly so that her little sister didn't see it.

"The thing about money is not that easy, Runa."

"But… can't they just stay here?"

"Yes." Majbritt nodded and she looked mild. "They are welcome to stay here, but they want to move on now."

"But… what about little brother?" Runa had a thoughtful look on her face.

"Eystein is so big now and he can eat real baby food. He will be okay, otherwise they would not have gone." Majbritt looked sincerely at Runa, who began to understand that this was serious.

"But… will they not be back?" Her voice sounded weaker now and her eyes were wet from tears.

"Yes, they want to come back one day…"

"But, when? It might not be for a long time." Runa was about to cry and Majbritt put a comforting hand on her cheek.

"You see, Runa, they don't want to live like us. They are travellers, this is their life. They go from place to place because they want to. It's their way of life."

"But, I will miss them." Runa began to cry and Majbritt gave her a warm hug.

"Yes dear, we're all going to miss them."

Olava had been quietly listening to Runa's many questions and Majbritt's explaining words. From the sound of her little sister crying, her own eyes filled with tears and she looked down. The three of them were quiet for a while and not until Eystein began to cry impatiently for food, did they leave the kitchen and walk out to Malou and the others.

Malou hugged them warmly, Runa first and then Olava, and when she got Eystein in her arms, tears began to run down her golden cheeks. She tried to dry her eyes again and again, but in vain, and when she first surrendered to her tears, she couldn't stop crying. Olava and Runa looked in surprise at Malou and didn't know what to do, but the other women came over to comfort her. They made a close circle around her so that she could cry. Even the children came to hold her. Runa and Olava had never seen a grown-up cry like that before and they were standing in the background, uncertain what to do. Raya was the one who invited them to join the circle and when they had gotten used to the unusual situation, it felt so good to stand there together with the others to comfort and be comforted.

The only one who did not take part in the sorrow over the forthcoming farewell, was Eystein. He was by now so impatient that he had to wait for food that he let out a cry so loud that they all looked at him. They were so surprised that they began to laugh, and when he responded by crying even louder, they laughed even more. When he was finally lying by the breast, he continued to have little bursts of anger whilst nursing, and in the end everyone was laughing so much that tears filled their eyes. The women's heartfelt laughter and the children's happy giggling seemed to have no end, and finally, Olava and Runa had to take the little children outside whilst Malou took little brother to a quiet room where he would calm down enough to drink.

When Olava and Runa came out to the barn, the men were busy packing their wagons with all their belongings and the things they had made in the course of the winter. The two girls stopped for a moment and stared at the packed wagons and in that moment, they fully realized that they were leaving soon.

Back at the farm the news that Malou and her family were leaving was received with calmness. Everyone had known that it was only a question of time before they would leave and the most important thing now was the knowing that Eystein was well. Karin even said that she was surprised they had stayed for so long. But Runa was inconsolable and the grown-ups tried to comfort her. Olava on the other hand kept her feelings to herself. She knew that no one else on the farm would feel the loss in the same way that she and Runa felt it, and most of all, she wanted to spend time with the horses. But she had to wait until the evening came.

While they were clearing up after breakfast the next morning, Anna said that she wanted to meet Malou and the rest of the family. The others in the kitchen stopped in the middle of their chores and looked at her.

"Will you be able to?" A look of surprise crossed Karin's face. Anna was still weak and couldn't handle too much strain.

"Yes, I think it will be okay." Anna nodded. "If the girls and Lukas come along, I'm sure it will work out just fine."

"What about...?" Gudrun looked a little worried and Anna nodded.

"Tormod is going to town in two days. He will

be leaving early in the morning and will stay one night at his sister's house."

If anyone on the farm had an errand in town, they used to spend one night at Aunt Barbro and her husband, Uncle Knut's, house. The town was almost one day's journey away and it would be late night before they were back. First they had to row over the fjord in their boat. After that they had to travel by foot or horse carriage and finally there was the ferry to town. Their aunt, who was their father's sister, lived together with Uncle Knut on the other side of the fjord where they had their own smithy. They had never had children of their own and Olava and Runa had always been a little scared of their aunt. A few times when they were younger and their aunt was visiting, they played in the hay that Barbro was bewitched by an evil sorcerer who had stolen her smile.

Olava tried to imagine what it would be like when her mother met Malou and the others. The thought was both good and a little frightening at the same time.

"Will you tell Majbritt and Malou that I will come with you the day after tomorrow?" Her mother smiled mildly at her.

"Yes, I will." Olava nodded.

"Can't we all go?" Runa lit up in an expectant smile.

"Well, I'm not so sure that's a good idea." Her mother sounded hesitant.

"I would love to come." Their grandmother had been sitting in the chair by the fireplace with Eystein on her lap and had been quiet until now. At first they all looked at her with surprise, but then

Karin took the word.

"Yes, we can bring something to eat."

"It would be very nice." Now Gudrun agreed, too, and Runa looked hopefully at her mother.

"Please, Mum?"

"Well… I don't know. We must ask Majbritt and Malou first."

"Hurray." Runa clapped her hands and jumped up and down and the others laughed at her.

It was late afternoon when they walked through the forest towards Majbritt's farm two days later. Runa came first and was walking more backwards than forwards, stretching her neck to make sure everyone was coming. After her, Olava walked with little brother in her arms. She couldn't help but smile at her eager little sister. Then came Gudrun and Grandmother, each carrying a basket of food, and after them, Anna was walking with Karin and Lukas on each side. They helped her as much as they could, but where the path was narrowest, she had to walk on her own. They were right behind her, though, ready to grab her if she should lose her balance. Slowly but surely they moved ahead and before they knew it, they were there.

Out on the courtyard, the children were running around and playing. When the youngest boy saw Runa and Olava, he ran towards them with his arms in the air, ready for a big hug. The oldest boy, on the other hand, hurried inside and after a few moments, Malou and the other women appeared in the doorway. They walked towards each other a little hesitantly. It was difficult to say who was most nervous to meet the others. Majbritt had seen them from her kitchen window and came out to welcome them as well. This was how it happened that they all met in the middle of the courtyard.

There were a few seconds of confusion as they were all greeting each other, but then everyone became aware of Anna and Malou. They were standing a little to the side, away from the others, facing each other without words, both with their eyes resting mildly on the other. In that moment all boundaries burst and two hearts became one. No one was more or less than the other. It was only two women, touched in the very core of their souls in the meeting with the other. Words were unnecessary. The grateful smiles and the tearful eyes spoke their own language.

A silky soft silence surrounded the little group of people. Everyone was quiet when Anna took a small gift from her bag and handed it to Malou who accepted it a little hesitantly and dried her eyes as she carefully removed the paper. It was a painting of the Virgin Mary with her little child in her arms. Olava knew it well. It used to hang above her mother's bed and she knew that she had gotten it from her own mother. Malou held her right hand to her heart and nodded to Anna in gratitude.

Olava could easily feel her own heart beating as she was standing there among the others. Breathing deeply and calmly, she filled her lungs with air as she let her eyes wander from person to person and all of a sudden it struck her that little brother had several mothers. It was their own mother and Malou, it was Karin and Gudrun, it was Grandmother and Raya, it was Aishe and Nadya, and then there were Runa and herself. Olava smiled a little to herself. If her little brother had many mothers, then he also had a caring and loving father and that was Lukas.

Even many years later, when Olava was a grown

woman, she remembered the episode on Majbritt's courtyard with a rare feeling of gratitude and joy.

It was a night of farewells. Inside the house, the fire crackled merrily in the fireplace. They had set the table and found extra chairs so that there was room for everyone. The men came in from the barn with their instruments and when they had eaten, they began to play and sing. Marko on his accordion, Nanosh on the violin and Stevo and Shandor on their guitar and harmonica. The women played an instrument that Olava had never seen before and Lukas told her that it was a tambourine.

As the twilight fell and the afternoon turned into night, they were all gathered in the warm kitchen, listening to the melancholic tones from the music. The children were dancing until they exhaustedly crawled onto a lap where they fell asleep. Soon it was dark outside and the only light came from the fireplace. Olava knew that she would never forget Malou and her family who had done so much to help them, and there, in the light from the dancing flames, it struck her that these people had the same deep look in their eyes as the horses.

8

Underneath the last traces of snow and ice, the creek chuckles. Joyful tunes sing of spring. The warmth from the sun gives life to the earth. The sun-yellow coltsfoot peeks up from the ground. Happily stretching in ditches and on slopes. The silvery blue anemone mirrors the sky in its adorable dress. New life is emerging everywhere. The forest floor is transformed into a bright green carpet. Heavenly white anemones pop up everywhere. Then the leaves begin to sprout. Silky green buds simmering with life. The long angel wings of the silver birch dancing gracefully in the wind. Two butterflies fly lightly over the meadow. Together they join in the dance of life.

Little brother's new discoveries had no end. He was chattering and talking and every day he discovered new sounds. Sometimes his eyes widened in surprise at hearing his own voice and Olava and the others enjoyed every moment with him. Soon the sounds became little words; "Da, da, da" and "mam, mam". With a little help, he began to roll over, first from his tummy to his back and then back again. He also began to sit by himself without support. After some time he found out how to move by using his arms, to begin with he got more backwards than forwards, this to his own frustration, but then he discovered that he could move forwards by using his legs. Soon he would be rocking back and forth on his hands and knees and after a while his arms and legs began to work together and he learnt to crawl.

A whole new world opened up to Eystein and soon he would be cruising happily around the floor, exploring the kitchen. All the things that he could find in drawers and cupboards were exciting and they had to keep a constant eye on him. After some time, he began to stand up by holding on to the furniture and everyone on the farm was watching the day that he took his first small steps on his own. They were sitting by the breakfast table when Eystein suddenly let go of the bench.

"Look at little brother." It was Olava who first noticed that he was standing by himself. They all became quiet and everyone was watching as he took his first few wobbly steps out on the floor before he fell.

"But Eystein, you can walk." Karin was totally taken by surprise, but then she smiled proudly. Lukas was the only one who looked more at Karin than at Eystein.

"My sweet little child, you are so clever." Grandmother clapped her hands in excitement and looked warmly at her grandchild.

"Did you see that, mummy, little brother can walk." Runa looked expectantly at her mother.

"Yes." Anna nodded and smiled, touched by the little scene. Olava noticed that she wiped her eyes quickly with the palm of her hand.

"Well, I'm sure you'll become a decent worker after all, little man?" Tormod smiled smugly where he was sitting at the end of the table.

Eystein revelled in the attention from the grown-ups and, quick as a lightning flash, he crawled back to the bench to try again. Soon he found his balance and before Eystein turned one, he mastered the art of walking.

With the coming of spring, school started again. Olava had finished seven years' schooling last year, ending with her Confirmation. She felt a bit sorry for Runa, who, every other morning, ran off on her own to the little school house close to the church. Olava remembered last year with dread. She had been able to answer the minister's sharp questions without problems, but she could still remember how she had kept repeating herself out of fear of not passing. In the weeks before the test, she would sometimes wake up in the middle of the night with a nightmare. She was standing in the front of the church and had forgotten a word in a psalm and the minister and all the parents were staring at her with angry eyes. She could still remember the psalms and the stories from the Bible that they had to learn by heart. Sometimes stanzas and lines would pop up in her head, often when she least expected it, as if they were printed in her memory forever.

Spring turned into early summer and the time came when they would take the animals to the mountain farm. Olava would normally go, but this year it was natural that she stayed back at the farm to look after Eystein. He was too little to come along and Gudrun, Lukas and Karin could manage the work on their own. It was decided, however, that Runa could come. She was running around, beside herself from pure joy when she was told, mostly because she knew that now she would have the three grown-ups all to herself for many weeks.

  The farm was situated almost three hours' walk into the mountains, and every summer they brought the cows and the goats so that they could eat from the fresh grass and drink from the clean mountain water. On the first part of the road they walked past two farms, after which they turned and walked along a path through the forest and further up into the mountains. Gradually the forest became thinner, and the higher up they came, the trees were fewer. At some point, it was only the small mountain birch that could survive in the altitude.

There was one place where the path was so narrow that only one animal could pass at a time. On one side there was a steep cliff wall and on the other a deep gorge. There was a story from the time when Olava's great grandfather had run the farm. They had lost a cow which had fallen into the gorge. Lukas and Karin always walked first and stopped the animals long before they had to cross the narrow place. Lukas stayed behind and sent one animal at a time whilst Karin walked ahead and received them on the other side to make sure they continued to walk.

Olava was always a little nervous when they got to the place and, yet, she also found it somehow exciting. When she was younger, Lukas would always carry her on his back over to the other side, but for some years now, she had been old enough to walk by herself.

It was one of the highlights of the year when they were going to the mountain farm, but this year, Olava was happy to stay home. She knew that it wouldn't be the same to be there and that she would be thinking about Eystein all the time. Instead, she enjoyed the mild days back at the farm. Lukas had made a baby swing which he had put up in the big apple tree in the garden and Eystein squealed in delight every time he got a ride. Olava taught him how to put his hands up in the air to show how big he was and she would sing the same children's songs for him that she had learnt when she was little. Eystein listened to her with big eyes and soon he began to clap and move to the familiar melodies. Every time Eystein learnt something new, Olava would show it to her mother. There was always something special about the moments when the three of them were alone in the kitchen and their mother was happy and relaxed.

The tense atmosphere between her parents bothered Olava and it became more obvious now that the others were gone. During the meals they would normally avoid eye contact, and if they finally did talk, it was in a distant, cold tone and only about practical chores around the farm. Sometimes her father would say things to criticise the food or something else Anna had done. They were mostly little, hidden comments or questions.

"Mother, is it not you who has made the potato cakes today?" He knew very well that it was Anna who had made them and it was all it took before the atmosphere around the meal was ruined. Olava cringed when she heard it and Grandmother started to get some of the old tight look on her face again. Anna, on the other hand, tried to ignore most of it and mostly, she avoided answering. But as she got stronger, she could also answer back in her own way. This happened one day at the breakfast table.

"Who made this bread?" Tormod had taken a bite and then put it aside. "I have." Anna sounded friendly at first and pretended as if it were nothing.

"I see."

"Do you not like the food?" Anna sent her husband a quick glance.

"I did not say that." Tormod was immediately on guard and they were quiet for a moment before Anna continued.

"By the way, when is it that you're leaving with the fishing cutter?" It was her way of telling him that she wished he would leave and Tormod knew.

"You know very well that it's not until the fall." He got up.

"Yes, but one can always hope." Anna was completely calm when she said it and Olava could hardly believe her own ears. She had never heard her mother be so direct and rude before and she held her breath out of fear of the consequences. Grandmother was quietly staring at the table-top. And sure enough, Tormod got up from the table and left the room with a furious look on his face. Olava's heart felt heavy as she noticed the cold in her mother's eyes as her father disappeared behind the door.

Tormod's response was a piercing silence that lasted for many days. He walked around like a hungry tiger who had been let out of his cage and whom no one dared to come near. After that episode, it was as if Anna gave up any attempt to answer back to her husband. The consequences were too big and it was easier to keep quiet and avoid confrontations.

A couple of days later, Tormod walked to the mountain farm to get cheese and butter which they made there in the summer. Even though it was mostly Lukas who came down to the farm with supplies, Tormod decided to go. He was gone for two days and for Olava it only got more obvious that her mother was much more relaxed when he was not there. Sometimes she tried to remember what it had been like when her parents were still fond of each other. She could vaguely remember a Christmas Eve many years ago when they hugged each other and one time when they had laughed at something Runa had said, but it seemed such a long time ago.

Olava began to look forward to the day when the others would be back from the mountains and the atmosphere was remarkably lighter the day that they came walking over the courtyard, tanned from the sun and happy, bringing all the animals. The cows and goats were bursting with health and well-being after all those weeks with free pasture.

Eystein turned one and they celebrated the day with cream cake and birthday songs. When they lit the single candle on the cake, they all fell silent. The room filled with the kind of softness that comes when many people share the same thoughts. Karin smiled warmly to Anna whose eyes were wet from tears. Grandmother coughed a couple of times and Gudrun folded her hands under the table. Runa smiled at little brother with sorrowful eyes and Olava had a big lump in her throat.

Lukas searched the room with his eyes and made small talk with Tormod about Storm, who needed shoeing soon. When the light had almost burnt down, Karin took the cake and held it in front of Eystein. They blew at the light to show him what to do, but he was too little to understand. Instead, he planted one hand in the cream and when he tasted it, his face lit up with a surprise of delight. Runa giggled and the others laughed, too. Grandmother quickly found a cloth and cleaned him up. And then, in one, two, three, they all blew at the candle. It was time for cake.

The summer was coming to an end and soon the garden was full of berries and fruits that had to be gathered and made into juice and jam. Olava helped as much as she could, mostly when Eystein was asleep or sat in his swing. Autumn came and Tormod and Lukas were busy with the harvest. Two seasonal workers stayed on the farm for a couple of weeks to help. Autumn turned into winter and Christmas came with lots of snow. Eystein looked in wonder at the shining Christmas tree and could not understand why he was not allowed to touch the glimmer. Christmas Eve he fell asleep in Olava's lap while they were opening presents. Winter turned into spring and Lukas built a soapbox car for Eystein who drove around the courtyard the fastest he could. Spring turned into summer again and Eystein began to talk. Single words became little sentences and soon he could make himself understood.

Everyone on the farm followed Eystein's development with joy and interest. Still, they were all thoroughly tested when he, at the age of two began to throw himself on the floor and scream out loud if things didn't go his way. It took Olava a while to get used to holding him tight on her lap until he stopped kicking and screaming in rage over a seemingly small detail. It was a long period where everyone's patience was tested until Eystein finally understood that it didn't work.

"You can go on the swing again tomorrow, Eystein." Olava held him in her arms while they were standing by the window looking at the swing in the garden.

"Swing swing tomorrow?" Eystein looked sad, but Olava smiled at him and nodded.

"Yes, it's late now and it's time for you to go to bed." She pointed at the window to show him that it was getting dark.

"Sleep now." Eystein had understood that he could not go on the swing anymore that day and then it was time to say goodbye to the others in the kitchen.

"Sleep tight, my dear child." Anna was combing Runa's hair. She got up and kissed him gently on his cheek.

"Nighty nighty, little brother." Runa yawned.

"Good night, my little gold nugget." Grandmother put down her knitting and caressed his head.

"Sleep tight, little troll." Gudrun stroked him gently on his cheek.

"Sweet dreams, little prince." Karin took his hand and smiled warmly.

Then Olava took him into the room and sat him on the changing table where she took off his sweater and trousers.

"Me sleep now?"

"Yes, but first you need a clean nappy." Olava took off his old nappy, washed him and gave him a new one.

"Lala sleep now?"

"Yes, I'm going to bed soon, too." She put on his pyjamas before she lay him in his bed and tucked him in. Eystein hugged his teddy bear and Olava kissed him tenderly on both cheeks and on his forehead. She sat down next to the bed and sang the same song that her mother had always sung for her and Runa when they were little. "I am little, but I will, child of Jesus always be. He can hear and see me, too, when I pray." Eystein was so tired that he was nearly asleep when Olava tiptoed out of the room and closed the door quietly after her.

The seasons came and went and the bond between Olava and Eystein grew stronger. Together the two of them would lie in the tall summer grass, arms and legs stretched, finding figures in the pearly white clouds in the sky. A long fish, a dangerous troll, a big teddy bear. When the forest was full of blue berries, they would walk for hours, eating the juicy berries until they were full. Together they would run outside when the first snow fell. With their faces turned towards the sky, they would turn round and round, trying to catch the feathery light snowflakes with their tongues.

Christmas Eve morning they would tiptoe quietly out to the barn with a big wooden plate of porridge which they placed in the hay by the far wall. And quite right, when they went to check the next morning if Father Christmas had been there and eaten it all, the plate was empty. Olava almost felt a little guilty at Eystein's big, surprised eyes when he saw the empty plate and when he, with great enthusiasm, told the others in the kitchen.

Together they would spend time in the stalls with the horses, patting their muzzles whilst talking to them softly. Sometimes when Olava was riding Odin, Eystein would sit in front of her, at first a few slow rounds in the courtyard, and later they would take longer trips in nature. Olava taught Eystein to climb trees and often they would sit in their favourite tree, a gigantic willow, singing and laughing. Together they would walk in the spring forest, picking flowers for their mum.

Anna was always happy for the flowers and she'd put them in a vase on the table so that everyone could see how pretty they were. Eystein was never disappointed by the joy of giving. Eystein and Olava also had their own secret place with lots of little, wild strawberries which they ate in the heat from the first summer sun. Sometimes they would put them on long straws which they took home and shared with the others, but they never told anyone about their secret strawberry place.

The day came when Olava turned 17. Eystein had seemed very secretive in the days before her birthday and sometimes Olava was not allowed to come along if he and Lukas were in the barn. She pretended as if she didn't understand anything but was aware that they were up to something. On the day itself they celebrated with cream cake and birthday songs in the afternoon as they were used to and when it was time for Olava to open her presents, Eystein was standing in front of her, a little shy, hiding his arms behind his back. She looked at him with a gleam in her eye.

"I wonder what you've got there?"

"Choose one hand." Eystein smiled bright in anticipation.

"I choose that one." Olava pointed at the right one.

"Wrong." Eystein showed her an empty hand.

"Okay, then I would like that one." Olava pointed at the other, but Eystein was quick and showed her another empty hand.

"Oh no." Olava pretended as if she was giving up and Eystein laughed happily.

"Try again, try again." He jumped in anticipation.

"Nooo, I'm not sure I want to." She hung back.

"Yes, yes, try again."

"Okay then… that one there." Olava pointed again and this time there was a small present in Eystein's hand. It was beautifully wrapped with a ribbon tied on top.

"Is that really for me?" Olava looked at Eystein in surprise and he nodded eagerly. He gave her the present and she opened it carefully. First she pulled both ends of the ribbon and then she removed the paper. Inside the present there was a little necklace with a leather cord. It was made of wood and had the shape of a heart. Olava held it in her hand and looked at it in wonder.

"But Eystein… is it really for me?" She hardly knew what to say.

"Yes, Lukas helped me." Eystein smiled happily.

"Not much, and it was Eystein's idea." Lukas patted Eystein's hair and winked at Olava.

"It is beautiful." She was still admiring the necklace and then she smiled at Eystein. "Come here, my dear." He crawled into the lap of his big sister and got a warm hug. "Thank you so very, very much, it's the best gift I have ever had."

While the others praised Eystein for the beautiful gift, Olava slipped the necklace around her neck. She wore it every day for the rest of her life.

One late winter evening after Eystein had fallen asleep, Olava went out to the horses, something she still did when she wanted time to herself. She went from stall to stall, making small talk with all of them before she went into the barn and lay down in the hay by the far wall. She was chewing absently on a straw when Karin and Lukas all of a sudden came tiptoeing through the door from the stalls and closed it quietly behind them. She was just about to get up, but there was something in the way they were giggling and laughing that made her lie absolutely still. With a mixture of surprise and dismay, she saw how they were standing close, holding each other's hands.

Her heart was beating fast in her chest when they closed their eyes and their lips met in a kiss. At first gently, but then long and dearly. Olava turned away. It felt so wrong that she should see this. The two people that she cared so much about. They were lovers. Her eyes filled with tears. She looked up again and to her horror, Lukas' arm disappeared behind Karin's blouse and up her back. "Oh no, not that." Olava was lying absolutely quiet, thinking about the cows and the ox in the field in spring. It must not happen. Karin sighed heavily and Olava's heart was beating fast. What was she going to do if they... oh... no. Olava knew the words from the boys in school, but it felt so wrong to think about those words now. Soundlessly, she lay down, hiding her face in the hay and covering her ears with her hands. She prayed dearly that they would stop.

In the time after the episode in the barn, Olava acted as if nothing had happened, but still she tried to avoid Karin and Lukas. Even though they had never got further than kissing that night, Olava felt as if she knew a secret which was not hers and, in a way, she felt ashamed. A few times Karin and Lukas looked at her questioningly, and maybe, they guessed what had happened because it wasn't long before they made a surprising announcement.

It was Lukas who got up at the table one evening some time before Easter. They had just finished eating supper.

"I have something to say." He rushed his hand through his hair and down his neck. "Karin and I..." He paused and took Karin's hand. They smiled warmly at each other and Lukas looked at Karin when he continued. "Karin and I, we're getting married." Everyone was staring at the two.

"Are you getting married?" Runa was the first to speak and she sounded very happy.

"But?" Grandmother, on the other hand, looked utterly puzzled.

"Yes, we're getting married in the spring." Karin's eyes were radiating.

"This spring?" Grandmother sounded confused.

"Yes." Karin nodded happily.

"Congratulations, both of you. You deserve all the best." Anna smiled, touched.

"Thank you." Karin sent her a grateful smile.

"Congratulations." Olava wanted to say something as well, but it was difficult for her to find the words.

"Thank you, Olava." Karin tilted her head to the side and looked almost a little sad when she smiled at Olava. Lukas, on the other hand, winked at her. Olava smiled a little. She didn't know if she had managed to seem surprised at the news. She had guessed that they would tell them all at some point and most of all, she was relieved that she didn't have to keep the secret to herself any more. She also noticed that Gudrun didn't seem very surprised, either. Maybe she knew about Karin and Lukas, too.

"In the spring?" Tormod hadn't spoken until now, but he didn't seem overly surprised.

"Yes. After we've ploughed and seeded." Lukas had already thought about that.

"I see." Tormod smiled a little. "You are, of course, very welcome to have the wedding here." Karin and Lukas looked at each other and Karin nodded.

"Thank you, we would love that." She smiled at Tormod.

"And I want to give you a piece of land as a wedding gift if you want to build your own house." Everyone around the table looked at Tormod in surprise, as if they wanted to make sure they had heard him right.

Grandmother looked bewildered, maybe most of all because she had not been asked about such an important decision when it came to the family farm. Anna looked surprised as well, but only for a short moment, before she smiled and nodded a little to herself. Olava looked at her father. She felt a kindness towards him that she hadn't felt in a long time. Karin and Lukas, on the other hand, seemed to be completely bewildered and their eyes met as if they were trying to communicate without words.

"But... it is all too much. Thank you so much." Karin looked from Lukas to Tormod and to Lukas again.

"Thank you." Lukas had a worried frown between his eyes and looked down." It's just that... we're going to America." It was silent as the grave around the table.

"America?" Gudrun looked horrified.

"Is that far away?" Runa looked serious.

"Yes, my dear, it's far away." Anna answered Runa, but looked mostly at Karin and Lukas. Runa began to cry and Anna held her close.

Olava couldn't believe it. Getting married was one thing, but going to America? She knew that there were others from the community who had gone. The big ship sailed from the city and she had heard that the trip took many days, maybe weeks, and that it was expensive. She also knew that many never came back. She began to stare emptily out of the window.

"America?" Gudrun was still speechless.

"Yes." Karin nodded to her friend and was close to crying.

"When are you leaving?" Tormod sounded unaffected, but his heavily bent shoulders revealed something else.

"We'll be leaving this summer." It was obvious in the way Lukas spoke that the decision was final.

"I see. I want you to know that you are always welcome back. The offer will always hold good." It was the greatest acknowledgement they would ever get from Tormod and they knew.

"Thank you." Lukas nodded seriously.

"Thank you so much." Karin began to cry and Lukas held his arm around her. The others could only stare at the two. The way Karin let Lukas comfort her whilst crying at his shoulder was the only explanation they needed.

"If we make waffles when you're getting married, then you won't cry anymore, will you, Karin?" Eystein had a serious look in his eyes. He had been listening quietly to the grown-ups and observed what had happened around the table. Now he came with his own solution to the problem. It resulted in hearty laughter, but it made Karin cry even more.

The wedding was held on one of those spring days when heaven and earth merge together on the horizon and when the calm pulse of the soul beats in every living being. Karin was wearing a lovely, silky white dress, which in all its simplicity made her shine like the mild spring sun. She had made it herself and Lukas could hardly take his eyes from her. A small wreath made of fresh spring flowers lit up her face and Eystein whispered to Olava that he thought she looked like a princess. He was sitting next to his big sister in the church and found it a little difficult to sit still while the minister gave a speech about the obligations of marriage.

The more he spoke, the more Karin smiled, and

in the end, he looked at her firmly and described in sharp phrases what the consequences had been when Eve lured Adam to eat of the apple. But Karin only shone more and it didn't seem as if Lukas heard one word of what was being said. Finally, the minister was done and Karin and Lukas gave each other their "Yes."

Majbritt was there with her sons and she looked at Karin almost as much as Lukas did. The immediate happiness between the two people awoke a distant memory from her past. When they were gathered outside the church after the ceremony, she came over to congratulate them. Olava and Eystein were standing nearby with their mother.

"What you have together. Remember that every day is a gift." Karin and Lukas became aware of the sincerity in Majbritt's words and knew that she spoke from experience.

"Yes, Majbritt, we... will." Karin looked thoughtfully at Majbritt and nodded slowly. She dried her eyes.

"Thank you, Majbritt." Lukas put his arm around Karin and smiled warmly. Olava noticed that her own mother bent her head, her face was calm but sad.

"We'll miss you." Majbritt spoke in a low voice as if not to disturb the joy on a day like this.

"We'll miss you, too." Karin looked sincerely at Majbritt and they gave each other a hug.

"We hope to be back one day." Lukas shook Majbritt's hand gently.

"Yes, I hope you will, too." Majbritt smiled. Then she walked home with her boys.

The time after the wedding went fast. Everyone

knew that the parting day came closer but no one mentioned it with one word. In the days before Karin and Lukas were to leave, everyone found themselves walking around in a vacuum. They were polite and considerate to each other, in fact, almost gentle, so that no one should trigger the endless grief they all felt. Tormod spent much time by himself, but one night he suggested that they should all go to the city to say goodbye.

Per and Berit were the new employees and even though they had only been with them for a few days, Tormod was sure they could manage the farm while they were gone. Grandmother said that she would stay home and look after Eystein. The moment she had said it, she pulled out a handkerchief from her apron and dried her eyes.

Olava wept bitterly the day at the harbour when they were waving goodbye to Karin and Lukas. They were standing by the railing of the big ship together with hundreds of other people seeking their fortune on the strange continent. Olava was standing close together with the others on the crowded harbour. Gudrun, Anna and Runa cried, too. Tormod was the only one who didn't cry, but he avoided looking at the others and didn't say one word while they were standing there. After what seemed like a long time, the ship sailed. Karin and Lukas were standing close while they waved and Olava could see that Karin was crying. She wondered if she would ever see them again, but tried to push the thought away. It was unbearable.

9

Everything is simmering with life. The bumblebee flies from flower to flower. Melting together with the flow of summer nectar. The sun touches all life with its warming rays. The grass blinks cheerfully in the light. Caressed by the gentle breath of wind. Quiet puffs rushing through the tree crowns. Silky soft clouds, hand in hand in the sky. Linking eternity. The enchantment of the long summer nights. Heaven and Earth breathing together. The warm, velvety nights. Only the Northern Star is a tear in the sky.

It was quiet on the farm in the days after Karin and Lukas had left. They had promised to write as soon as they could, but it was scant consolation. Weeks could pass, maybe months, before they heard from them and it wouldn't change anything. They were not there anymore and even though they had said that they would come back one day, no one knew when or if it would be to stay. They hadn't made any promises and it was no good to hope in vain.

In the following days, Olava often went out to the stalls to spend time with the horses and be alone with her thoughts. A few times she managed to sneak out so that Eystein didn't see her, but most times he would come along. Olava didn't have the heart to say no and in a way it was good that he was there. He talked and played like he used to and made Olava forget about her loss, at least for a while.

Per and Berit quickly became part of the daily rhythm on the farm. They neither could nor wanted to replace Karin and Lukas, but as time passed, they won a place in everyone's heart. Per proved to be quite an acrobat and impressed everyone with his tricks. He could do a perfect cartwheel and a handstand without losing his balance. Runa was the one who was most eager to learn and she could practice for hours in the garden. Eystein found it exciting, too, and with the help from Olava, he could do both a cartwheel and a handstand.

Berit was a little shy to begin with, but after some time, she proved to be a master in the kitchen. She could make the most delicious meals and she loved to mix and cook, swing the casserole spoon, taste the gravy and experiment with new recipes. Olava followed her work with interest, especially if she was baking cakes. Both Gudrun and Anna were grateful for the unexpected help. Grandmother was a little sceptical to start with and it was probably the words of praise from Tormod that in the end made her accept the new times in the kitchen.

Berit was also given the title of world champion in pancake baking. It happened one afternoon in the kitchen as they were gathered around the table, enjoying the pancakes she had made. They were perfectly baked, thin and delicate and tasty. Eystein had his mouth full of food when he suddenly exclaimed that they were the best pancakes in the world. The laughter around the table had a freeing effect and Berit smiled happily. As the days passed, they all realized that life continued without Karin and Lukas and slowly the loss felt less painful.

Summer came and it was time to take the animals to the mountains again. It was the year that Eystein turned 5 and for the first time, it was decided that he could come. Last year he and Olava had gone with their father and stayed there for a couple of days, but this year they would be there the whole summer with Gudrun, Runa, Per and Berit. Olava had stayed on the farm for four summers to look after Eystein and now she was looking forward to spending time in the mountains with him. Eystein remembered the mountain farm well from last year and was eager to go. When they had to postpone the trip due to much rain, he was greatly disappointed. In the end, he placed himself by the window whilst looking out on the pouring rain with a serious look on his face. Then he walked over to Olava with firm steps.

"Who is in charge of the weather?" Eystein was standing with his arms crossed and Olava was careful not to laugh. The question was seriously meant, but inside she was smiling.

"In charge of the weather? She didn't always know what to say when Eystein asked one of his wondrous questions. She paused a little before she answered. "It's no one really who decides what the weather will be like. It just is the way it is." Eystein looked as if he accepted the answer but didn't look happy at all.

"Are you excited about going?" Olava smiled at him.

"Mmm…" He nodded.

"Me, too, and as soon as the rain has stopped, we'll go."

"The rain is stupid." Eystein looked disappointed and Olava looked mildly at her little brother.

"But the rain also makes everything grow so that the animals can have something to eat." Eystein looked a little puzzled and Olava took him on her lap. She remembered how their mother had once explained it to her and Runa and now she passed it on to Eystein.

"Everything we eat comes from nature and it needs both rain and sun to grow. When the grass grows in the earth, the cows get something to eat, and from them we get milk which we use to make cheese and butter. When the grain grows in the fields, we get flour so that we can make pancakes." Eystein listened to Olava with big, questioning eyes.

"I think maybe I like the rain anyway." He pulled his shoulders up to his ears, bent his head back and smiled from ear to ear.

"That's good my clever little brother." Olava laughed and gave him a warm hug. From the kitchen table Anna was watching the two. She held her right hand over her heart and smiled, touched.

"Yes, it's just like us humans. We also need sun and rain to grow." Olava looked at her mother and nodded slowly. She hid the words somewhere in the treasure chest of her memory which she was going to open many years later.

Three days later, the sun came out and they could finally leave. Anna was standing in the courtyard waving goodbye as they left. Eystein turned around many times and waved back. He wasn't feeling too safe among the big cows and kept close to Olava making sure he held her hand. Olava turned around, too, and waved. For a short moment she felt a twinge of guilt at the sight of her mother standing alone, but Anna was smiling happily and the feeling disappeared.

They enjoyed the trip to the mountains. Eystein walked the whole way by himself without getting tired and they all praised him. When they could see the farm, he began to run, but he didn't let go of Olava's hand, so she ran, too, and Runa followed. Olava had a wonderful feeling of peace at the sight of the familiar houses, the calm lake surrounded by the fertile valley with the fresh grass and the majestic mountains in the background.

Everything was the way it used to be. The log cabin where they lived with three little rooms, a cosy kitchenette and a small living room with a fireplace. The barn with the stalls for the animals. The little wooden house where they made cheese and butter called the creamery. The little boat house down by the lake and the outdoor toilet with room for two people. The adult animals felt at home right away and began to graze in the area. The calves were jumping and dancing out of pure joy at the unexpected freedom.

The days in the mountains were a welcome respite from the life on the farm even though they had to work hard much of the time. The animals needed milking morning and evening and sometimes they had to go look for them. After the milking, the milk had to be sieved and put into pails, cups and plates. Then they had to make butter and cheese. The equipment had to be cleaned regularly in the creek that ran into the lake and every now and then they had to do all this without Per when he was down on the farm with the finished food products.

When Olava was milking the animals, Eystein would often sit next to her and observe. A couple of times, he tried to milk one of the goats, but although he got a little braver each day, he didn't dare to touch the cows.

They swam in the lake, did gymnastics on the grass and played hide and seek. Sometimes they went with Per out in the boat to catch fish which they cooked on the fire the same night. Olava showed Eystein how to make a farm using stones, sticks and cones. He spent several days building a huge farm with almost a hundred different animals. He showed it proudly to the others and was almost inconsolable when one of the cows stepped on the farm and ruined it. Olava tried to comfort him the best she could, but nothing helped. It was not until she helped him build a new one that he got happy again. One day followed another and in a way it was as if time stood still.

Just a few days before they would go back to the farm, a storm began to brew. The dark clouds in the sky warned of the approaching rain, wind and possible thunder. They had to gather the animals and get them into the stalls before it all broke loose. Olava and Eystein had to go and look for one of the goats who used to go some distance away from the farm. They walked along the path and down towards the river whilst scouting in all directions. Eystein was jumping happily next to his big sister and tried to copy her by holding his hands over his eyes while looking in all directions with a serious look in his eyes.

"Kamma. Kammma." Olava began to call.

"Kamma, kamma. Where are you, little goat? We cannot find you, sweet little Kamma goat." Eystein was singing more than calling and Olava laughed. They walked for some time whilst calling and scouting.

"Look!" It was Eystein who saw her first. He pointed eagerly towards the other side of the river where Kamma was standing on the hillside eating from the fresh green grass.

"Kamma!" Olava called, but the goat didn't

react.

"Kamma, Kamma!" They called together, but Kamma continued to eat without taking any notice of them.

"I have to go and get her." Olava looked around. There wasn't that much water in the river, but it was steep here, almost two meters straight down to the water and many stones and rocks. She wouldn't be able to get over here.

"Come." Olava took Eystein's hand and walked a little further down to a place where there was a huge stone. It was so big that it made it possible for her to jump over. The place was called "the leap."

"Wait here, I just need to go and get Kamma." Eystein nodded happily and sat down by some rocks a little further down. He began to play and Olava smiled at him. "Be careful of the edge. I'll be back in a few minutes." Then she jumped over to the other side.

It only took a few minutes to get Kamma, but when Olava came back, Eystein was gone. She smiled a little to herself. He had probably hidden somewhere. She began to call his name, but got no answer. Then she began to look behind the nearest bushes and trees, but he was nowhere to be found. When the first raindrops fell, she called out loud that they didn't have time to play, but he didn't answer. She couldn't understand it. Had he hidden so far away? The nearby bushes were the most natural hiding place, but he was not there. Olava looked in all directions whilst calling his name. Where could he be? Had he run back to the farm? No, why would he do that? Olava stood completely still for a moment when something made her go down to the rocks where he had been sitting. She was puzzled whilst searching for clues when all of a sudden she noticed something moving between the rocks. She got a shock when she saw that it was the tail of a viper. Instinctively she pulled back and nearly stumbled and fell. A wave of fear flushed through her. Had Eystein seen the snake and panicked? The rocks. They were so close to the edge. Then she saw him. In a split second she was paralysed. The fear felt like an iron grip on her heart. He was lying completely still.

Without thinking Olava jumped out into the river and was by his side in a few seconds. She pulled him up and turned him around. His clothes were completely wet and he was so pale. Eystein was bleeding from a wound in his head. She knelt by his side and put her ear towards his heart. Olava could not feel his pulse. His body was heavy and unmoving. She had to stay calm, but inside she was fighting against insanity. She fumbled helplessly over his small body. Breathed air through his mouth. Pushed his chest. Again and again and again. Olava didn't know for how long she tried to revive him. Finally she hid her face in her hands and screamed. She hit her own head with all her power. Put her face down into the cold water to stay sane.

Then Olava disappears to a place where everything is peaceful. Everything around her melts together. Eystein is so beautiful. She takes his head carefully with both hands and puts it in her lap. She caresses his hair and cheeks gently. She takes his hand and squeezes it softly. She holds him close to her body. Close, close, close while she's rocking him to and fro. Her own little brother. She sits like this until the storm breaks loose. She must go home to her mother. She lifts him up in her arms, carefully. Then she begins to walk the long way back to the farm.

Time and place do not matter. She takes no notice of Eystein's weight. The rain and the wind grow stronger, but she cannot feel it. She sings. For her little brother and for herself.

When Olava got back on the farm, she fell down from exhaustion in the courtyard. She continued to hold Eystein in her arms. The following minutes were like a bad dream, a nightmare. It was their mother who saw them fist. Her screams made their father and grandmother come running. The panic and the shock cut deep scars in Olava's heart. Still, she was the only one who couldn't cry.

The dream continued. The others came down from the mountains. They did not understand what had happened until they saw Eystein with their own eyes. He was lying in his bed with his hands over the quilt. His face was calm and peaceful. They took turns watching over him. Olava did not move from his side and didn't sleep for two nights. Tormod came into the chamber many times, but left almost immediately. Runa couldn't stop crying. Gudrun did her best to comfort her. Anna cried and prayed, lit candles and prayed. Grandmother cried. Per and Berit did their best to take care of all the practical chores on the farm. The minister came. Together they gathered around Eystein's bed. They prayed and cried. Olava had a feeling of being outside everything that happened. The only thing she really noticed was that her father didn't look at her at all.

Olava was watching over Eystein the second day when Anna came in. She hardly noticed that her mother looked pale and thin and that her eyes were red and swollen. She sat down and caressed Eystein's cheek with her hand.

"Olava?"

"Yes." Olava looked quickly at her mother through a veil of tears.

"Have you cried at all?"

"No." Olava shrugged her shoulders a little.

"Olava? There is something I want to tell you." Her mother sounded serious and Olava tried to listen when she continued. "There are certain bonds that can never break. Not even in death." Olava looked at her mother, but didn't understand what she was talking about. Anna dried her eyes and now her voice was a gentle whisper. "There is a bond between you and your little brother. Between you and Eystein. It will always be there."

"Okay..." Olava smiled faintly, but her mother's words didn't matter. They were only words.

The funeral in the church. Everyone paralysed by grief. Quiet crying everywhere. The minister's speech. Eystein who was with his Father in Heaven. Majbritt who supported Anna on the way out to the grave. Tormod with his head bent. Grandmother's face, apathetic from grief. Gudrun who held Runa who was crying and crying. Olava who walked by herself and who shied away if anyone tried to come close. The minister's words by the grave. The soil on the coffin. The whole community who was there. The uncertainty in some eyes, the sympathy in others. The brief handshakes and the hesitant words after the ceremony. Anna's words by the grave before they went home. "Thank you for all your joy. I will see you, my son." Majbritt by her side. Their crying.

The heart-breaking silence when they came home.

10

The fog hangs like heavy curtains. Shivering ghostly in the scanty wind. A dim silence hides in the mist. The darkness overshadows all light. Dense clouds hanging near the water surface. Drinking and rising up. The wind shows its power. Rips and tears in everything. Leaden grey clouds massive in the sky. The rain hammering down. Little beings bend their heads. Some succumb to the heavy forces. Threatening sounds in the distance. Then the furious roar. The shining scar in the sky strikes the tallest tree. Creating deep wounds.

Olava opened the front door carefully and walked soundlessly into the hallway. She had been wandering aimlessly around in the forest for hours without noticing either time nor place. It was way past bedtime and she was surprised to see that there was still light in the kitchen. Through the crack in the door, she could see her mother and father. Her father was standing by the window with his back to her mother.

"You must not do this." Olava stiffened when she heard her mother's voice. The sound of unfathomable despair scared her most.

"Do what!" Her father remained in the same position.

"You must not do this to her."

"What do you mean!" He sounded cold and dismissive.

"Won't you please talk to her. She is hurting so much…"

"It is difficult for all of us." He sounded angry.

"But she is completely broken… and you are rejecting her."

"What do you mean?"

"You do not talk to her and you do not look at her."

"HE IS DEAD. DON'T YOU UNDERSTAND?" His voice shivered.

"But she… Olava… she loved him." Olava's eyes filled with tears at her mother's words.

"She was supposed to look after him."

"Tormod… it was an accident. She has always looked after him. Don't you understand… This is ruining her."

"She left him and let him sit by the river by himself. There is nothing more to say." In the hallway Olava bent her head and closed her eyes.

"NO! OH GOD. IT'S NOT HER FAULT. TORMOD!" Her mother sounded desperate now.

"Be quiet!" Her father's voice was low and threatening.

"YOU MUST NOT DO THIS. DON'T YOU UNDERSTAND? SHE CANNOT TAKE IT ANYMORE."

"You are behaving like a mad woman. You need help." It sounded almost like a neutral statement. It was quiet in there for a moment.

"Yes, you are right. If I am to live with you, I need help." It was scary to hear the little laughter in her mother's voice when she answered.

"I am warning you." Her father's voice was ominously low.

"She loved him more than life itself."

"BE QUIET, DO YOU HEAR!" He turned around. His face was hard as stone. He grabbed Anna's hands and shook her.

"Tormod, it hurts. LET GO!" The pain in her mother's voice.

"WE WILL NOT TALK ABOUT THIS ANYMORE. DO YOU UNDERSTAND!?"

"I AM BEGGING YOU. YOU MUST NOT DO THIS." Her mother was crying.

"BE QUIET!" Her father was furious.

"No! I will not be quiet, not this time... You are ruining your family."

"AAAHHHH!" Unaware of his own strength, Tormod threw Anna over the kitchen floor. Olava's heart was hammering in her chest, but she froze on the spot. From her hiding place behind the door, she got a glimpse of her mother. She was lying on the floor with her hands before her face and cried. When she spoke again, she sounded almost mild.

"There will always be an unbreakable bond of love between those two children. Nothing is stronger than that. Nothing you say or do can ever destroy that."

"She has to leave. The sooner the better." Her father walked towards the door, but although Anna was shaky, she managed to get up and stood in his way. Her voice was trembling with anger.

"I curse the devil that lives in you, Tormod. Do you hear me?" She squeezed the words out through her clenched teeth. "DO YOU HEAR WHAT I'M SAYING? I CURSE THE DEVIL THAT LIVES IN YOU." She was shouting now.

"I AM WARNING YOU." Her father sounded threatening and he tried to pass Anna, but she moved so that he couldn't get past her.

"I CURSE THE DEVIL THAT LIVES IN YOU, TORMOD."

Olava didn't see it, but the sound of the blow

and the thump on the floor told her what happened. She had a sickening feeling in her stomach. She had to get away, but it was too late. Halfway up the stairs, the door to the kitchen opened with a bang. Olava backed away when their eyes met. Her father's eyes wavered in despair.

"THIS IS ALL YOUR FAULT." He tore open the front door and walked out. The words hit Olava like a deadly lightning. She was paralysed with only one thought in her head. If only she were dead. She walked up the stairs in a daze, but stopped outside the room. Runa was asleep in there. She had to be quiet. How strange. Someone was walking in the hallway downstairs. Was it mother? Now the front door opened. Olava walked quietly into the room and over to the window. It was her mother. She stumbled as she walked with one hand on her head. In the middle of the courtyard she stopped. Olava was staring at her mother. The pain and the grief was written in both their faces.

The wind tore at Anna. The rain whipped against her. But she didn't notice. She took her wedding ring off her finger. Held it in her hand for a moment. Stared at it. Then she threw it away with all her strength. She stumbled. Fell to her knees. Bent her head. Her arms were hanging limply at her sides. Then she lifted her face towards the sky. Slowly. The sound of pain from a bottomless pit and grief. Her eyes wild like a wounded animal. Again and again she screamed. Slow, terrible sounds from the bottom of her soul.

A tear found its way down Olava's cheek, but she was unable to move. Every cell in her body was filled with fear and horror. She had heard the same sounds once before. It was the night when Eystein was born.

"What is it with Mum?" Olava hadn't noticed that Runa was awake until all of a sudden she was standing next to her. Runa rubbed her eyes, at first a little puzzled.

"She..." Olava didn't know what to say, but the sight of their mother spoke for itself.

"MOTHER!?" Runa rushed out of the room.

"Wait." But Olava's voice was only a whisper and Runa was already on her way down the stairs. From the window Olava could see that her little sister ran out to their mother.

"MOTHER!" Runa yelled, but her mother took no notice of her.

"MOTHER! MOTHER!" She yelled with all her strength, but Anna was in another world. A world of unfathomable grief and pain.

"MOTHER, MOTHER, MOTHER!!!" Runa grabbed her mother's shoulders and shook her and now Anna looked at her daughter. Then she bent her head towards the ground and cried helplessly. Runa sat down on her knees in front of her. She was crying as she put one hand uncertainly on her mother's arm. Then they held each other tight and cried together.

Olava pretended as if she was asleep when Anna and Runa came in a little later. Runa was crying soundlessly when she took off her soaking wet clothes and lay down in her bed. Their mother whispered a few comforting words to her and tucked her in. Then they sang the goodnight prayer silently together and said goodnight.

"Goodbye Mum." Olava whispered the words softly to herself when Anna left the room and closed the door behind her.

She stayed awake until everything was quiet in

the house and she was certain that Runa was asleep. When she sat up on her bed, she was staring emptily out into the air for some time. Then she got up, took a bag from the closet and packed some of her clothes and her savings. When she had finished, she walked over to Runa's bed and stood there for some time looking at her. Little sister. A wave of grief flushed over her, but she held back her tears.

"Goodbye..." She bent over Runa and whispered in her ear. Runa moved a little but continued to sleep safely. Olava walked quietly out of the room and down the stairs. She walked soundlessly and quickly into the kitchen and took some bread and a bottle of water. In the hallway she put on her shoes and jacket. Then she walked out of the door of her childhood home.

It took a long time before Olava's eyes got used to the darkness. The rain had stopped, but the wind was still strong, and not until a bright shining moon could be seen behind a fleeing storm cloud, was she able to see the path that she was walking. On the hilltop towards the north, the church towered like a silhouette towards the living sky. The sight of the dark building frightened her and she avoided looking at it. Instead she began to find flowers that were growing along the path. One by one she picked them until she had a beautiful bouquet. She walked slowly. The weariness was almost a blessing. Now and then she stopped and listened. It was as if the silence blocked out the wind.

Finally she was by the church. It seemed even more frightening now that she was close by. She looked around to all sides. The small gate into the cemetery creaked as she opened it. While she walked slowly, her eyes wandered from one headstone to another. So many names.

Olava stopped a few meters from Eystein's grave, almost as if she was waiting for someone. It was the first time she had come here since the funeral. The grave was covered with soil and the headstone was up. Slowly she walked closer. Both hands holding the bouquet with the wild flowers. By the grave she stopped and paused. Then she knelt. She read the words carved in the stone. Her hand was trembling slightly when she caressed his name. Eystein. Gently she took the flowers, one by one, and put them on the grave. She took some soil in her hands. Sensed it between her fingers. Closed her eyes and felt the scent from it. Caressed her face with it. First her cheeks, then her chin, her mouth, eyes and forehead. Then she put her head on the earth.

"Goodbye, little brother." She was whispering.

Then Olava went into the darkness.

PART II

11

In the darkness old fears awaken. The shadows of the night grow large. The mist moves slowly over the water. A veil of tears covering the ocean. The silence from the depths. A brutal hope of peace. Dark clouds fleeing from the wind. Escaping without any goal. Silencing the moon's gentle light. Hiding all stars. A lonely bird flies high above. Each beat of the wing a soft goodbye.

Olava had only one thought in her head as she walked from the church downhill towards the boat house. She had to get away. As far away as possible. The thought was the only safe point for her now. The only thing that could make her stand upright. A kind of hope. Like a numbing veil around her heart. It was as if she was walking in an unreal dream. If only she could be far enough away, then maybe she could forget

The boat house looked lonely and abandoned where it stood, close by the water's edge. Immovable in all kinds of weather. Gazing peacefully at the horizon. Olava stopped by the little stone steps in front of the door. The silence was so strange and everything looked different in the darkness. She let her eyes wander from the little, narrow path leading up to the house, to the large, flat stone by the wall. The old gnarled tree trunk by the water's edge surrounded by seaweed and mussels. Every little bush and stone. She knew the place so well, but in the darkness, everything seemed to be a shadow of itself.

    The last time she had been here was earlier in the summer, some time after Karin and Lukas had gone. They had been out fishing with a net, Eystein, Per and herself. Eystein had been sitting next to her in the back of the boat telling her a story about a huge fish that lived down in the water. She had been listening to him with big eyes while Per was rowing the boat and smiling at them. Olava closed her eyes and the memory disappeared. She felt a sickness rise up within her. Stumbling she found the wall with one hand and very carefully she glided down on the stone step. She tried to control the feeling of sickness by breathing deeply and slowly, but she couldn't stop it. Crouched forward with her hand on her forehead, she threw up. Over and over again until she was completely empty. Afterwards she sat completely still with her head in her hands, dizzy and exhausted. The nausea was gone, but her head still felt heavy. She took a handful of soil and put it on her forehead and slowly she began to feel better. She couldn't stay here. She had to move on. Her legs were trembling when she got up and it took her some time to find her balance. Then she lifted the solid hook of the door and went into the boat house.

    The darkness was heavy in the small house. Olava knew that there was a kerosene lamp on the table in the corner and she fumbled her way through the dark. She found the matchbox and after several attempts, she managed to light the lamp with the wet matches. In the glow of the light she could see that the boat was lying the way it used to, leaning over to one side. The oars were standing by the wall and the net and other fishing gear was placed over the beams in the ceiling. She walked past the boat and opened the doors in the gable that were facing the water. The wind was quieting down and the last remaining fog was about to disappear. The moon looked out from behind the scattered clouds, half full and surrounded by little, shiny stars here and there.

Olava remained standing in the doorway for a while gazing towards the other side. She had no plan, but if she managed to get into town, she might be able to travel further by ship or horse carriage. It felt all wrong to take the boat, but she had to move on. The walk around the fjord would take at least two days. If she moored it by Aunt Barbro and Uncle Knut's boat house, they would find it later. She was certain about this. Maybe her father would get mad. She lowered her shoulders at the thought of that but pushed it away. She didn't have the strength to think about that now. Had to move on.

Olava knew well what to do to get the boat on the water. She had done it many times before, never all by herself, though. She put the bottom stopper in the hole and fastened the oarlocks on the sides. Then she placed the oars on the planks of the boat. She paused for a while, uncertain what to do. There was a thick, woollen carpet and a tarpaulin on the shelf under the roof. Should she take it with her? Her conscience said no, but her reason told her it might get cold. Maybe even very cold. She decided to take it. With quick movements she took the tarpaulin and the carpet from the shelf and put it in the front of the boat together with her bag.

Normally there would be at least two people to push the solid wooden boat out on the water. Fortunately, it was ebb tide, so if she could only get it out of the house, it was almost in the water. Olava began to push, but the boat hardly moved. She pushed again, but it was almost as if it was stuck. Olava's hope began to vanish. Everything seemed so impossible. For a moment she considered whether she had to give up. But no. The boat had to get out.

Olava clenched her teeth and pushed with all her strength. Slowly but surely, centimeter by centimeter, the boat glided over the wooden beams in the floor. Every muscle in her body was tight, the sweat ran down her face and with one last effort, the boat was out and in the water. Olava grabbed the rope in the boat and tied it to the hook on the outer wall. Exhausted after the effort, she sat down for a while to rest. In a way it felt good to be completely drained.

When she had caught her breath and rested for a while, she went back inside the boat house and closed the doors in the gable. The kerosene lamp was still lit and she walked over to the corner and sat down on her knees by the table. As she turned the knob, she followed the flame with her eyes as it slowly vanished. When it was completely gone, the house was again engulfed in darkness. Olava walked out the small door and put the hook back on. Then she loosened the rope from the hook on the wall and walked out on the big stones in the water while she carefully pulled the boat a little closer to herself. With one foot on the planks in the back of the boat and the other on one of the stones, she pushed to get away from land. She found her balance, sat down on the thwart in the middle of the boat and placed the oars in the oarlocks. First one, then the other. Her heart was pounding hard and her arms shivering when she took the first strokes. She was on her way.

Olava had come some distance from the shore when her thoughts began to wander to those back home. When would they discover that she had gone?

She had been walking a lot in the woods since the funeral. Sometimes from early morning till late at night. Would they think that she had gone out when they woke up the next morning? It had happened a couple of times before that she was gone before they got up. What would they think when she didn't come home in the evening? Would they begin to look for her? Maybe they would ask for her on the other farms or go to the mountain farm? When would they realize that she had gone further away? They would at least understand that she had rowed over the fjord when they discovered that the boat was gone. But when would they find out? She thought about her mum. And what about Runa? All of a sudden she felt overwhelmed by guilt. What had she done?

Olava stopped rowing, pulled in the oars and let the boat float by itself. Her eyes rested on the calm water. The dark surface looked almost velvety in the dim moon light. Both frightening and soft at the same time. Almost peaceful. In that moment everything seemed so simple. Olava closed her eyes and took a deep breath. She saw herself sink to the bottom, slowly, almost gently through the water. Further and further down towards the bottom. In a strange way it felt so good. So right. And so simple. She opened her eyes. The possibility was so close and yet so far away. She couldn't do it. She knew that. She had to get away. She couldn't stay home any more. Not after what had happened. She had to move on. As soon as she got the chance and when she had come far enough away, she would write to her mum and Runa.

Olava took the oars and began rowing again. She fell quickly into the familiar rhythm. The oar blades moved soundlessly through the water right under the surface, and when they were above water, little drops fell off the wet wood and created circles. Olava watched how they got bigger and bigger until they melted into each other.

After some time, she got closer to the shore on the other side. She looked over her shoulder to make sure she came in as close to Aunt Barbro's boat house as possible. When she was almost there, she took the rope and walked out on one of the big stones in the water. She pulled the boat past the stones on the outside so that it came in next to the boat house. Then she pulled it up on the shore as far as she could and tied it to the house.

Olava took her stuff from the boat and put the carpet and the tarpaulin on top of her bag. For a short moment she let her eyes wander over the water towards the other side to their own boat house. It was so tiny and looked almost helpless from this distance. Olava swallowed a lump in her throat and turned away. Then she took her bag over her shoulder and began to walk. She did not look back.

In the east the sky had begun to grow lighter and Olava decided to hurry. It was at least a couple of hours' walk to the ferry that sailed into town and she wanted to get there as early as possible. She felt her inner pocket where she had put the money that she had saved since her Confirmation. It wasn't that much but enough for the ticket, food for some time, a carriage or ship from town and lodging for some days if she found a cheap place. When she was far enough away, she would try to get a job, maybe as a servant on a farm or in a house in town.

As the sun slowly rose over the hill and began the day's journey towards the west, Olava walked along the narrow country road. She was deep in her own thoughts when she suddenly heard the sound of a horse carriage in the distance. She turned around but couldn't see it and ran as fast as she could over to some bushes on the roadside where she hid. She breathed a sigh of relief when it drove past. No one had seen her and she didn't see anyone she knew. She was more alert when she continued to walk, but no one else came.

Some distance away, she could see the ferry that merged with the shiny morning fjord and the rich mountainside in the background. It was coming closer to the port and Olava walked fast. A short distance away from the ferry, she stopped to see if there was anyone she knew. She recognized the carriage she had met earlier and saw one more carriage. A man and a woman were standing next to it. She had not seen them before. Should she go any closer? No. Someone might come at the last minute and some passengers would be leaving the ferry. She didn't want to take any risk and remained where she was until the ferry was in port. When the coast was clear, she walked on board as the last person. She found a seat in a corner and sat down facing the wall. She placed the bag under the table together with the carpet and tarpaulin. Someone might begin to wonder.

Not until now did Olava feel how tired she was. She tried to stay awake but slowly her eyes closed. She was fast asleep when she suddenly woke at someone talking to her. For a few seconds she felt paralysed, but then she realized that it was only the ticket man.

"Oh my, I'm so sorry, my dear friend, I didn't mean to frighten you." He was smiling at her.

"It... it's okay. I must have fallen asleep." Olava was still confused.

"This is not the best place to sleep." He smiled good-naturedly and Olava looked at him, puzzled. It felt so unreal that someone could look so happy and be so friendly.

"No..." Olava tried to smile and sat up straighter on the narrow, wooden chair.

"You must have been tired. Are you going into town?"

"Yes..." Olava gave him money for the ticket.

"Are you going into town all by yourself?" He opened his purse, put the money in and gave her the ticket.

"Yes... I..." Why did he have to ask about this? Olava's brain worked fast to come up with a story. Why hadn't she thought about this before? "I... I'm going to stay with some family for a while... they have small children and need some help."

"I see... well, have a nice trip." He lifted his cap and nodded a friendly goodbye.

"Thank you." Olava felt guilty as she watched him go. He had believed the story without a doubt. She hated to lie.

When the ferry was in port, Olava tried to get off without being noticed. She didn't know anyone who lived here, but it was best to be careful. She knew that people from her community often went into town with different errands. Olava looked around. The port was full of life. Some fishing cutters were going out whilst others came in with the morning catch. Barrels with fresh fish were carried off the boats and sold at the market a little further up in town. She knew where it was but wanted to wait before she went up there. There was another place she wanted to see first.

Olava began to walk along the harbour towards

the port where the ship to America had sailed from. It was where they had said goodbye to Karin and Lukas that day in spring. It was before… It was before the mountain farm. It was before everything changed. She wondered if they would get to know about it. Maybe her mother would write a letter. But they had not heard from them yet, and it had been several months. Olava shrunk at the thought that Karin and Lukas would know what had happened. About what she had done.

At the ferry port, she stopped on the very same spot where they had been standing and waving that day. She wondered how they were doing now. They had been talking about saving money before going west. Had Lukas gotten a job in New York as they had planned? Maybe they had already gone off in search of land. She wondered if they thought about them back home? About her? Olava's chain of thought was interrupted by two boys with fishing rods who came walking towards her. She decided to walk on.

On her way to the market square, Olava found the well. She took her place in the small queue and found the water bottle in her bag. An elderly woman was pulling up water and just before Olava, a mother was standing with her small child in her arms. Next to her a girl was looking curiously at Olava from her mother's skirts. She was probably around 4 years old. A little younger than… Olava looked down. A little younger than Eystein. Olava whispered his name in her thoughts. Her eyes filled with tears and the pain in her chest made her dizzy. She straightened up. It was no good. He wasn't here anymore. She had to be strong.

Olava avoided the little girl's eyes while she was waiting, but when they left, she watched her go. She was so alive as she danced next to her mother.

Olava couldn't understand it. It was so unreal that someone could be so happy. She took the rope and lowered the bucket into the well. It sank slowly and when it was filled with water, she hoisted it carefully back up. Olava filled her hands with the cold, clear spring water and drank. Again and again until she had quenched her thirst. Then she filled the water bottle and continued to walk towards the market.

There was a myriad of people at the many stalls selling everything from fish and meat to vegetables, potatoes, eggs, bread, flour, salt and sugar. Olava took her place in the queue for bread. The noise from all the people felt like an unpleasant buzz in her head and after she bought a loaf of bread, she hurried away. She decided to walk up to the church which was situated above the town and had a good view. She thought she would probably be able to find a place there where she could rest and eat in peace.

Olava walked with slow steps uphill and when she was finally there, she fell onto the grass behind a large birch tree. She had only eaten a few pieces of the bread when she fell asleep, and when she woke up, many hours had passed. Above her the huge tree crown bathed in the light from the late afternoon sky. The leaves were sitting close to each other on the long, gently rolling branches. For a couple of minutes Olava remained unmoving, just watching. After a while she sat up slowly and took the carpet from her bag and put it around her shoulders. She rested her back against the tree trunk and for a long time she sat completely still whilst eating the rest of the bread.

The sun was low in the sky and Olava decided to stay where she was for the night. It wasn't likely that someone would come here and she was well hidden behind the large tree. The night was also mild, and with the carpet and the tarpaulin, she would be okay. Besides, she would save money not having to pay for a room and it was probably a good idea. She didn't know how much time it would take her to find work. The next day, she would find out how to travel further. There were some posters about transportation at the telegraphist office and she would go there.

The fog is thick. Olava runs through the empty streets. Around the corner of a house. Something is after her. It wriggles. What is it? She is frightened. Turns around. Where is it? She runs again. It is there somewhere. She knows it. Something is following her. She runs again. It's coming closer. It's right behind her. Then she wakes up.

Olava sat up breathing heavily. It was a dream. It was just a dream, a nightmare. She tried to calm herself down and think about something else, but the distress and fear was still in her body. She didn't dare to go back to sleep. Instead she stared into the darkness and listened to the sounds of the night. A dog barked somewhere in town and another answered. A bird whistled in the distance, long and lonely sounds. Something rustled quietly in the bushes behind the tree. Not until late in the night did Olava fall asleep again and when a cock welcomed the day with a long doodle-do, she felt as if she had only slept for a few minutes.

The telegraphist had not asked her any questions. He had only received the money and given her the ticket. Now she was on her way to Christiania, the capital, which she had only seen pictures of and heard about in school. First with a ship the long way along the coast, and then with a horse carriage.

Olava stayed most of the time in the small cabin. Every now and then she walked out on the deck to get some fresh air but never for very long. She slept most of the time, a heavy dreamless sleep. Other times she would just lie in her bed and stare at the ceiling. Sometimes she thought about her mother, Runa and Grandmother. She wondered if they were looking for her now? Were they worried about her? Maybe they were afraid something had happened to her. She decided to write as soon as she got to Christiania.

Everything felt so unreal when they arrived in Christiania. Olava held her right hand before her eyes when the chauffeur helped her out. The strong sunlight hurt after so many hours in the carriage. Olava politely said goodbye and began to walk. The city was bigger than she had thought and she spent the rest of the day getting to know it. She found a cheap hostel where she could stay, the market, a well and a shop where she bought some letter paper and a pen. The same night she sat down by the small desk in her room and, after a long time, finally found the words:

Dear Mother,
As you know by now I have left home. I travel from place to place and my plan is to find work on a farm or in a house. I am sorry I took the carpet and the tarpaulin and I hope you've found the boat by Aunt Barbro's boat house. I am sorry, Mum, for everything that has happened. You should not worry about me. I'm okay and will manage just fine. Say hello to Runa and Grandmother and Gudrun from me. I will write again later.

Love from
Olava

Olava read the letter again and again. What would it be like for her mother to read it? Should she write something more? Something about Eystein. About the accident. No. And she didn't want to write that she was in Christiania. Then they would know where she was. She wasn't even sure if she would stay here. She wondered if her father would read the letter. She read it one last time before she folded the letter and put it in the envelope. It was time to go to bed. Tomorrow she would post the letter and ask for work.

It was late in the night and the narrow streets were almost empty when Olava walked back to her small room the next day. She had been walking from house to house the whole day and asked for work. Some places she was met with a polite "no thank you", other places with a frown and blunt rejection. In one place they had begun to ask her about her family and where she came from. Hesitantly, she had told them the story she had come up with: that she came from one of the neighbouring communities to her own, that her father was dead and that they had been forced to sell the farm and go search for work. Olava thought they had looked suspicious and was almost relieved when they said no thank you.

When the same thing happened the next day and one more day, Olava got really worried. What had she been thinking? That it would be easy to find work. What should she do now? Leave the city and ask for work at farms? She decided to give it a try. There had to be someone who needed extra help.

Two days later Olava was back in the city. Every cell in her body ached from tiredness. She had taken a carriage out of the city to the country and walked from farm to farm but no matter where she came, she was met with rejection. In the last place she had asked for work the woman in the house had told her that if it weren't for her blond hair and blue eyes, she would have thought she was a gypsy girl. With her words Olava's last remnants of courage and hope disappeared. She had washed her face and tried to comb her hair and shake her clothes to look decent, but she had had to spend the night in a barn in shelter of some heavy rain, and it showed. She might as well give up.

Unruly thoughts filled Olava's head as she walked through the streets of the city. It was almost a week since she had left home. What should she do now? And what about money? She didn't have much left. Her thoughts were interrupted as she noticed a poster on a wall. It was information about the ship for America. She walked closer to read what it said. Next departure was in a few days. Olava hadn't considered America. What was it Karin and Lukas had called it? The land of opportunities? But it was so far away and they spoke a completely different language there. Besides, it was probably expensive. She dropped the thought right away, but her head was full of worries as she went back to her room. What should she do now?

12

The wind grows stronger. Sending lonely howls through the night. The cold comes sneaking in. Raw and damp on the open sea. Leaden grey clouds roll heavily over the sky. Dark roars from above. In short glimpses the shining scar. The ocean in wild dissent. Fighting in turbid chaos. Whipping rain from all directions. Chilling gusts of wind. Huge waves fighting each other like giants in a merciless battle of life and death.

It was a cold evening two days later. Olava was standing at the harbour with her bag over her shoulder staring at the big ship to America. It sailed early next day. The last couple of days she had been walking from house to house from early morning till late in the evening asking for jobs. Finally, she had given up and a desperate plan had begun to take shape in her head. She had spent her last money on bread and some extra bottles of water. She had also filled her bag with apples which she had picked from a tree whose branches hung outside the fence and no one could see her from the windows in the house.

In the dark the ship looked like a huge, silent shadow and it seemed to grow bigger the closer she came. Two large chimneys towered up towards the gloomy night sky. The boarding gangway was down, ready for the passengers the next morning. There was a rope in front of it, but she could easily jump over. Could it really be that easy? She walked slowly closer to the gangway. When she was almost there, she looked quickly in all directions. Her heart was hammering, but everything seemed calm and peaceful. She jumped quickly over the rope and ran as soundlessly and fast as she could up the gangway. Up on the deck she hurried over to the nearest lifeboat where she quickly hid under the tarpaulin. She was in hiding. Had anyone seen or heard her? She listened, tense, but everything was quiet. After a while she was certain that no one had seen her. She tried to find a comfortable position and put her own tarpaulin under her body and the carpet around her. She used her bag as a pillow. Olava was so overwhelmed from exhaustion that she hardly noticed the hard wooden floor beneath her before she fell asleep.

The next morning she woke at the sound of voices and steps close to the boat. The fear that someone might find her made her lie completely still. Hopefully no one would look under the tarpaulin. Soon there was a whole crowd of grown-ups and children on the deck. There were talking, shouting, crying and comforting voices. She knew that they were standing by the railing waving goodbye. Finally, there was the sound of a long honk and Olava felt the ship begin to move. She was on her way.

The time felt endlessly long and it became more and more difficult for Olava to lie still. Her body was aching and she felt increasingly sad and discouraged. She had read that the trip would take a little more than a week. She wondered if there might be somewhere else on the ship she could hide. She had to try but didn't dare to leave the lifeboat until it was night. Olava dozed a little during the day but couldn't really sleep. It felt as if an eternity had passed when everything quieted down around her.

After some time she drank a little water and ate some of the bread. Finally she could no longer hear either voices or steps around her and it got darker under the tarpaulin. When everything was quiet, she lifted it so that she could see the deck through a little opening. It was night. Carefully she removed the tarpaulin so that she could look in all directions. There was no one to be seen. Olava's joints and muscles ached and it hurt to get out of the boat. She left her bag in the boat, put the tarpaulin back on and tiptoed over to the railing where she was in hiding from the deck. In the light from the moon she could see the ocean. Dark waves in all directions. She breathed in the fresh ocean air and with her eyes closed she stretched her neck and back. For a short moment she forgot to be afraid of getting caught.

The thought of staying in the lifeboat for the rest of the trip was unbearable. She had to go inside and see if she could find somewhere else to hide. Not far from the lifeboats there was a door which led into a long living area. There were tables and chairs by the windows and in the middle of the room there was a staircase to the lower decks. Maybe she could find a cabin which was free? She walked down one staircase, then one more and one more. She continued through a hallway with cabins. Should she try and open one of the doors? She could always apologize and say that she had gone wrong. Then she stopped. The sound of steps coming closer made her freeze. Someone was walking straight towards her and before she knew it, he was standing right in front of her.

"Hi. What are you doing here in the middle of the night?" It was someone from the crew.

"I... I'm just out walking." Olava stammered.

"Can't you find your cabin?" He did not seem

suspicious and Olava tried to smile.

"Oh yes... I can... I'm on my way back there now..." She walked one step further and nodded as if to say goodbye.

"Let me take you there. Which number are you in?"

"No... no, it's not necessary." Olava froze. This must not happen.

"Yes, of course. I know this ship in and out." He only wanted to help, but Olava could feel how the panic grew in her chest. Now she would get caught. All kinds of thoughts rushed through her head. In the corner of her eye she could see the number on the door next to her. It was 121.

"I live in number 137." She was almost certain that there had to be a cabin with that number a bit further down the hallway.

"Okay then, it's this way. Just you come with me." He began to walk.

"Svenn, is that you?" There was a voice from the other end of the corridor.

"Yes, it's me." The man in front of Olava stopped and answered.

"The shift changes now." At the end of the corridor she could see the shadow of a man.

"Okay, I'll be right there." The man turned towards Olava and pointed down the hallway.

"I have to go now, but you are almost there. Only a few more doors further down."

"I see... thank you..." Olava swallowed a lump. The man was already on his way in the other direction. She didn't know what to think. Could it really be true? But she couldn't remain here. She had to get back to the lifeboat as soon as possible. She walked fast and quietly back the same way that she had come, on guard in case someone should come.

Back in the boat she breathed a sigh of relief. That was close. She wrapped herself in the blanket, pulled her legs up to her chin and curled up into a bundle. Unruly thoughts were running through her head. What would happen if she got caught? It was illegal to be a stowaway. Maybe they would leave her with the law enforcement or send her back. It must not happen.

Olava drifted in and out of sleep. It was as if the cold slowly crept into every cell of her body, and even though she had put on all her clothes and wrapped herself in the blanket, she was soon trembling with cold. The wind was getting stronger and she could feel how the sea got higher. The ship rocked rhythmically back and forth, up and down, and soon the waves hit the hull sending cascades of water up on the deck. Hard drops fell on the tarpaulin over her and it was flapping ghostly in the wind. She didn't dare to go out on the deck in this weather. If only she could sleep all the time. But it was hard when she was freezing so much. Shivering with cold and grief she cuddled up under the blanket. She had to stick it out. It would probably get better in the morning.

But the storm continued and no one came out on the deck the whole next day. Olava thought about giving up and going inside into the warmth, but in the end she was so exhausted that nothing seemed to matter. She began to cough. She held the carpet before her mouth to lower the noise, but it only got worse. Gradually, she became more distant, feeling fatigued and hot from fever when she was awake. A couple of times she tried to raise her voice and call out for help, but she couldn't utter a sound. Nothing mattered any more. Her thoughts became more and more unclear. Mother? Can you hear me? Mother? I'm going outside to play with little brother. Soon she was far away and she couldn't feel the cold any more.

The next thing Olava remembers is voices, anxious and loud. The tarpaulin is torn away. The rain and the wind whip her face. Two strong arms lift her out of the boat. She has no strength to resist. She loses her consciousness. The next time she wakes up, she is lying in a bed. Someone is holding her head and trying to give her something to drink. She coughs violently. They put her head carefully back on the pillow again. Behind a blurred veil she can see people in the room. Far away she can hear their voices.

"Did she drink any water?"

"No, I'm not able to wake her up. She is very warm."

"We must try again."

"We need more blankets." Someone opens the door and enters the room.

"Is this the girl?" A deep, authoritative voice fills the room.

"Yes, we found her in one of the lifeboats."

"I see. Has anyone seen her before?"

"No, not that we know."

"Has she been awake?"

"No, her fever is very high and she is confused and distant."

"I see, I want to talk to her when she wakes up."

"Yes, Captain."

A little later Olava woke up in a haze. She tried to gather her thoughts. Slowly glimpses began to appear before her. First the ship and the lifeboat, then the storm and the cold. All of a sudden she realized what had happened. They had found her. Instinctively she felt her neck with her right hand. She froze. It was gone. No, it couldn't be true. She felt everywhere around her neck, over her chest and stomach. It had to be there somewhere. She began searching the bed. The necklace. The necklace from Eystein. The heart. The one that she got from little brother for her birthday.

"No no..." Olava wanted to get out of bed to search.

"Wait... stop." A couple of strong arms grabbed her and pushed her gently back into bed.

"You cannot get up."

"Yes, the necklace... from little brother."

"What is she talking about?" Someone else came over to the bed.

"I don't know." Olava could feel the desperation grow. They didn't understand what she was talking about.

"It's from Ey... little brother... it's my necklace." She was crying.

"Easy... everything will be fine."

"She is in a state of delirium."

"NO NO, IT'S MY NECKLACE." Olava tried to get out of bed, but they held her tight. She struggled to get free but had no strength.

"STOP. What is wrong with you?"

"It's gone... it's from my little... Eystein..." Olava was struggling to find the words. She cried profusely.

"Try and talk calmly so that we can understand you." The other voice sounded mild. Olava tried to control her crying.

"It's my necklace... a heart, it's a heart of wood ..."

"A necklace?" A worried face looked at her.

"Yes... yes, it's my necklace." Olava nodded several times. Then a third voice.

"She had this around her neck."

"Is it this one?" A hand took hers and gave her the necklace. She looked at it through a veil of tears. She closed her hand around it and held it to her heart. Carefully she lifted her head from the pillow and put it around her neck. Within a few seconds she was gone again.

Olava didn't know how much time had passed when she all of a sudden opened her eyes. A man was sitting on a chair by her bed looking seriously at her. She tried to sit up but the movement made her dizzy and she had to give up.

"Good morning. I can see that you're feeling better."

"Who are you? I mean... I'm sorry..." All of a sudden she realized that she might sound rude.

"My name is Petter Jensen. I'm the captain of this ship." His dark blue eyes in his strong face looked at her questioningly. "But who are you?"

Olava swallowed a lump.

"I am... my name is... Olava." Now she realized that there was another man in the room. He was standing in the background listening to the conversation. She looked at him shortly.

"This is our doctor." It was as if the captain could guess her thoughts.

"I see..." Olava felt shy.

"Where do you come from, Olava?" She had to think fast.

"I come from Christiania."

"I see." He paused a little before he continued. "We sailed from Christiania, but your accent tells me that you come from out west." Olava felt caught.

It was as if he could see straight through her.

"Yes." She avoided his eyes but noticed that he shook his head worriedly. He didn't say anything for a while.

"You have been very sick, Olava. I don't know what would have happened if we hadn't found you."

"Thank you..." She didn't know what to say. The captain was staring emptily into the air for some time. He wore a furrowed brow.

"Do you know that it's illegal to be a stowaway?" His voice was even deeper than before and Olava lowered her eyes.

"Yes... I'm sorry... I want to pay..." She could hardly hear her own voice and he looked at her, concerned.

"You're not a girl who has any problems with the law enforcement, are you?"

"No..." Olava looked away.

"But what were you thinking... and what were your plans in New York?" Puzzlement was written all over his face.

"I... I wanted to see if I could get work as a housemaid." Olava could hear for herself how weak she sounded.

"I see." The captain sounded tired and not very convinced. "But how were you planning to get into the country?" Olava didn't answer and he sighed heavily. But then he smiled and shook his head.

"Do you realize that you are my first stowaway?" Olava couldn't take it any more. She broke down and began to cry.

"I'm sorry... so sorry... I've never been a problem to anyone before. I didn't mean to. I'm sorry... I'll pay when I get some money. I'm just so tired..." She hid her face in her hands and cried.

"It's okay... don't you cry, everything will be

fine. Just you wait and see." He put a comforting hand on her shoulder and sat like that without saying any more until she had calmed down.

"I would like to pay you back…"

"Don't think about that now." He looked at her sincerely.

"But will you please tell me what has happened?" Olava could hardly take it that he was so friendly. Tears were running down her cheeks, but she only shook her head. He paused for a while before he spoke again.

"I see. It's okay." His voice was mild and it was as if he talked more to himself than to her. "It must have been tough." For a short moment, Olava could see a glimpse of vulnerability in his eyes. He let his right hand run down his face a couple of times, as if he was considering what to do.

"I have to take you back with me. You need to be registered to get into the country. We'll sail again in a couple of days."

"I see…" Olava nodded slowly. It was not until now that she realized that they were actually in New York, the city that Karin and Lukas had talked so much about.

"But there is one thing I would like to know, Olava." The captain tilted his head. "Do you have a place to stay when we get back? A home?" Olava shook her head almost imperceptibly.

"But do you have any family?" Olava was staring emptily in front of her. Somewhere in her thoughts she knew that she couldn't lie now. In a way it was a relief.

"Yes… but I cannot go home." Her voice was just a whisper.

"I see." The captain nodded his head slowly and sent her a worried look. He got up from his chair. "I'll leave now so that you can sleep. You look tired and you've had a bad pneumonia and you are still sick." He lifted his cap and left the room. A few seconds later, Olava was fast asleep.

Slowly Olava got her strength back. She ate a little more every day. To start with only a few small bites, which she chewed thoroughly, then a little more, and after a few days she could eat a small meal. Her fever disappeared and she coughed less and soon she could stay awake for longer periods of time. Eventually she managed to sit up in her bed and take a few small steps around the room. Still she hurried back to bed where she crawled under the quilt. This was where she felt best.

Sometimes Olava pretended to be asleep if someone came in. Then they would leave quickly and she could be alone. It felt almost wrong that everyone was so friendly and helpful towards her, especially after what she had done. The doctor came in to check on her every day and the kitchen helper came with food, morning, midday and evening. And the captain. He had been so kind. Olava didn't think he would inform the police. But they were on their way back and although she tried to avoid bad thoughts, it got harder and harder as the days passed. She no longer believed that she was able to get work. Those kind of employments were agreed upon in advance. At least that was how it was done back home. Olava no longer knew what to do. Everything felt so uncertain.

Sometimes glimpses from the last weeks popped up in her head, short, incoherent glimpses. The furious look. The accusation. Her fault. She jumps over to the other side of the river. Why did she do that? The blow. Mother on the kitchen floor. The sight of little brother by the river. Why did she have to see that? Why did she have eyes so that she could see that? Why wasn't she the one who died? If only she were dead. If only she had never jumped over the river. The funeral. The small coffin. Her father not talking to her. The row boat. The silence out on the water. The soft surface. She sinks towards the ocean floor. The necklace is gone. The panic. Her mother in the rain. Runa is running. She is shivering from cold. The fluttering tarpaulin. When Olava felt like this she crawled, exhausted, back under the quilt. Sleep was the only blessing against the heavy thoughts.

Two days before arrival, Olava was strong enough to go out on the deck. She stood by the railing, a spot where she was alone. There weren't many passengers on the ship and she tried to avoid meeting any of them. The weather was mild and calm and for a short moment she enjoyed standing with her eyes closed feeling the sun and the wind on her face. But the peaceful moment disappeared quickly. Worried thoughts came sneaking in on her as if they had a will of their own. Restless and uneasy she went back to her cabin. She sat down by the little table and tried to concentrate on a book, but the words made no sense. After she had read the same sentence again and again, she put the book away. She was just about to go to bed when someone knocked on her door. As always when someone came, Olava felt a pang of anxiety, and instinctively she straightened her back before she said "come in". It was the captain. He nodded kindly at her and sat down in the other chair.

"Hi, Olava. I hear that you're doing much better?"

"Yes, thank you, I feel much better."

"That's good." Friendly wrinkles formed a pattern around his eyes when he smiled. "We're in Christiania in a couple of days. You've probably been told."

"Yes." Olava nodded a little shyly.

"Have you thought more about what you want to do?" He looked at her questioningly.

"Yes... but I don't know." Olava hesitated. "I'll probably try and see if I can get work again."

"I see." He smiled encouragingly. "Listen to me. I might be able to help you get a job. There is a place in town which has some job advertisements. We can always see what they've got and I'm sure you can get a job somewhere and see how it goes. I'll put in a good word for you."

"I... but..." Olava looked confused.

"It's entirely up to you, of course."

"Oh?" Olava found it difficult to speak. She could hardly believe her own ears.

"It's only if you're interested, of course." He looked a little hesitant and Olava realized he might think that she was not interested.

"Oh, but thank you. Thank you so much." She nodded several times.

"Good. And you can stay with me and my family until everything is settled. And Olava..." There was a glimpse of compassion in his eyes. "I won't tell anyone anything about this, you know..."

"Thank... you." Olava lowered her head.

"Very good, that's a deal then." He smiled happily and went out of the room. When he had left, Olava was puzzled. She had so many questions, but most of all she was surprised. He really wanted to help her.

13

The dew falls over the evening land. Little drops on every leaf and straw. Shiny, silvery, they blink sadly. Silent tears from yesteryears. The mist falls. Slowly over grassland and meadow. Covering woods and fields. Hovering like ghosts over the water. Blurring the true voice of the depths. Masking the pain of the soul. Little breaths of wind sing of a way. Sending messages through the tender wings of hope. But only for a short moment. Then the veil comes back.

Almost two years had passed since Olava had come to the hotel in the small town which was a little more than an hour's train ride from Christiania. She had stayed with the captain and his family for a few days until everything was settled and she had gotten the job. Olava could still remember how he stood on the platform with a serious look on his face and with his hand in the air waving goodbye when the train left.

The captain had helped Olava with money for the train ticket and new clothes, and in the first months she had put aside money from her salary so that she could pay him back as soon as possible. He had told her not to think about it, but she had insisted and was looking forward to the day when she could send the letter with the money. Even now, after such a long time, she often wondered at how much he had helped her. He had not asked her more about what had happened, but the last thing he had said to her was that if she ever needed help, she was more than welcome to contact him.

It felt like an eternity since Olava had been sitting on the train with her forehead resting against the window, staring absently at the mild, gently rolling countryside so different from what she knew from home. Her thoughts had been occupied with the family she was going to work for. She didn't know much about them, only that the couple were running a small hotel together with their two children, who were about the same age as her. They had applied for help in the kitchen and with the cleaning. Olava felt uncertain about everything. What if it didn't work out? And what about the family? What were they like? Her nervous thoughts made her instinctively pull up her shoulders and sit restlessly on the seat.

When the train drove into the station, she could see a white-haired man, tanned from the sun, gazing at the sky. He had his hands solidly planted in his pockets. On the platform they had approached each other carefully and with a friendly smile, he had asked her if she was Olava. She had nodded politely and held out her hand to greet him. Her first thought was that he seemed kind and when he took her hand in his and wished her a warm welcome, she could sense how some of her worries disappeared.

The trip to the hotel in the horse carriage went slowly. Ole had pointed in different directions and told her about the area; the names of the mountains, where to find hiking trails, the locations of good fishing waters and the names of the families on the different farms. Olava had nodded and looked in the different directions where he was pointing, but it was hard for her to pay close attention. She was soon going to meet the rest of the family. If only they were like Ole.

The white-painted hotel was beautifully situated by the country road some distance away from the actual town. In front of the building there was a small yard and to the right there was a solid log house where Ole lived together with his family. He told her that he and his father had built the house with the help of carpenters from town. This was before they had taken over the hotel from his parents.

Ole and Olava had just stepped out of the carriage when a tall, slim, and yet, strongly built woman came walking towards them with long steps, welcoming arms and a big smile. Underneath the white apron, which she took off while she was walking, she had a dark blue, well-fitted women's suit. She wore her hair in a tight bun and was an impressive woman.

"You must be Olava. Welcome to us." Her overwhelming welcome and rich voice made Olava take a few steps backwards, but she smiled politely.

"Thank you…"

"This is my wife, Gerda." Ole was holding the reins of the horse in his hands.

"Yes, Gerda Marie, but I only use Gerda." The tall woman took Olava by the shoulders, turned around and walked towards the hotel without looking at her husband. "How was the train ride?"

"Very well, thank you." Olava looked over her shoulder to Ole who remained with the horse. His fresh smile had disappeared from his face.

"That's good. I want to show you the hotel." Gerda walked quickly and soon they were going up the stairs.

"This is the reception. It is mostly me or my

son, Steinar, who works here." Gerda walked behind the front desk.

"This is the guest book and this is the shelf to the keys, but I will introduce you to all this if it becomes relevant." She continued to walk and opened a door a little further into the entrance area.

"You can come with me." Olava followed her quickly. They entered the kitchen where a short, pleasant woman with round, smiling cheeks was stirring in a casserole pot. She nodded and smiled at Olava.

"This is Gunnhild. She is our permanent chef and has been with us for almost 16 years." Gerda hung her apron on a hook behind the door. "Thanks to her our kitchen has a very good reputation among our guests." She gave Gunnhild a satisfied smile.

"And this is Olava, our new assistant in the kitchen."

"Hi and welcome." Gunnhild put down the wooden spoon and dried her hands lightly in the apron. She blinked and Olava thought she looked kind.

"Thank you." Olava took her hand.

"Mmmm... delicious." Gerda seemed pleased with the scent from the meat casserole.

"It only has to simmer for a little while before it's ready." Gunnhild's eyes became small over her round, smiling cheeks.

"That's good. I'll be back as soon as I've showed Olava around." Gerda threw a quick glance around the room.

"This is where you will be working most of the time."

"Okay." Olava nodded.

"At least to start with and then we'll see how it goes." Gerda raised her eyebrows a little when she looked at her. Then she continued.

"We serve three meals a day, morning, midday and evening. Gunnhild will introduce you to everything tomorrow morning." Gunnhild nodded kindly and Olava smiled, grateful.

"We're going this way." Gerda continued out another door, through a corridor and further into the dining area. Olava had to walk fast to keep up with her.

"This is our dining room. Our most important job is to make sure that our guests always get the very best service. They always come first." She looked questioningly at Olava.

"Yes, of course." Olava nodded and tried to seem perfectly okay with the expectations, but she had a bad feeling inside. She looked around at the tables by the windows, beautifully decorated with clean, white tablecloths, crocheted napkins, fresh flowers and candles. In the middle of the room was a long table decorated with the same white tablecloths, two beautiful flower decorations, a five-armed candle holder of silver and three baskets with fresh fruit. Everything looked so perfect.

"We arrange breakfast and lunch on the long table. Dinner is served at the small tables. We always make sure that there is fresh fruit in the baskets." Gerda took a pear from one of the baskets and examined it closely before she put it back.

"Well." She clapped her hands. "I think I want to show you the rooms now. If you have any questions, don't hesitate to ask."

"Yes." Olava thought everything went so fast and couldn't think of anything to ask about.

They walked back to the entrance area and continued up a staircase into a corridor. Gerda took a large key ring from her pocket and quickly unlocked one of the doors to a room.

"This is one of our double rooms." There was a white-painted double bed in the middle of the room with two small tables on each side. By one of the walls there was a washstand with a beautifully decorated washbasin and a shelf for cups and a soap dish. Next to it was a large closet and in the corner by the window a small round table with two armchairs. Everything was light and spotlessly clean.

"Do you have any experience with cleaning?"

"No... yes, a little..." The question came as a surprise to Olava. "From the farm... where I come from." She swallowed a lump. It felt so strange to talk about something from back home.

"I see. I might need you for cleaning as well. I will teach you." Gerda let her eyes wander around the room, moved the vase in the window sill a little and adjusted the bedspread.

"Okay. Now let me see. I will be going to the kitchen soon, but we just have time for a walk outside first. I will show you our fruit orchard." There was a touch of excitement in Gerda's voice.

Back in the corridor a girl came walking towards them with heavy steps. She had a washing cloth in one hand and a bucket with warm water in the other.

"Hi. Now there you are."

"Hi, Mum." The girl looked at them with a sullen smile.

"This is my daughter, Elin." Olava guessed that the girl could be one or two years older than herself.

"And this is Olava." Gerda walked a step to the side so that the two of them could say hello.

"Hi." The girl put down the bucket and held her hand out.

"Hi." Olava could hardly feel her handshake.

"Olava is our new kitchen assistant, but you know that of course." Gerda sounded sharper now.

"Yes."

"Good. We are on our way out. Mr. and Mrs. Jacobsen will be leaving tomorrow morning. Their room needs cleaning and there will be a new family arriving. They will be staying in room number 19. It must be ready for tomorrow morning." Gerda sounded anxious.

"Yes, Mum." Elin answered almost without looking at her mum.

"Okay. I will see you in the kitchen when you have finished with the rooms."

"Yes." Elin nodded and Gerda gave her a quick smile before she continued down the corridor. Olava and Elin's eyes met for a short moment before Olava followed Gerda.

Outside, the autumn sun was setting, mild and round in the west, and a couple of milky white clouds were floating lazily across the sky. It was getting late in the afternoon. Gerda and Olava were walking down towards the creek that ran clearly and silently all the way along the edge of the property of the hotel and ended in a small lake close by. Gerda told Olava that there was a nice place with a swimming jetty by the lake which was used by their guests in the summer. A huge, strong oak tree stood down by the creek, spreading its long arms in all directions. Under the branches there was a white-painted bench with a view to the creek and the fields behind it. Olava stopped. A swing hung from one of the largest branches of the tree. The sight made memories flood back into her mind. Eystein had loved his swing. For a moment she lowered her head and closed her eyes. A heavy pain in her chest grew for every breath she took and she felt overwhelmed by a sudden tiredness. In the distance she could hear Gerda's voice as she talked about the different rose varieties in the flowerbeds and about the beautiful water fountain that they had been given by a prominent politician and his wife who had visited the hotel three summers in a row.

"Are you tired?" Gerda's sharp voice made Olava wake up.

"No… no, I'm fine."

"Good. I want to show you the fruit orchard then."

On the southern side there was a big garden filled with berry bushes and fruit trees. Olava struggled against tiredness. She must not seem rude and dutifully she tried to concentrate on Gerda, who was pointing and explaining.

"As you can see, we have apples, pears, plums and cherries. In the bushes over there we have raspberries, blackcurrant and gooseberries, and there is the bed with strawberries. The vegetable garden and potatoes are over there and in that corner we have rhubarb." Gerda put her hands to her side and breathed in deeply.

"The season is coming to an end but we had a good harvest this year. Most of it goes to the cooking, of course." She smiled and Olava nodded. There was still some fruit hanging on the trees whilst some was lying on the ground half rotten or partly eaten by the birds.

"Okay. Now let me see. I have to go to the kitchen now. Our guests will be having dinner in an hour, but I will show you to your room first. You are probably tired after the journey." It sounded more like a fact than a question.

"Yes… a little."

"You can rest before dinner. We eat at 9 after the guests have finished."

"Okay… thank you." Olava was relieved. Now she would have some time to herself.

Olava stood in the middle of her room as Gerda closed the door behind her. Her room was the first of three rooms in a narrow hallway. One door at the end of the hallway led to the living room in the basement and the other led to the garden.

Her room was light and simply equipped. The bed stood by one of the walls and a washbasin with a mirror was by the other wall. The closet stood to the left of the door and in the corner by the window was a small desk with a chair. Olava put her bag on the floor, took off her shoes and hung her jacket on the hook by the door. She sat on the bed feeling exhausted, closed her eyes and rested her forehead in her hands. Her head was heavy with thoughts. Little brother. Why wasn't she the one who was dead? She held her chest in pain. It hurt so much to breathe. Why did she leave him alone by the river? It was her fault. Everything was her fault.

She lay down carefully on the bed. For what seemed like a long time, she lay motionless staring at the ceiling. She tried to breathe deeply and calmly. Her eyes rested on a crack in the white ceiling paint right above her. It wasn't very big. Maybe a little longer than her forefinger. She dwelt on the little mark for a long time. After a while the pain in her chest began to disappear and she became more and more drowsy. Finally she fell asleep.

Swing swing. We'll go on the swing tomorrow. Swing swing tomorrow. Yes, you're going to sleep now. Little brother? She's calling his name. Where are you? Has he hidden somewhere? She's looking behind the nearest bushes. Eystein? We're going home now. She's looking in all directions. Walking down to the stones. The snake. The next second she's paralyzed. NO. NO. NO.

Olava woke up with a start. The pain in her chest was back and she was breathing heavily. Why should she live? Why? Slowly she lay her head back on her pillow again. Why had they found her in the lifeboat? Why did little brother have to die? She took the necklace that she was wearing around her neck and held it gently in her right hand. A little tear ran down her cheek, but Olava could not cry.

It was getting dark outside when she got up a little later. She had to gather her strength to go up for dinner. Her body felt tired and heavy, but it helped a little when she put some cold water on her face and put on clean clothes. She stood for a moment staring at herself in the mirror. She closed her eyes and opened them again. Was it really her standing there? She breathed in deeply a couple of times and went up the stairs and into the kitchen. Gerda and Elin had just finished cleaning up after the guests' dinner and were about to prepare their own. Gunnhild had gone home for the day.

"Hi, now there you are." Gerda disappeared into a room next to the kitchen with a bowl of potatoes in one hand and vegetables in the other. Elin followed her with plates and cutlery.

"Hi." Olava nodded politely to the back of the two women and felt a bit uncertain what to do.

"Hi Olava. We're eating in here." It was Ole coming in from the reception.

"Hi." She followed him into the next room where there was a big dark-stained dining table with the dinner on it, almost ready.

"Do you think you could possibly bring the gravy?" Gerda's sharp voice startled them all. Olava, confused, looked at them all one by one. Who was she talking to? It was Ole. With a frozen expression on his face he went back to the kitchen and when he came back, he put the gravy on the table without looking at his wife.

"Okay, then everything should be ready." Gerda sounded all normal again, but the others sat down in silence. Olava avoided meeting anyone's eyes.

They were just about to start eating when a tall, slim boy with a big smile came in through the door.

"Hi." He seemed restless and rushed his right hand quickly through his heavy, dark blond fringe.

"Oh, there you are. Come and sit down with us." Gerda smiled enthusiastically and pulled out the chair next to her own. He was expected because there was a plate for him.

"Good, I'm so hungry I could eat a horse." He was just about to sit down when he became aware of Olava.

"This is Olava. She arrived by train today." Gerda smiled.

"Steinar." He held out one hand across the table and his strong fringe fell into his eyes.

"Hi... Olava." She got up a little hesitantly and nodded shyly.

"Steinar is our oldest son." Gerda smiled proudly and gave him the potatoes.

"Did you get it all?"

"Yes, but the honey wasn't ready, I can pick it up in a couple of days."

"I see, that's all good then."

"We get our honey from a farm about two kilometers from here." Ole turned to Olava with his good-natured, characteristic smile. She smiled and nodded politely back at him.

"Yes. We have agreements with some of the farms in the area where we buy different commodities." Gerda raised her eyebrows and looked at her husband. "Did you by any chance talk to Linn about the meat price?"

"Yes."

"And what did he say?"

"It's the same."

"I see." Gerda shook her head in disbelief. "This is the second time in two years that he has put the price up. If this continues, we'll have to find another supplier."

"We won't get it cheaper anywhere else." Ole's answer came abruptly and he sounded slightly irritated.

"It is unacceptable that he puts the price up now, again." Gerda's angry voice kept Ole quiet, but he sent his wife a cool look and she stopped. There was a moment of silence, but then they continued to eat and no one mentioned the case again that night.

The rest of the conversation was about the next day. How many guests they had, who was leaving, who was arriving, and how long they would stay. Gerda led the conversation and distributed the tasks. She went through the menu, which groceries they needed and who should get them. Olava sat quietly and listened to it all. She had been worried that they would ask her about her family and her home and was relieved that they only addressed her with practical information.

Olava was excited and nervous when she woke up the next morning. Breakfast had to be ready for the guests at 7 and she had to be in the kitchen half an hour in advance. Even though she had lots of time, she dressed quickly and hurried up the stairs from the basement living room. In the reception, Steinar was about to show a couple of the guests a hiking trail on a big map on the wall. The two men had already packed their rucksacks and were wearing hiking boots and anoraks and were obviously leaving early. Olava hurried past them not to disturb.

In the kitchen Gunnhild was in full swing by the stove. She was busy but looked up and smiled at Olava when she entered.

"Good morning, Olava."

"Good morning."

"Did you sleep well?"

"Yes, thanks…" It wasn't completely true. Worried thoughts had kept her awake for a long time before she finally fell asleep.

"Good. Now, let's see. There is a clean apron behind the door. You can wear that." Gunnhild continued to work whilst Olava took the white, newly ironed apron, pulled it over her head and tied it behind her back.

"We are a little busy before breakfast, but afterwards we'll have more time. I'll show you how things work around here then."

"Thank you." Olava nodded. She stood for a moment and observed Gunnhild's movements as she quickly and effectively cracked one egg after the other, added milk, salt and pepper and stirred the mix with a hand whisk. Afterwards she took a bundle of chives and cut it with surprising speed. Olava had never seen anyone work so fast before.

"Can I help you with anything?" She wanted to help and felt comfortable around Gunnhild.

"Yes, please… let me see. You may take the roller table over there and take it into the dining room." Gunnhild sounded calm and friendly in spite of being busy. Olava went over to the table. There were two baskets with bread and rolls, little plates with butter, small, elegant glass bowls with different kinds of jam, a big cheese bell with different sorts of cheese in it, dishes with cold meats decorated with green salad, small tomatoes and rings of onion and cucumber. There were boiled eggs wrapped in a delicate embroidered cloth, slices of tomato and cucumber on plates of their own and dishes with fruit and small cakes. Everything was beautifully garnished.

"Gerda is about to make everything ready in there. She will show you where to put it."

"Okay, thank you." Olava nodded and left with the roller table.

In the dining room, Gerda had just finished setting the small tables by the windows.

"Good morning. It's good that you're bringing in the food." She seemed to be in a good mood.

"Good morning." Olava walked over to the long table with the food.

"Okay, now watch what I'm doing. Everything has its specific place." Gerda took the different dishes and bowls and put them on the table in a particular order. Olava followed her closely so that she would remember how it was supposed to be done.

"Good." When Gerda was done, she walked around the table and adjusted a couple of the dishes a little. "Scrambled eggs and bacon seems to be the only thing we're missing. Otherwise it all seems to be ready." She looked pleased.

During breakfast Gerda walked in and out of the kitchen and the dining room serving coffee and tea. If something was missing, Gunnhild made sure to fill up the plates and dishes. Olava was standing by the large sink doing the dishes as the guests finished eating. Elin came up from the washing basement with newly ironed tablecloths, clean kitchen towels and washcloths. She didn't say much but seemed happier than the day before and helped Olava dry.

When the last guests had gone, Gerda went to replace Steinar at the reception desk while the others cleaned up. Afterwards it was time for their own breakfast. Ole came in and sat down by the table with a large cup of coffee and a satisfied sigh. Steinar came in from the reception and made everyone laugh when he gave Gunnhild a big and tender smack on the cheek. She laughed surprisingly and chided him gently whilst shaking her head. Olava couldn't help but laugh, too. It was a long time since she'd done that.

The days went by with hard work from early morning till late at night and Olava soon learnt all the daily routines. Gunnhild was friendliness herself. Effectively and calmly she showed Olava how things were done and introduced her to all the different tasks. She was also the only one who had asked her about her family and past, but Olava always responded elusively if she felt that she was being asked too much.

During the days when she was busy, Olava almost managed to keep the heavy thoughts at a distance, but it was harder in the evening and at night when she was alone in her room. Then they would often come sneaking up on her and keep her awake. They were meandering restlessly in her head. There were nights when she had nightmares. Always the same. The escape through the foggy streets. The fear of something chasing her. Something that wriggles.

The frantic escape around the corners of houses. The panic which grows. She knows it's there but cannot see it.

Olava always woke up when she was most scared and afterwards she was afraid to fall asleep again. Sometimes she got up and when she did, she would take the chair by the desk and carry it over to the closet by the door. When she stretched, she could just reach the little wooden chest with the lock that she had put at the back of the top shelf. It was where she hid the letters from her mother. Back in bed she would take the key that she had hidden by one of the bedposts and open the lock on the chest. She'd take the first letter and unfold it carefully. Olava had written to her mother a few days after she'd come to the hotel and had received an answer shortly after. It was especially the first letter from her mum that she would read again and again.

Dear Olava,
I cannot describe in words how good it is to hear from you. We have been so worried. Thank you for writing. I think about you every day and pray that you are fine. I hope you have come to a good family. I am so sorry for everything that has happened. You must not feel guilt, Olava. It was a tragic accident. Our dear Eystein has peace where he is now. I pray that you will find strength and comfort with God in your grief. We miss you here. The sorrow is deep. Majbritt is a blessed support and Runa and I visit little brother's grave almost every day. It is so beautiful up there. Do you remember how the two of you used to give me flowers? Now it's us that pick flowers for him. I so wish that you would come home.
Love from
Your Mum

Sometimes Olava cried quietly when she read the letter. She remembered very well how they used to pick flowers for their mum and little brother's joy when he gave them to her. It was a good thought. The only thing she didn't understand was this thing with God. Did her mother really believe in Him after what had happened? Olava had not prayed one single time since the accident. It didn't make any sense. It could almost make her angry.

14

The feeble evening sun disappears behind the hillside in the west. Slender rays wave the day goodbye. Twinkling faintly in the forest lake. Then it's gone. In the twilight dark, other creatures awaken. A myriad of mosquitos. Large swarms just above the water. Forever buzzing. Forever searching. Looking for food. Imperceptibly they find their prey and sting. Inject poison and suck nourishment. A breath of wind sends them off into hiding. Just as fast as they came. A moment of blessed peace. Then they are back again. Ceaselessly swarming. Tirelessly searching. Round and round.

The days turned to weeks and the weeks turned to months. Olava never told anyone about the accident or about how she had left her home. If anyone asked about her family, she told them briefly about her mum, dad and Runa and that she had had a younger brother who died when he was little. By hiding her story, Olava tried to forget and this was how life went on. Sometimes when she thought back at what had happened it was like an unreal dream. Like a distant past that had nothing to do with her. But even though time drew a veil over the memories, the grief lived on in her heart.

When Olava had a day off, she would often go for a walk by herself into the mountains. With a lunch pack and extra clothes in her backpack, she would leave early in the morning and sometimes be out the whole day just walking and walking. It wasn't long before she knew all the hiking trails in the woods, past the waters and marshlands, along ridges and mountain tops. Olava could walk for hours. Sometimes she'd sit down to eat, but it wasn't long before she continued to walk. When she came back after a day like that, she would always feel better than normal and often she'd sleep through the night.

Olava also began to observe Gunnhild when she made cakes and desserts. To begin with she stayed in the background, but Gunnhild invited her to join in. There was something touching about the way Gunnhild worked with and prepared the food. She treated everything with the greatest care, as if they were small living beings she was protecting. Sometimes she even sang and talked to the fresh berries, the sun-ripened fruits and the tasty chocolate.

Olava had never seen such delicacy or tasted such good cakes and desserts before. She observed Gunnhild closely when she explained her techniques and showed her how to follow them. She also began to read recipes in the evening before she fell asleep and soon she was allowed to assist. The day came when Olava made her first dessert cake for the guests, one of Gunnhild's famous cheese cakes with fromage filling and cherry jelly. Gunnhild had helped her a little with the jelly, but apart from that, she had done everything by herself.

Gunnhild clapped her hands enthusiastically when she saw the great result and said that from now on the name of the cake should be "Olava's cheese cake". Olava laughed shyly but was quite surprised herself to see the beautiful cake when she put it in the cooling room.

The next evening when the cake was cut into pieces and arranged on small dessert plates for the guests, Olava felt a twinge of pride and expectation. After this episode her wish and courage to learn grew and in time it became her regular task to bake and make desserts. Gunnhild was thankful for the help and even Gerda seemed pleased with the arrangement. A couple of times Gunnhild asked her if she had considered becoming a confectioner and even though Olava had never thought about that, the words kindled a little flame of hope and joy in her.

Gerda came by the kitchen several times in the course of a day but never for very long. Olava always felt best when she was alone with Gunnhild. Elin came by the kitchen when dinner was to be served and Gunnhild had gone home for the day. Apart from that she mostly stayed away. Steinar often came by with groceries or to get something. Other times he came by just to have fun with Gunnhild or taste the food. A couple of times he had sent Olava a half smile and winked at her, but she had looked down right away. She felt uncertain about the restless boy, but still in a way, she was also fascinated with him. Steinar was cheeky and charming at the same time.

Ole came by the kitchen when something needed fixing or they were eating. Olava had seen and heard how Gerda could scold him over little details if he was there, so he stayed as far away from the kitchen as he could. Sometimes Ole could be gone for several days without anyone mentioning where he was. Gerda was always especially restless and impatient during those days and the atmosphere was heavy and tense. Dinner was eaten quickly without anyone saying much. Elin looked tormented and even Steinar was quieter than he usually was. When Ole came home he looked tired and unwell and it would always take a few days before he was his usual self. Olava couldn't understand what was wrong and one day she gathered her courage and asked Gunnhild. They were standing by the kitchen counter peeling potatoes and cutting vegetables.

"Do you know if Ole is sick?" Gunnhild gave her a worried look. She looked around the kitchen and waited a few seconds before she answered in a low voice.

"You see… we don't talk much about it…"

"Oh… I didn't mean to…" Olava regretted that she had asked.

"No, no. It's okay. I think you should know." Gunnhild shook her head and sighed heavily.

"There is a farmer not far from here who makes his own liquor… Ole spends time with him."

"Oh?" Olava shook her head blankly.

"Yes, you see, they drink together." Gunnhild had a sad look in her eyes.

"Oh, I see…" Olava nodded slowly. She understood now.

"Yes, it's a shame. He's a good man, Ole."

"Yes, he is." Olava nodded in agreement. They continued working in silence and didn't talk more about Ole's drinking.

It wasn't long after one of Ole's trips to the farmer that one day Gerda came rushing into the kitchen from the dining room with a fruit basket in her hands. Both Gunnhild and Olava stopped in the middle of their work and looked at her with surprise when she placed the basket hard on the kitchen table with both hands.

"Who put fruit out today?" The tight look on her face told them that something was wrong.

"I did." Olava looked at Gerda and the basket with the fresh fruit.

"Look here!" Gerda took an apple from the basket. Olava had never seen her like this before. Her face was twisted from frustration and her voice was trembling with intense rage.

"But...?" Olava could still not understand what was wrong.

"What is this?" With a fierce movement Gerda pointed at a small spot on the apple. Her staring eyes demanded an answer. Olava froze.

"It is... a spot."

"Do you think I can run a hotel like this?" Gerda threw the apple in the bin.

"But..." Olava was speechless. In the corner of her eye she could see that Gunnhild had stopped kneading the dough.

"I have to be able to trust my employees. Haven't I said it time and time again that you must check every fruit before you put them in the basket to the guests?"

"Yes... but I..." Olava could forget all about telling her that she had checked every fruit. She must have overlooked the small spot.

"Fruit with spots are to be used for juice and jam."

"Yes..." Olava could feel tears filling her eyes.

"Good. Don't ever let it happen again." Gerda took the basket and walked quickly back to the dining room. Olava continued doing the dishes. Her hands were shivering when she took a cup from the water. How could Gerda get so mad? And what was it that she had said? She couldn't run a hotel this way. Couldn't trust her employees? How could she say that? Olava was buried in her own thoughts when Gunnhild came over to her, grabbed a kitchen towel and began to dry.

"Gerda doesn't mean it so bad. Sometimes she's just got too much to do." Olava nodded quickly but avoided looking at her. The rest of the day she was quiet and when it was time for dinner, she excused herself from the table saying she was tired and went down to her room. Olava could still feel the discomfort in her body after the confrontation. Over and over again she relived the episode in her thoughts.

After that day Gerda began to comment on her work. It started with small remarks and criticism but in time it only got worse. In some periods hardly a day went by without Gerda having some kind of opinion and critique of her work. Involuntarily Olava became more on guard and was afraid to do something wrong. She also began to avoid Gerda if possible.

Olava had been with the family a little more than a year when one day Gerda asked her to come over to the reception desk. Olava was on her way down the stairs to her room. She had a break before dinner.

"There is a letter for you." Olava walked over to the desk and received the letter. She could see that it was from her mother.

"Thank you." She continued towards the stairs to the living room in the basement.

"Olava!" Gerda called again and Olava turned around, instinctively on guard against Gerda's moodiness.

"Yes?"

"Is something wrong?"

"No, everything is fine."

"Is it a letter from your family?"

"Yes, it's from my mum."

"How wonderful. It's a good thing she writes you every now and then, isn't it." Gerda smiled briefly and Olava nodded.

"It's not much you've told us about your family, really, is it?" Gerda was looking through some documents. "But that is entirely up to you, of course." Olava didn't know what to say.

"And you haven't really been home on a holiday since you came here either, have you?" Gerda was staring at her questioningly.

"No, it's a long journey."

"Yes, of course it is. Well, I hope she's writing something nice." Gerda took a quick look at the letter. "And we'll see you in half an hour, right?"

"Yes." Olava nodded and Gerda continued doing the paperwork.

Olava waited to open the letter until she was in her room sitting on her bed. It was always sad to read the letters from her mum. In the beginning she had written and asked her if she wanted to come home, but Olava neither could nor wanted to. Most of the time she would send her a short answer saying she was doing fine and that she was thinking about them, but that she didn't want to come home. Now she was sitting on her bed reading that her mother would come and visit her.

Three weeks later Olava was waiting at the railway station in the little town. Ole had taken her there and was waiting for them by the station building. She squinted against the sun as she was looking for the train which was supposed to arrive any minute. She held her hand to her heart when it pulled up to the platform and her mother came out. At a distance she looked the way she used to, but when she came closer, Olava could see how much older she looked. She had tired wrinkles around her eyes and had become so thin. But her smile was warm and hearty like Olava remembered it.

"Hi Olava." They gave each other a gentle hug.

"Hi, Mum." Olava nodded and smiled faintly.

"It's so wonderful to see you." Her mother had tears in her eyes.

"Yes... it's good to see you, too." All of a sudden Olava felt absolutely powerless. Her mother seemed so frail.

"Ole is waiting for us over there." She pointed in his direction.

"That is very kind of him." Her mother smiled wearily.

"Mother?" Olava knew that there was something she had to tell her.

"Yes, what is it?"

"I haven't told the family anything about... you know... the accident." Olava looked down. It was hard for her to speak about it.

"I see, I understand." Her mother nodded sadly.

"Do you want me to help you with your bag?"

"No, it's okay. I'm fine." Her mother took her bag and they began to walk.

Olava had taken three days off to be with her mother. They would sleep in the hotel the first night and then take the train to Christiania and stay there for two days before her mother would go home. Olava had felt uncomfortable at the thought of her mother meeting the family but thankfully she and Ole began to talk right away. Gerda was also in a good mood and whilst they were having dinner, she described Olava's work in the kitchen in laudatory terms. She also told Anna that it was Olava who had made the strawberry tart that they got for dessert.

Her mother smiled proudly, but Olava was quiet. It was the first time she heard Gerda say anything good about her work and in a way it felt wrong and strange. It was hard to trust what she was saying. Olava felt relieved when they said goodnight a little later and went down to the room.

"They seem nice." Her mother sat on the extra bed that had been put in for her.

"Yes." Olava nodded. She didn't want to tell her what Gerda could be like.

"Are you happy to be here?"

"Yes, I'm fine."

"I'm so glad to hear that."

"I like to bake and make desserts. It's Gunnhild who has taught me. It's mostly me who makes desserts for the guests." It felt nice to share this special joy with her mother.

"That is so wonderful." Her mother smiled.

"Yes." Olava nodded. They were quiet for a moment.

"Runa says hello." Her mother's voice was mild and soft and Olava swallowed a lump.

"Thank you... how is she?" The feeling of having let her little sister down went deeper than she realized.

"She's been crying a lot. That's good. And she misses you. We all do. Gudrun and Majbritt say hello, too, and Grandmother."

"How is grandma?"

"She's okay but she spends much time by herself." Her mother sighed quietly.

"And father?" Olava couldn't hide the bitterness in her voice. Her mother was quiet for a moment.

"He thinks I'm visiting Aunt Mathilde." Mathilde was her mother's sister, younger by two years.

"I see." Olava looked down and avoided her mother's eyes. She had difficulties hiding her disappointment.

"He's not well."

"What?" Olava looked at her mother with surprise in her face.

"It's something with his stomach."

"But... what's wrong with him?"

"We don't know. He's been to the doctor in the city but they don't know what it is."

"Is it serious?"

"It's hard to tell. Some days he just lies in bed." Her mother shook her head sadly and they didn't say more for a while. Olava stared emptily into the room. Her father was sick.

"I wish you would come home."

"No, Mum. I'm not coming home." Olava shook her head. Just the thought of that felt impossible.

"But will you come and visit us?"

"Yes maybe... I don't know." Olava was staring absently into the air.

"What happened with little brother was an accident." Olava avoided her mother's eyes. Her throat felt thick with tears, almost like a big, painful wound. She paused for a long time before she answered.

"I let him sit alone by the river."

"But... Olava, it was an accident."

"Stop it. Stop it, Mother. I don't want to talk about it."

"But is there anybody here that you can talk to?"

"No! And I don't want to talk to anyone. Do you understand?" Why couldn't she stop? Olava lay on the bed with her back towards her.

"I see…" Her mother's voice was mild and calm.

"I want to sleep now." Olava pulled the quilt up to her face. She could feel her mother's eyes on her back but didn't want to turn around.

"Would you like to pray together with me?"

"No, Mum. I do not pray anymore." Olava could hear how her mother became quiet, but she didn't turn around. She could feel her own heart-beat.

"Okay. I see… Sleep well, dear Olava." Her mother came over to the bed and gently caressed her hair. Tears filled Olava's eyes from the little touch, but she didn't want to cry.

A little later she could hear her mother's quiet prayer like a soft whisper in the room.

The days in Christiania went fast. They stayed in a small guest house in walking distance from the city center. Olava knew the city well from the days when she went from house to house asking for work. It was strange to see some of the same streets and houses again. Had she really walked here? Was that really her? Had she stood and knocked on all those doors? She didn't tell her mother much about her time in Christiania and didn't mention the ship to America with a word. It would only make her even more worried.

There was one place that Olava remembered especially well from the days in the city and that was a small café with a pastry shop. She really wanted to go there and when they were standing by the counter about to order, she looked at all the cakes with entirely new eyes. It was the first time she was in a café with her mother and they were both a bit uncertain, but also excited, when they sat down by one of the small tables by the window. They ordered coffee and chocolate cake with nut cream and it wasn't long before a friendly woman came with the coffee and cake on a tray. They thanked her nicely and enjoyed the delightful moment when they took the first bite of the cake. It was delicious, but it struck Olava that Gunnhild and her own chocolate cakes were just as good if not even better. She would tell that to Gunnhild when she got back.

Her mother told her different things about life back home. They had heard from Karin and Lukas who wrote that they had bought land in Minnesota and had begun to cultivate the land and build a house. She also mentioned little episodes with Eystein which made them both smile, but they didn't talk about the accident or the time after. One time her mother asked her if she wanted to come home for Christmas, but Olava only shook her head. The last thing Olava saw from her seat in the train was the sorrow in her mother's eyes when she waved at her from the platform. In her bag Olava had a letter from Karin and Lukas.

15

The curtains of fog are thick and grey leaving the land silent and deserted. Heavy clouds shut out the light. Every road has a blind end. The trees stand like naked silhouettes. Trapped in a prison of gloom. Lonely in the dim silence. Caught in a world without colour. Thickets of thorns are hiding in the mist. Sucking the sap and strength from everything around it. They will sting if you come too close. Large shadows blurring and distorting. Appearing from the depths of forgetfulness. Like a burden all too heavy.

Olava didn't notice the rhythmical sound of the train, the gilt-edged clouds over the hillside or the young lovers a little further ahead in the compartment. Heavy thoughts filled her head. When would she see her mother again? It could be a long time. But Olava didn't want to go home. She knew that. Her father didn't even know that she had visited her. But he was ill. What if it were serious? Some days he just stayed in bed. It was hard to imagine. Olava couldn't remember that he'd ever been sick before. She was wondering if he ever thought about her. Never mind. But what about Runa? Her mother had said that she had been crying a lot, and that the two of them often visited little brother's grave. She was wondering what it looked like there now.

In a glimpse Olava remembered the soil between her hands when she said goodbye. A shooting pain hit her in the chest. He wasn't here anymore. Oh no. Little brother. Eystein. Why had she left him? Why had she let him sit all alone by the river? Olava closed her eyes. She had to think about something else or she would break down.

It was late in the afternoon when the train arrived at the station. Olava walked back to the hotel and would be back just in time to help out with dinner as they had agreed upon. She was wondering what Gerda would be like when she got back. She had given her some days off without any questions and had been very kind towards her mother, but one never knew.

When Olava entered the reception, Gerda was welcoming a new family that had just arrived. Olava didn't want to disturb them and hurried down to her room with her bag and jacket. She went up to the kitchen right away. Gunnhild had gone home for the day and Elin was preparing dinner. Olava put on her apron and started working. Not long after, Gerda came into the kitchen.

"Hi Olava."

"Hi."

"Have you begun making desserts?"

"Yes." Olava smiled and nodded.

"Good. Well, there is one thing you should know. You seem very rude when you just walk by the reception without saying hello." The discomfort of Gerda's intense look made Olava freeze.

"I... didn't want to disturb."

"It's not about disturbing, it's about you showing politeness and respect to our guests."

"But... I am always polite..." Olava simply couldn't understand Gerda's accusations. They hadn't even looked at her when she came in.

"You walked by without greeting. Don't you think that's rude? What exactly do you think the guests might think?" Gerda raised her voice.

"But, they didn't even see me." Olava wouldn't put up with it.

"You don't know that, do you? You walked straight past. That is very rude." The tight look on Gerda's face and the contempt in her voice made Olava keep quiet.

"Now get started with the work. We've been very busy while you've been away and two new families have arrived." Gerda went over to the kitchen counter and began cutting bread.

Olava continued with her work but couldn't let go of the discomfort she felt after Gerda's words. It was true that she tried to avoid too much contact with the guests, but did Gerda really think that she was rude? It's about showing respect. How could she say that? Olava tried to understand her reaction but only got more confused.

When the guests had eaten and they were having dinner a little later, Olava was quiet and spoke only if they asked her about something. It was Ole who especially wanted to know how the days in Christiania had been, but it was hard for Olava to share anything from the trip. She found it difficult to raise her voice and she had begun to feel uncomfortable in the presence of Gerda.

A little later Olava was sitting on her bed staring emptily at the wall. She felt tired. Gerda was so often after her and she didn't understand why. She would often have thoughts about leaving the hotel, but couldn't see how. What would she do then? She couldn't go home and she had nowhere else to go. It had been impossible to find a job and here she had both work and a place to live. Besides, Ole and Gunnhild were always kind to her and she learnt so much in the kitchen. Gerda could be nice, too. She was just too busy sometimes. It was also because Ole drank and he would go away more and more often. In a way Olava could understand that Gerda was stressed.

Olava felt a growing headache and was massaging her temples. Round and round in slow movements. She remembered the letter from Karin and Lukas. How could she forget? It was still in her bag. She was wondering what they'd written. They knew what had happened. The thought filled her with an endless feeling of sorrow and emptiness. Olava waited some time before she took the letter out of her bag. Back in her bed she leaned her back against the wall and wrapped the quilt around her. The letter hadn't been opened and her name was on the envelope. She opened it slowly with her forefinger and waited a little before she took the letter out, afraid of the feelings the words might arouse in her. Carefully she unfolded the letter in front of her.

Dear Olava,
Your mother has promised that she will give you this letter. Lukas and I have cried so much. We cannot understand that our dear, little Eystein isn't here anymore. The last time we saw him he was standing in the courtyard holding Grandmother's hand and waving goodbye. We have talked about him and you so often. You and Eystein were inseparable and the loss and grief is indescribable.

Your mother has written and told us that you've left home. We're so glad to hear that you've come to a good place and a good family. We have bought land now and Lukas will have finished building our house soon and the first harvest has been good. In the midst of grief there is also something wonderful happening as we're expecting our first child this spring. If it's a boy we will name him Eystein, and if it's a girl we will call her Olava. You are in our thoughts every day and we pray dearly that you will find strength and comfort in your sorrow.

Much love from
Lukas & Karin

Olava read the letter a couple of times. They were going to have a baby who they would name either after Eystein or her. That was kind of them. She smiled a little to herself but felt no joy. It wouldn't change anything anyway and they were so far away. Maybe she would never see them again. Nothing really mattered.

Slowly but surely Olava sank deeper and deeper into a hole of heavy thoughts. It was as if she had a blanket over her head, unable to see anything clearly. Gerda just got worse and worse and Olava was inevitably on guard all the time. Steinar and Gunnhild were the only two that Gerda didn't target with her comments and criticism and since Elin and Ole stayed out of the kitchen most of the time, Olava got most of it. It was always worst when they were alone. Gerda also had periods when she was calm and nice and it could be almost impossible to imagine what she could be like otherwise. Olava did her very best with everything she did and couldn't understand how Gerda could be so displeased. She never knew if her work was good enough and the unpredictability was exhausting. Sometimes she tried to defend herself against the accusations, but it only made everything worse and finally she completely gave up answering back.

Olava's unsettled myriad of thoughts got worse and worse. She was caught in a cage with her own thoughts as bars. Thoughts about herself, thoughts about others, thoughts about the past, thoughts about the future, thoughts about yesterday, about the day tomorrow, about what had been said, about what had happened and about what might happen. In the end the bars had become so thick that she couldn't see clearly. But the thoughts were invisible. Olava began to think that this was how it should be.

It was late one afternoon after a busy day with several unannounced guests. Ole had been gone for five days and the atmosphere in the house was heavy and irritable. Gunnhild had just gone home and Olava was about to make roses and leaves of marzipan when Gerda came in from the reception bubbling with frustration.

"Olava."

"Yes…" She hunched her shoulders instinctively and met Gerda's eyes, uncertain about what Gerda wanted.

"In the future I want you to clean the living room in the basement and some of the rooms."

"Okay…" Olava nodded.

"This means I won't be needing you to make desserts and cakes anymore."

"But…" Olava was speechless. Gerda knew how much she enjoyed this work. She had to know.

"Gunnhild can do it like she's always done." Olava didn't know what to say. What if she couldn't bake anymore?

"I…" She tried to think fast. "Would it be okay if I use the kitchen to bake in my spare time? I will buy the ingredients myself, of course."

"No, absolutely not. The kitchen is for cooking food for our guests and ourselves, nothing else."

"But... I would bake for all of us."

"No. You should concentrate on your work. We all have a common responsibility, right?" Gerda smiled knowingly and went into the dining area. Olava looked after her, surprised and confused.

A little later Gerda asked her to go down to the basement to clean the living room and when she was done, she came to check on her work. Olava had cleaned the whole room thoroughly, but Gerda pointed out several places where she should clean again. When she disappeared up the stairs, Olava looked after her with a tormented look. Her aversion towards Gerda was boiling up inside her.

Later that night Olava was lying on her bed staring at the crack in the ceiling right above her. It was as if it had become bigger. She couldn't let go of the thought that she wouldn't be able to bake anymore. Why had Gerda decided that? Gunnhild had mentioned several times how grateful she was for Olava's help. She wouldn't even be able to bake in her spare time. Olava tried to convince herself that it didn't matter, but it wasn't easy.

Gerda got more and more unpleasant. Always in disguise so that the others didn't know what was going on. Olava couldn't understand what she had done wrong and she got more and more desperate. If only she would stop. Be quiet and leave her alone. Sometimes she'd think about leaving the hotel, but as time went by, it seemed more and more impossible.

One night Olava was sitting on her bed. She was beating herself in the head over and over again with clenched fists, so hard that she couldn't really feel the pain. She was bubbling with irritation and her disgust for Gerda made her feel like she was choking. She had been hysterical because of a tiny crack in a plate that one of the guests had gotten. Olava was beating herself until her scalp was aching. In spite of the pain, it felt good. She buried her face in the pillow. Most of all she wanted to scream, but her voice was paralyzed. Finally she sat up and knocked the back of her head against the wall, again and again, but quietly so that no one would hear her. Her own thoughts kept her imprisoned and her body was heavy and restless. Not until late in the night did she fall asleep.

Olava runs through the streets. She's all alone. The silence is scary. She's fleeing desperately. Something is after her. It wriggles along the house walls. She runs again. Turns around. She knows it's there. It must not find her. She's running blindly. Catching her breath. It's coming closer. She cannot see it. Where is it? She wants to call for help but cannot utter a sound. The fear chokes her. She's so scared.

    Olava woke up abruptly. A throbbing headache made her dizzy and she felt sick. She just managed to get over to the washbasin in time before she threw up. Oh no. What if someone found out? She had to hurry. Quickly she opened the window, put a towel over the wash bowl and ran through the hallway towards the door to the garden. It was almost dark outside and she hurried down to the creek where she washed the bowl.

    Back in her room she sat on her bed, exhausted. Luckily, no one had seen her. Olava couldn't sleep more that night. It was that dream again. It would come more and more often and so did the fierce headache.

One more year went by and another one. Olava sank deeper and deeper into a depression. She struggled to manage the routines of her daily life, afraid that if she let go, she would sink into a bottomless void. The day came when she had to force herself to get up in the morning. Sometimes she could both see and feel Gunnhild's worried looks, but she no longer asked her how she was doing and Olava didn't say anything. Gerda had begun to comment that there must be something wrong with her and in time the family dinners had become a torment. Olava's body was stiff and heavy and she didn't have the strength to raise her voice. Mostly she would sit quietly, grateful to be left alone.

On the inside Olava fought against Gerda's accusations, but the day came when she began to doubt herself. Maybe she was right. Maybe there was something wrong with her. Slowly her aversion towards Gerda became indifference. She was probably right. There was something wrong with her and more and more often she felt that the others thought so, too.

Slowly Olava forgot who she was. Controlled by hidden thoughts of guilt, loss, sorrow and fear, life became something she had to survive. Loneliness blighted her life and worst of all there was a haunting feeling of being abandoned. Everything was meaningless. Somewhere deep inside, Olava had a feeling that this was not how life should be, but she couldn't see her way out of it. More and more often, forbidden thoughts appeared in her head. What if she was not here anymore? What if she died, too, like Eystein? But she couldn't do it. Not to those back home. Mum, Runa, Gudrun and Grandmother. And

Dad. And Karin and Lukas who had had a little girl that they had named Olava Ingrid. Olava after her and Ingrid after Karin's mother.

One early spring morning Olava packed her rucksack with food and extra clothes. Lately she'd just stayed in bed on her days off, but something made her get up and go out this day. The emptiness and fatigue felt like a heavy carpet as she dragged herself over the courtyard and up the road that led to the path to the mountains. With her head bent, she walked along the fields and further into the woods. If only she could cry. But she couldn't. Her chest felt tight and painful. Olava neither heard nor saw anything around her and didn't notice a woman who was gathering herbs between the trees some distance from the path.

"Hi…" Olava thought she heard a voice far away. She stopped. Did anyone call?

"Hello…" Yes, there it was again. But who could it be out here in the middle of the forest? She looked over her shoulder but couldn't see anyone.

"Olava?" Now she saw her. Between the trees a woman came running towards her with small, quick steps and a big hearty smile. But who was it?

"Olava, is it really you?" The big and gentle woman embraced her and gave her a warm hug as if it was the most natural thing to do.

For many seconds Olava was staring into the familiar eyes, unable to utter one word.

16

The sun stretches its morning rays. Lights up the day with love from the east. Warm thoughts melt frost and snow. The sluices of heaven open. Heavy tears of rain. Pouring down for days. The river flows over its banks. Washes winter away. Then quietly it eases up. Little drops drum lightly in the trees. Touching the leaves with gentle strokes. The sun breaks through the mist. Sending light and warmth to the earth. Dries up the forest floor. Where the heather grows. The hope in the green leaves. The light in the gentle flowers. The strength from the deep roots. The power from Mother Earth. New winds sing of hope.

Olava stood completely still and wasn't able to utter a word.

"Olava, is that really you?" The woman's face lit up in a surprised smile. She took a step backwards and looked at her from an arm's length distance so that she could see her properly.

"Malou?" Olava's voice was a weak whisper. She stared in wonder at the familiar face, older now, but with the same heartfelt smile and the warm eyes. She still had her foreign accent.

"Yes, it's me. I can't believe this. But what are you doing so far away from home…" Malou stopped in the middle of the sentence. She looked at Olava with worried eyes and the smile disappeared from her face.

"But Olava... what is wrong?"

"I... everything is... okay." Olava swallowed a lump and looked down. She felt endlessly tired.

"But... what has happened?" Olava looked into the mild, open eyes. The next seconds felt like an eternity.

"It is... little brother..." Malou tilted her head, her dark eyes loving and serious at the same time.

"Little Oystein?"

"Yes... he is not here anymore..." Olava nodded almost imperceptibly. For a moment Malou looked as if she wanted to say something, but then she closed her eyes and bent her head. When she looked up, her eyes were filled with tears.

For a long time they stood still, two people on a path in the middle of the forest one early spring morning. Only a cool breeze whispered quietly in the tree crowns. Finally Malou spoke again. "What happened, Olava?" Her voice was mild and comforting. Olava bent her head. The pain in her chest felt like a big, open wound.

"He... he fell into the river and hit his head... there was a viper... I was supposed to look after him." Olava could no longer hold back those tears that she had tried to control for so long.

"I let him sit alone by the river... and when I got back..." She shook her head despairingly.

"I called for him... I thought he had hidden somewhere..." Her words were blurred by tears. Olava no longer had any choice. She fell apart and cried.

Malou didn't say anything. She only stood quietly by her side and helped her when she needed it. Finally, Olava curled up on the path, rocking back and forth. Everywhere around them the branches were waving softly in the golden spring breeze. Olava didn't see it. She was in deep mourning.

The sun was getting stronger. Olava had stopped crying but remained curled up on the path with her knees pulled up to her chest and her arms wrapped around her knees. She felt completely empty inside.

"I'm sorry..." Olava didn't know why she said it. The words just came out by themselves.

"Sorry? For what?" Malou sounded surprised. Olava waited a few moments before she answered.

"You gave him milk... when he was a baby... he was so sick. You saved him..." Malou was quiet for a long time and when she spoke again, her voice was serious.

"It was you who saved him, Olava." Olava swallowed a lump. Tears filled her eyes again. This time she cried quietly.

"I miss him so much." The words whispered in the wind.

"Yes..." Malou took her hand and held it carefully in hers.

"Come." She helped her up and over to a tree some distance away from the path. They sat down leaning their backs to the trunk and whilst tears were running down her cheeks, Olava told her story for the first time. About Eystein's first summer on the mountain farm. About Kamma who was gone. About the accident by the river. About how she had carried him home to the farm. About the funeral and the time after. About her mother and father's fight. About the blow and her father's words. About her mother in the courtyard. About the farewell at little brother's grave. About the journey to Christiania. About the days when she tried to get a job. About the ship and the lifeboat. About how sick she got and about the captain who helped her.

Malou sat completely still and listened to Olava while she told her story and when she had finished, they remained quiet for a long time. The silence together with Malou felt light and peaceful. It was as if it gently embraced the words of sorrow.

The sun was high in the sky by now. Mild rays found their way through the leaves and warmed their faces. Olava could feel how tired she was and for a short moment her eyes closed. All of a sudden she became aware of the life in a sunbeam. She looked in wonder at the fine grains of dust that were dancing in the middle of the beam. They were dancing like little angels. There were endlessly many of them. Olava looked and looked. All of a sudden she felt wide awake. They were dancing close, round and round, twinkling in the light from the sun. A little smile touched her lips.

"Look at the angels... they're dancing."

"Where?" Malou sounded surprised.

"There... in the sunbeam." Malou was quiet. Olava didn't see it, but she smiled, moved.

"Yes, they do." Their eyes rested on the dancing angels for a long time. It wasn't until a long time after that Olava understood that it was a gift from the moment.

Later that same night, Olava tiptoed out of her room and out the door to the garden. The others were gathered for dinner, but she had excused herself on the pretext that she wasn't feeling well and wanted to go to bed early. Gerda had neither answered nor looked at her when she said goodnight and Olava tried to shake off the discomfort as she walked through the garden and out on the road. She had left the window in her room slightly open so that she could get in if they locked the door to the garden.

Olava felt nervous as she walked up the road from the hotel and past the first two farms before the road turned and she continued down a dirt road. Malou had explained to her where to go to find the camp which was situated some distance away from the town. At first Olava had hesitated when Malou invited her. She had told her that they were going to make a fire ceremony to honour little Eystein and asked her if she wanted her to come. At first Olava had felt uncertain about it all but in the end, she had said that she would come.

Olava stopped when she saw the wagons that where standing in a circle in an open area near the edge of the forest. She counted them. There were 10, many more than Malou's closest family who had lived at Majbritt's farm that winter many years ago. The camp was full of activity, little kids ran around playing, some of the men were feeding the horses, and in the midst of the circle, the women were preparing the fire. Olava remained at a distance, a little uncertain. The thought of leaving again came to her mind, but then she saw Malou who was waving happily and came to greet her.

"Hi, Olava. Welcome." Malou smiled warmly and behind her a young girl came running towards them.

"You probably don't recognize her… it's Emilia…" Olava looked at the girl. Last time she had seen her she was only a baby, a few months older than Eystein.

"And this is Olava who I have told you about." Emilia looked at her with big, serious dark brown eyes. For a moment Olava remembered how she had been sitting on her lap while she fed her porridge and little brother got milk from Malou. She smiled carefully.

"Hi Emilia."

"Hi." Emilia's eyes got softer and she smiled shyly back.

"Come and say hello to the rest." Olava walked with Malou and Emilia towards the camp where they were met with gentle smiles and friendly nods. Malou's closest family greeted her warmly with quiet compassion. There were Aishe and Nadya, Marko, Stevo, Shandor and Nanosh. Although the years had left their marks, Olava recognized them. She greeted them all in silence. It was too difficult to speak. Almost to her relief the children gathered around her. Olava could hardly recognize them after so many years and Malou told her who was who. When they ran off to play, Olava looked around, searchingly, and Malou guessed her thoughts.

"Raya left our world almost two years ago." Olava nodded sadly, but Malou smiled warmly.

"She left quietly in her sleep. She has peace now."

"I see..." Olava tilted her head. Malou's words felt good and made her thoughtful.

"Come, let's go and sit down." They walked over to the fire where the others were gathering with warm blankets and instruments. Children and adults sat in a circle around the fire, the little ones on their mothers' or older siblings' laps. Malou introduced Olava to a woman a little older than herself.

"This is Veronica. She will be in charge of the ceremony."

"Hi. You must be Olava." Veronica smiled and for a short moment she turned her eyes to look at the sky. When their eyes met again, she looked almost surprised.

"Hi..." Olava was puzzled. It struck her that the woman had the most radiantly clear and darkest eyes she had ever seen.

"Welcome to us." Veronica bent her head slightly.

"Thank you." Olava nodded, mystified at something she didn't quite understand.

"Veronica is our Shuvani." Olava and Malou sat by the fire which was surrounded by a circle of beautiful, round stones.

"What is that?" Olava looked questioningly at Malou.

"It's a medicine woman among our people." Olava didn't have time to ask anymore as the talking died away and silence descended.

The evening darkness fell slowly over the camp as everyone's eyes rested on the vivid flames that stretched elegantly towards the sky and melted together in a magical dance. The cracking from the fire was the only sound that broke the silence of the dark. For a long time they all sat quietly as the peace spread through the circle. Veronica started to walk around the fire. In one hand she held a rattle instrument. With slow steps she walked round and round while the rustling sounds rose and fell. Olava observed everything with wonder. The beautiful woman with the raven black hair and the radiant eyes looked almost as if she were in another world. One by one the others closed their eyes and began to rock steadily back and forth. Then Veronica stopped, looked towards the sky and spoke, at first once, then several times. She bent towards the earth and then towards the sky again. Olava didn't understand what she was saying. She looked at Malou who nodded warmly but didn't say anything.

When the ritual was over, Veronica sat down

in the circle with the rest of the group. She spoke again. Olava thought she could hear little brother's name and looked questioningly at Malou who whispered that it was a prayer for Eystein and everyone in her family. Olava listened to the foreign words, puzzled. What was she saying? Her thoughts were interrupted when all of a sudden she heard crying and she realized that it was Veronica. Olava tried to understand what was happening. The woman knew her story and was crying in deep grief. All of a sudden she realized that Veronica was crying her tears, she cried little brother's tears and she cried for her whole family. Olava was even more surprised when the crying began to spread in the circle. Malou, Aishe, Nadya and several of the women cried in silent grief. Not until a long time after did Olava understand that they were tears that came from love.

They were surrounded by an ocean of darkness when silence again fell over the circle and the only light came from the fire, a few scattered stars in the sky and an almost white new moon. Olava could faintly see the many faces in the light from the fading flames. It was no longer possible to tell who was who. One of the men started to sing, a slow melancholic mourning song from old times. For a long time he sang alone, then more joined in, and two of the men played quietly on their violin and harmonica. Olava held the necklace from Eystein close to her heart. Quiet tears ran down her cheeks. The foreign tones sounded in a strange way so familiar.

Olava could faintly see the road in the light from the sky beings when she walked home around midnight. The events of the night filled her with a sense of deep wonder. The circle, the fire, the ceremony, the prayer and the song. It was all so new and yet it felt so natural. Veronica and the others had shared her grief. The deep sorrow which she had tried to hide for so long.

Olava stopped and watched the hotel from a distance. It looked like a big, silent shadow and when she got closer, she became aware of her dislike of the place. She was relieved when she closed the door to her room, as if it gave her protection. Lying in bed she folded her hands over the quilt. Tears ran down her cheeks and her thoughts circled around what she had experienced. It took her a long time to fall asleep.

Olava walks through the streets. Slowly around the corners of the houses. She stops and looks around. It's the same place as always, but this time everything is peaceful. The light is breaking through the grey clouds. Something wriggles, but it dissolves quietly. Turns into nothing and disappears. The silence is light and peaceful. Olava wakes up. It is the last time she has this dream.

A few days later Olava was having dinner with the family at the hotel. She tried to sound as friendly as possible when she turned to Gerda.

"I would like to go home for some time." Olava was surprised at how easy it was to lie to her.

"I see?" Gerda hardly looked at her.

"Yes, my father is sick."

"That should be okay. We have a quiet time ahead of us." Ole spoke.

"Well... I don't know." Gerda hesitated.

"Besides, you haven't used any of your holiday yet." There was something quietly insistent behind

Ole's friendly words.

"I'll clean the living room in the basement while you're gone." Olava looked at Elin, happy and surprised at the unexpected support.

"Very well, then. It's okay and maybe it will do you good to go home for some time." Gerda continued to eat.

"When will you be leaving?" Ole smiled at her.

"I would like to go as soon as possible."

"I'll take you to the station."

"Thank you." Olava smiled but looked down. It was harder to lie to Ole.

Three days later Olava was standing by the station building looking at Ole as he drove away. When she couldn't see the horse carriage anymore, she took her bag over her shoulder and walked fast and with her head bent in the other direction out of town. To her relief there were hardly any people around. She had checked out where it was best to go without being seen. Just outside town she turned and followed a small dirt road until she got to a narrow path which led back through the forest and further along the road to the place where the camp was.

After the night around the fire Malou had asked her if she wanted to come and live with them for a while. Olava was both happy and surprised, but her first thought was that it was impossible. She had her work at the hotel and even though she was ashamed at the thought, she knew that she wouldn't tell Gerda or any of the others about her meeting with the Roma family. Hesitantly she had tried to explain that she would probably not get time off from work. Malou had smiled understandingly and said that she was always welcome.

It was after an episode with Gerda the next day that an idea had begun to take shape in Olava's head. Gerda had complained that the kitchen towel Olava used was too dirty and had made the usual comment that she couldn't run a hotel like that. The kitchen towel was newly washed, but Olava hadn't answered back, just looked at Gerda. In that moment she got the idea. She could say that she wanted to go home for some time.

In the next three weeks Olava lived together with Malou and the rest of the family. Like the time when they stayed at Majbritt's farm, she felt at home almost immediately. They received her like one of their own and from the first day, she helped out with the daily chores. Olava was happy and grateful to be of use. During the day she helped to get water, gather firewood, cook and look after the little ones. In the evening they gathered around the fire where they sang and played music often until darkness fell. For each day that passed, Olava experienced more and more how these people lived in peace and harmony, and it struck her how different it was from life at the hotel.

What was going to change Olava's life forever was the meetings with Veronica. Every morning she gathered three young girls, two of the youngest women and Olava in a circle in a clearing some distance away from the camp. Veronica was a treasure chest of wisdom and she poured out of her knowledge. She could be funny and serious, bubbly and facetious, and her words danced through the air when she spoke. Sometimes she spoke with passion, other times she asked questions, and she always listened carefully to their answers. Every now and then she would pause for a long time and sit quietly without considering either time or place. Veronica's eyes were deep and wide open. Like a mirror of her soul. She radiated with a glow that Olava had never seen before. Not until many years later did she understand that it was a glow that came from love to every living being.

Every morning Olava listened to the old wisdom which had been passed down from generation to generation for centuries and Veronica's words echoed in her soul. It was all wisdom that Olava already knew somewhere deep inside herself and which had to be found again.

Veronica talked about old traditions for healing and about finding our strength and power in order to live in balance and harmony. She talked about the circle as a symbol of our power and about which forces make the circle strong and healthy and which forces limit us as human beings. Veronica talked about fear and about what it does to our power.

"It is fear that keeps us from giving and receiving love." Veronica looked almost sad when she said it.

"Criticism and judgement are negative thoughts and feelings which take our power. When we compare ourselves to others or try to control others, there is this small voice inside of us which thinks that we are even better than or worse than others. Neither is true, of course." Veronica spoke as if it was the biggest truth.

Veronica also talked about change of fear.

"Everything that we deny are old wounds which show up in different ways. Some are angry or sad all their lives. Some blame others and some get sick. By getting everything that we deny up to the surface and giving it light and love and forgiveness, we get greater power."

Veronica spoke about the power in thoughts, body, feelings and spirit.

"We call them "The Four Daughters of Beauty." She sent them all a warm and heartfelt smile.

Veronica talked about being connected and about the power of the seven winds. About the power from east, south, west and north, Mother Earth, Grandfather Sun and Grandmother Moon. Veronica talked about our ancestors and about the legacy we pass on to the next seven generations.

"All our actions today have significance for the next seven generations."

Every night Olava went to bed with a lot of new knowledge that filled her head with many questions, but she'd also begun to feel a quiet joy and a careful hope for the future.

Some days Olava walked with Veronica out in nature to gather herbs and plants for tea and medicine. It was on these walks that she learnt to give something to Mother Earth and only take what she needed. Veronica also showed her how to bless the water and seek advice and guidance in nature. Sometimes they would just sit together in silence and it was often after these quiet moments that they talked. It was some of these conversations that were going to follow Olava through her life in many years to come.

It was one of those days when the spring breeze dances to the light and green tones in every tree and every bush. Veronica and Olava had gone further than they used to and it was soon afternoon when they stopped by a small forest lake. Veronica breathed in deeply and a peaceful smile spread in her face.

"This is so beautiful."

"Yes..." Olava looked around. It was really beautiful.

"Shall we sit for a while?"

"Yes." Olava nodded.

"Over there seems to be a good place." Veronica set the basket with plants and herbs on a big, flat stone where it was safe. They sat down in the grass close to the edge of the lake.

Olava was by now used to sitting in silence together with Veronica and the discomfort that she always experienced in the beginning had begun to subside quicker. She breathed in as deeply as she could, the way she had learnt, and every time she breathed out, she let go of all the tension in her body. She tried to let go of the thoughts that popped up in her head and slowly she felt more and more relaxed. This time she let her eyes rest on the light blue sky and the scattered lily white clouds which were mirrored in the silvery water. The afternoon sun was warm and pleasant and they sat for a long time before Veronica spoke.

"Olava?"

"Yes?"

"Do you feel guilty at what happened to your little brother?"

The question came unexpectedly. They hadn't talked about the accident before. She hesitated. "Olava, do you feel that it is your fault?" Veronica repeated the question. Olava looked absently at her hands. Her throat felt thick with tears.

"I let him sit alone by the river. I was supposed to look after him. My father... he said..." Olava couldn't say more. She shook her head despairingly.

"What happened to Eystein was an accident." Veronica's voice was mild but serious.

"He was just lying there… completely still… he had hit his head." For the first time Olava used words to describe the sight which was burned into her memory. She bent her head and cried.

"It was a tragic accident, Olava."

"But he was dead… I tried to revive him, but he was dead. I carried him home to Mum and Dad." Olava broke down, her tears fell to the ground. Veronica sat quietly next to her and let her cry.

"It was an accident."

"I shouldn't have left him. Maybe he was scared…" Olava no longer tried to stop her tears. She just let them come. Veronica waited a long time before she spoke again.

"What would you say to him if he were here now?" Olava looked at her questioningly through her tears. She let the question rest.

"I would say… I'm sorry…" Veronica tilted her head and nodded lovingly.

"What else would you say?" Olava looked at her mild face, mystified at the presence in her calm eyes.

"I would say… that I miss him… and… that I love him." Olava closed her eyes and bent her head towards the ground. The words rested in the air.

"What do you think he would say to you?" Olava looked bewildered at Veronica.

"He would probably say… that it was an accident… and that I shouldn't be so sad all the time." Olava hid her face in her hands and cried.

"Yes…" Veronica's voice was mild and gentle. "It's not your fault, Olava. It's no one's fault." Olava let her eyes rest on a small stone in the water. She nodded almost imperceptibly. Her face was red and swollen from all the tears and in the end she dried her eyes and nose in her sweater. In the midst of it all, they had to laugh. Veronica took her hand and Olava rested her head on her shoulder. They sat like that for a long time.

"Sometimes I just don't want to be here anymore, I just want to die." It suddenly felt so natural to say the forbidden words.

"Yes… I know…" Veronica nodded slowly.

"Do you?" Olava looked at her in surprise.

"Yes." Veronica's face was sorrowful and peaceful at the same time. "It's many years ago now. I lost my little daughter."

"I'm so sorry… I didn't know…" Olava lowered her eyes, uncertain what to say.

"Don't apologize." Veronica smiled at her. Then she told her about her little daughter.

"I was very young. About your age. She was born premature. She was with us for two days but then her little heart stopped beating." Veronica's voice sang with love for her little daughter.

"For a long time I felt guilty, that I could have done something to prevent it." Veronica paused for a while, looked over the water, closed her eyes and opened them again. She smiled.

"She was the most beautiful little girl you could ever imagine. We named her Viola." Olava nodded. Something happened inside her while Veronica told her story. She wasn't the only one who carried sorrow. How could she think that? They sat without saying more. Veronica's story filled the air with a heartfelt presence where words weren't necessary. After some time she spoke again.

"You see, Olava, it's through our wounds that we close our hearts." Olava was quiet and let Veronica's words sink in.

"It's also through our wounds that we open our hearts again." Olava removed a tear from her cheek and nodded slowly.

"And remember this, Olava, it's your story. Make it your story." Olava was puzzled. Her story? Make it her story? Once again Veronica's words had given her something to think about.

Olava was also introduced to a world of symbols. Like the morning when Veronica brought her cards and asked them all to take one. Olava pulled a card with the picture of a five-pointed star in a circle. Veronica smiled when she saw it and Olava paid close attention whilst she explained.

"It's a pentagram and it's an old symbol. We call it the star of wisdom. The tip pointing upwards represents the spirit and the four others symbolize earth, water, air and fire which are part of all life on Earth." Olava and the others listened in interest.

"You can also draw a pentagram like an unbroken, continuous line." Veronica drew the star with her index finger in the air. "It represents the connection between the spirit and the four elements." Olava smiled thoughtfully. When she was little she had often drawn the star without thinking about what it may symbolize. Veronica continued.

"The star also represents a human being." Veronica pointed at the five tips which could symbolize a head, arms and legs. She paused for some time whilst looking at the card seriously before she continued.

"The circle around the star symbolizes the cycle of life and nature. We are all part of this cycle." Veronica smiled warmly to each and every one of them and gave the card back to Olava who studied it with interest.

A few days later Olava walked in the forest alone. They were having a party later that night and she was gathering dry twigs and branches for the fire. She was lost in her own thoughts. It was as if these days had done something to her, as if her understanding of the world had been challenged.

She had learnt so much from Veronica and the whole family. They lived together in a completely different way, so close to nature, so uncomplicated and so peacefully. Once again it struck her how different it was from the busy days at the hotel and she realized that she hadn't missed it for a second.

Twilight had fallen over the camp when they gathered around the fire later that night. One of the youngest girls was already asleep in Olava's lap. She tried to take it all in. The golden-red flames danced beautifully against the sky. The women had dressed up in long, colourful skirts, beautiful dresses, shawls around their heads and rattling beads and pretty jewelry. Soon the first wistful tones sounded from the men's violin and guitar. The women formed a circle around the fire, some carrying a tambourine, others castanets. They began to dance and with light steps, swinging hips and waving arms they were carried away by the enchanting tones.

Olava was full of wonder. There was almost something magical about these women who stretched gracefully towards the stars in the light from the golden fire. That night all worries disappeared from Olava's thoughts.

The time with the family was coming to an end. Olava was going back to the hotel and in the camp they had begun to pack and get ready to move on.

Olava and Veronica were on their way back to the camp when they stopped on a hilltop with a view over the forest and lakes.

"Shall we sit for a while?" Veronica smiled but looked a little tired.

Olava hadn't thought about it before. Veronica wasn't so young anymore. They sat down to rest.

"This is our last walk together."

"Yes." Olava nodded.

"Are you looking forward to going back to the hotel?" Veronica looked at her questioningly.

"I don't know..." Olava hesitated.

"What is bothering you?" Olava was puzzled. Could Veronica tell?

"It is..." She looked down. Should she tell her about Gerda? In some ways it felt embarrassing.

"It is... the woman who runs the hotel... Her name is Gerda." Olava breathed in deeply.

"She's commenting on and criticising all the things I do... Sometimes she's complaining all the time and other times she avoids answering. I never know if she's in a good or bad mood." Olava shook her head.

"I've been thinking about leaving many times, but I don't know... The others are nice. Gerda can be kind, too... and all the guests like her... she's just too busy." Olava looked down. It felt strange to talk about Gerda in this way. Veronica paused before she answered.

"If you decide to leave one day, wait until you're ready. You will know when."

"I will?"

"Yes." Veronica nodded.

"But how..." Olava was confused.

"You see, Olava, our thoughts and feelings are important to how we experience our lives and how we view reality. Thoughts about ourselves and thoughts about others."

"But...?" Olava looked at Veronica questioningly. In a way this wasn't the answer she had expected.

"Do you remember that we talked about fear and where it comes from?"

"Yes." Olava nodded.

"Who decides who you are, Olava?" Olava looked at her a little uncertainly. She didn't quite know what to say.

"It's just that... I don't think I've done anything to her." She sighed.

"No, I know that." Veronica smiled warmly and gazed at the horizon. Olava pondered her words and was lost in her own thoughts when Veronica continued to talk.

"Is there anything in particular that you enjoy doing?"

"Yes." Olava nodded. "I like to bake and make desserts. Gunnhild has taught me. She's the chef at the hotel." Olava smiled at the thought.

"I see." Veronica listened with interest.

"I used to have the responsibility for making dessert for the guests... but not anymore..." Olava raised her shoulders a little.

"I see..." Veronica blinked lovingly at her.

"Well, it's Gerda who runs the hotel... she makes the decisions."

"Yes, I guess it is." Veronica smiled but her eyes revealed that she had more on her mind.

"What?!?" Olava laughed. She felt that she knew Veronica well by now and they could be cheerful and playful.

"Just remember, Olava, that you have a will of your own."

"Yes… but…" Olava shook her head. They both laughed. None of them said anymore and after some time they got up and began to walk back to the camp. They walked together in silence and Olava was grateful. Again she was lost in her own thoughts.

The next day Olava was standing in the doorway to Malou's wagon with her bag over her shoulder. She looked inside one last time. The wagon with the many symbols. She looked at stones, little figures, mussels, jewelry and feathers. Malou had explained to her about some of them, but she still didn't know the meaning of the others. On the wall was the picture of the Virgin Mary that Olava's mother had given to Malou all those years ago. Every night Olava had lain in her bed and looked at the picture before falling asleep. Olava smiled to herself, sad, but also grateful. Then she went outside to say farewell to the family.

The children and the women gave her a warm hug one by one. The men nodded politely for goodbye and Marko gave her a heartfelt hug. Nanosh gave her a small wooden bowl which he had decorated with beautiful patterns. He smiled shyly when Olava thanked him for the beautiful gift. She was both moved and surprised.

Malou waited until she had said goodbye to everyone. She removed some hair from Olava's forehead and held one hand lightly to her cheek. Her tear-filled, warm, brown eyes smiled at her.

"Goodbye, Olava…"

"Goodbye…" Olava swallowed a lump. "Thank you…"

"Thank you, too, Olava…" Both dried their eyes.

"Will you give my love to Veronica." Veronica

had left early in the morning.

"Yes, I will." They held each other close, both with their eyes closed. Then it was time for Olava to go.

In the outskirts of the camp she stopped and turned around. They were waving at her. Malou, Emilia and all the others. She dried her eyes and waved back. Her heart was filled with gratitude and for the first time in a very long time, Olava felt a spark of hope about the future.

17

The early spring frost bites hard. Cool nights form hoar frost on twigs and branches. Green sprouts defy the cold, break through old leaf. The first signs of new life. Squinting against the light. Stretching in the sun. Soon remnants of snow and ice melt. A little warmer every day. Streams trickle and trees shiver. The birds sing of spring. New buds shoot forth. Angel green in the golden breeze. The beating heart of spring beats with lush determination. The forest is celebrating. Green and light and wild and white. A redeeming power in roaring revolt. Mild winds sing of a longing. A song of peace and love. Where heaven and sea melt.

The first days back at the hotel seemed almost unreal. Olava felt as if she came from another world and even though she continued with her work as usual, her thoughts were somewhere else. The days in the camp and the conversations with Veronica filled her with wonder and questions. What was it that she had said? "Make it your story." What had Veronica meant by that? Her story. What had her story done to her? How could she make it her story? It's my story. The words followed Olava for a long time and she began to look for answers. Who was she? Where did she come from? What was her story?

At the hotel everything continued as usual and when Olava was off for the day, she went outside. She felt that she had to get away from Gerda and the heavy atmosphere. In the forest she found peace and calm and a place where she could be alone with her thoughts. It was on these walks that Olava began the journey back to her own past, her childhood, her mum and dad, Runa and Eystein and everyone on the farm. She began the journey into her own thoughts and feelings and into her sorrow. Back to the years with little brother, the accident and the time after. It was on these walks that Olava began to find herself again.

Veronica's words followed Olava wherever she went. "Your thoughts are not you. Your thoughts about yourself and others." Olava hadn't even realized that they were there. Her thoughts lived their own life. It was especially thoughts about Gerda and what she was capable of saying that whirled around in her head. Now Olava knew that they were there and slowly she began to recognize them, but it was like learning to crawl and walk again. She fell again and again and forgot that they were there. "Do not judge them, just observe them." That was what Veronica had said. But it was easier said than done.

 Olava also began to notice when her body reacted. It was mostly when Gerda was in a bad mood. Veronica had told her that old feelings sit in the body. "Some react by fighting while others freeze or flee." Olava knew that she only wanted to escape from Gerda's accusations. Did her body react like that because she had learnt it at some point? Olava remembered how her father had talked to her mother that time when she was sick and how his moods could make everyone on the farm walk around carefully, afraid of his temper.

 Most of all she remembered how she had frozen that night he had blamed her for the accident. Olava also began to look further back, to her grandparents. Dimly she remembered the bitter atmosphere between her grandmother and grandfather on her father's side, but she also recalled the warmth and joy in her mother's parents' home.

Olava's journey to her inner self became the most important journey in her life. She began to understand her story. It went far back, maybe even further than she realized. She began to understand her own pattern of fear and escape and how grief and depression had grown worse in all those years after the accident. First came the understanding, then came the acceptance, and after some time, Olava began to tell herself the things she hadn't heard from anyone else. This was how Olava began to make her story her own.

At the hotel everything got worse. Gerda's outbursts came more frequently and sometimes they all walked around as if they were afraid of stepping on a mine. The atmosphere was heavy and tense and no one said anything out of fear that it would make things worse. It didn't help when Gunnhild announced that she would soon retire. She felt that she had become too old to work in the kitchen. Olava was very discouraged when she was told. What would it be like to be at the hotel when Gunnhild was gone?

Gerda hired a new girl to take over Gunnhild's job. Her name was Silje and she was only a few years older than Olava. Silje had just finished her education as a chef and she began working at the hotel while Gunnhild was still there and could introduce her to the job. Olava observed how friendly Gerda was when she welcomed her and how relieved Silje was that she had come to a good place. Olava shook her head in disbelief. If only she knew.

Olava walked in the woods whenever she had the chance. This was where she found calm and peace. She had also begun to look at nature in a new way after the time with Veronica and the family. She found her own place, a beautiful little spot surrounded by birch trees, heather and grass and with a view over woods and lakes. She would often go to this spot and sit there with her eyes closed. She filled her lungs with air, listened to the sounds from nature, the hum of a bumblebee, the songs of the birds and the sound of the wind in the trees. She felt her own breathing, little breaths of wind against her cheek, her clothes against her skin and the sun's warming rays in her face.

Slowly Olava began to feel lighter in her body and her mind. She also began to deal with Gerda in another way and stopped answering her when she criticized her. But the more Olava tried to stay out of Gerda's way, the worse she got. It was like fighting herself out of a straitjacket. The more she tried, the tighter it got.

One night Olava came home late after a long walk in the woods. Everything was dark and quiet at the hotel and she got a shock when she tiptoed down the stairs to her room and all of a sudden heard Gerda's sharp voice behind her.

"Where have you been?" Olava turned around. She met Gerda's staring eyes but didn't answer her right away.

"I've been out for a walk."

"What are you thinking of? Staying out till late in the night and sneaking in like this?" Olava walked up a few steps so that she stood at eye level with

Gerda.

"Is there anything wrong?" Olava asked as calmly as she could.

"If there is anything wrong?" Gerda was fuming with frustration. "You stay out till so late without telling anyone where you are." Olava knew well that she had said she was going out for a walk. She avoided answering her.

"Are you not even going to answer me?"

"Do you have problems with any of the guests?" Olava was calm and casual and for a short moment Gerda looked at her, obviously baffled.

"If I have problems with any of the guests? I have never! What exactly is wrong with you? Ever since you went home to visit your family you have behaved like this."

"Like what?" Olava looked at Gerda questioningly.

"You do not answer when I ask, you stay out till late in the night without saying where you are. You are rude and irresponsible."

"I see." Olava nodded slowly. "I'm sorry you feel that way."

"I'm sorry you feel that way." This time it was Olava's turn to be surprised. Gerda was making faces when she repeated the words after her. That was something she had never seen before. In a way it was comical, but she answered her in a neutral and serious way.

"Yes, I'm sorry and I don't know anyone else who would say that about me, either."

"I don't know what others would say and not say, but maybe you should consider focusing on your work at the hotel instead of staying out all night. It is in fact what you get paid for."

"All night? It's a few minutes past eleven."

Olava smiled briefly. "Goodnight." She turned around and began to walk. She could feel Gerda's frantic staring eyes on her neck and was relieved that she didn't say more.

Olava was shaking when she sat on her bed. What was going on? She had never experienced Gerda behaving so rudely before. Olava took the pillow from her bed and held it tight over her face. She felt a sudden urge to scream out loud but she couldn't. Instead she made a quick decision. She crawled out of the window, tiptoed close to the house and walked quickly over the yard. She continued up the road and when she got to the path that led to the mountains, she began to run through the forest, along the fields and past the first lake. She ran until sweat poured off her and didn't stop before she was far away from the nearest farm.

She was surrounded by darkness and trees in every direction. Olava was gasping for breath, she put her hands on her thighs and clenched her teeth. And then Olava did what she should have done a long time ago. She screamed at the top of her lungs. First once, then again and again. She shouted in anger, despair and grief. Again and again.

Olava screamed like she'd never done before. Finally her legs collapsed and she fell on her knees. She began to cry. I am so tired. Her voice was only a weak whisper. Why did you have to die? Why did you have to die? Why? WHY? She shouted again. Olava was furious. WHY DID MY LITTLE BROTHER HAVE TO DIE? WHY? She cried. I'm so lonely. I'm all alone. AND WHY CAN'T THAT CRAZY WOMAN LEAVE ME ALONE? WHY? WHY? WHY? Olava hit her head with her fists. Again and again. WHY CAN'T THAT HORRIBLE WOMAN... Ouch. Olava felt her head. It hurt where she had hit herself. She lay down on the path, completely exhausted, and in the midst of it all, she had to laugh, a little silent chuckle. What if someone had seen her now? After a long time she got up and walked the long way back to the hotel. It was easy for Olava to find the way back in the dark.

After that night Olava began to shout when she needed it. It was mostly when there had been an episode with Gerda and she felt that she just had to get it out of her body. Olava began to bring a pillow when she walked in the woods so that she could scream into it whenever she felt like doing so. She also discovered that she could scream in her bed if she pushed her face hard into the pillow and covered her head with the quilt and the blankets she had in her room. Every time she felt a little lighter, but from then on Gerda was on her neck almost constantly.

Olava tried to pretend as if nothing was wrong and continued to do her work as usual. She was friendly to everyone. Also towards Gerda and somehow this seemed to frustrate her more than anything else.

Don't blame anyone and not yourself. Those were Veronica's words. Olava knew well that she couldn't blame Gerda that she chose to stay at the hotel. But why was it so hard to leave and what was it she was supposed to learn by staying?

The thought of leaving the hotel came more and more often. Sometimes Olava counted her money which she had put aside from her salary. She had saved enough to get by for some time, but she still had doubts. Where would she go? What would she do for a living? She needed work. What would happen if she came to a place where things were the same? When Gerda was at her worst, Olava only wanted to pack her stuff and leave, but something inside her made her stay.

Karin sent a letter from America with a picture of Olava Ingrid, a beautiful little girl with the same dark eyes and wild hair as Lukas. She also sent an old poem that she had found. "I hope you will find comfort in these words from a poem that I found," she wrote.

I am Alive

Seek my peace in the gentle breeze
Seek my fun in the rising Sun
Seek my light in the beauty of night
Seek my love in the Stars above
Seek my heart, we are not apart
I am with you, right by your side
I never died, I am alive.

Olava read the poem again and again. Tears ran down her cheeks and afterwards she sat for a long time, just holding the poem in her hands. The next day she put it in a frame and hung it on the wall above her bed. Olava read the poem every night before falling asleep.

Time went by. The thoughts in Olava's head had begun to quiet down. She could recognize them now and they had gotten a friendly but determined opponent, Olava herself. Sometimes she would talk to them and sometimes she joked and fooled around with them. Hi there, how are we today? It took a long time, but slowly and surely they no longer decided who she was. Olava also began to challenge all her convictions, first about herself and then about others. She began asking questions about everything she believed to be true. Who said that she was like that? Who said that guest was like this? She began to discover new sides to herself. It became easier for her to talk to the guests and she rediscovered the joy of singing, mostly when she was out walking. She began to read again. There was a little library in the town and in the books she found many answers.

Olava began to feel stronger. She no longer dwelt so much in her past. She had been through it so many times and the fact was that she could continue doing that forever. She no longer froze when Gerda accused her of something. Sometimes she tried to ignore her, other times she answered back. She had even practised in front of the mirror in her room how to stare back while making her eyes look hard.

"I want you to stop bothering me."

"Bothering you? I'm only telling you the truth. You are not doing your job well enough." Gerda fumed with frustration when someone talked back to her.

"If you are so dissatisfied why don't you fire me? I'm sure there are many people who would like to work for you."

"You cannot stand to hear the truth."

"What truth?" Olava could be almost unyielding.

"That is the most ungrateful..."

"Who of us is most ungrateful?" Olava learnt how to make herself hard and to shut down her emotions. But it was exhausting to live in Gerda's war and she never seemed to stop. It was as if she got nourishment from the conflicts.

One day Olava had had enough. She felt bone-weary and only wanted to get away, but the uncertainty of leaving filled her to the breaking point. All day she had felt how her throat was thick with tears and when she was off, her only thought was to get away from the hotel. That night Olava wandered aimlessly for hours and hours without thinking about either time or place. She cried like she had never done before. She neither wanted to nor could she stop it any longer, she just cried and cried. She had had enough and now her tears had a will of their own. If only she could hide, shut the world out forever. She walked and walked and muttered to herself through snot and tears. Never meet another human being ever again. Just live by herself in a small cabin far out into the wilderness, hide under a blanket and never go out. I don't want to be strong anymore. I don't want to. I'm so little. I'm just a human being. Olava fell apart. Nothing mattered. She didn't take any notice of the tears that ran down her cheeks. Nothing mattered anymore. She couldn't take it anymore.

Not until it was completely dark did Olava go back to the hotel. She didn't dare to think about how she looked and when she was back in her room, she stood in front of her mirror staring at herself. Her eyes were two tiny cracks and her face was red and swollen to the point where she was almost unrecognizable. What was she going to do to look normal the next day? She lay down with cold cloths on her face but continued to cry until late in the night.

She still looked ravaged the next morning. She couldn't show herself like that. Quickly she took the wash bowl, placed it by the bed, and opened the window. She went back to bed and waited until somebody knocked on the door. Olava turned her face to the wall and pulled the quilt over her head.

"Come in."

"Hi. Mother is asking for you." It was Elin.

"I've been sick all night." Olava muttered from under the quilt. Elin was quiet.

"Do you think you'll get better during the day?" Oh no, why couldn't she just go away. Olava made some sounds as if she was about to throw up again.

"Okay, I'll let mother know. Get well soon." Thank goodness, it made Elin leave immediately.

"Thank you." Olava whispered from under the quilt, but she also smiled a little to herself.

Olava stayed in bed the whole day. She couldn't remember that she had ever felt so relaxed in her body before. She lay completely still for hours without moving a single muscle. She only stared emptily into space and rested. Everything seemed so peaceful and it felt so natural to just lie there. She slept a little every now and then, a calm dreamless sleep, but most of the time she only lay completely still. Sometimes she looked at the crack in the ceiling above her. It had become even bigger.

After that day Olava began to feel a longing. She didn't know quite after what, but it was a feeling that came from inside and that grew bigger in time. A longing to surrender to life and live without fear and in peace and harmony with herself and others. She became stronger and it took more and more to get her out of balance. Slowly Gerda began to leave her alone and she almost completely stopped her accusations. Only now she targeted Silje instead. Olava didn't hear it, but she could see it in her face, the uncertain look in her eyes, and the way she was always on guard when Gerda was in the kitchen. Finally, Olava chose to talk to Silje about it and from that day they became each other's support. In time they came to trust each other and became friends.

Silje told her about her father whom she had never met and Olava told her about Eystein and the accident.

On Saturdays they began to go to dances. Olava got her first real kiss. She had kissed one of Majbritt's boys when they were little but that didn't count. Johan came from one of the farms in the neighbouring community, a shy, young man with a charming smile and an eye for Olava.

Silje had told her many times, but Olava had only laughed at it. Finally he gathered up his courage and asked her to dance. Afterwards he asked her if she wanted to go for a walk. Olava had hoped he would ask and when they were by themselves he stopped and took her hands in his. He bent forward and kissed her, at first gently. Olava closed her eyes and a pleasant sensation spread in her body. He kissed her again and Olava kissed him back. Soon they were standing close kissing each other long and tenderly. On their way back to the hotel that night Silje and Olava danced and laughed and the rolling tones echoed in the darkness of the night.

One day Ole's old parents, Thorkild and Majken, visited the hotel. They lived in Sweden, not so far from the border, but it was still a long journey for the two elderly people. Olava noticed the polite but tense relationship between Gerda and Thorkild. Majken on the other hand was the epitome of friendliness and tried to smooth things over with smiles and good words. It was mostly Steinar and Elin she talked to and it was easy to tell that they were fond of their grandmother.

Olava was on her way to bed one night when Thorkild was sitting in the living room in the basement smoking his pipe. He looked worried but smiled when he saw her. Olava nodded politely.

"Hi."

"Hi, Olava, would you like to come and sit for a while?"

Yes..." Olava hesitated but walked over to the sofa and sat down in one of the arm chairs next to it.

"Have you been out walking?"

"Yes." Olava nodded.

"You seem to be doing that almost every night, don't you?"

"Yes, I do." She smiled a little.

"Are you happy here?" Olava looked down. She wasn't sure what to answer and before she had time to say anything, Thorkild muttered to himself.

"Yes, I thought so..."

"Sorry?" Olava looked at him questioningly.

"Well, that woman is only here on earth because hell didn't want her." Olava looked at him in bewilderment, uncertain whether she had heard him correctly.

"I'm not sure what you mean...?"

"I'm talking about Gerda, of course, and she's only getting worse." Olava was slightly baffled, but in a way it was good to hear someone say it so directly.

"She's possessed and she cannot see it herself. It's like a disease which affects everyone else but herself." Thorkild shook his head sadly.

"Yes, she is... not always easy..." Olava pulled up her shoulders a bit.

"That is to say it mildly."

"Yes, I guess it is." Now they both had to smile.

"Did you know that we used to live here?"

"Yes." Olava nodded. She knew that Ole's parents had started the hotel and that Gerda and Ole had taken over when they got married.

"It was good for the children that we were here when they were little. It was my wife especially who looked after them much of the time." Olava nodded understandingly.

"But at some point we decided to move... the atmosphere got so bad and Gerda took it out on Ole." There was something sad about Thorkild when he talked about it.

"Why doesn't he move?" Olava felt that it was okay to ask.

"It's easier said than done. This is where he has his life... it's his childhood home. The children are here, too. And who knows, maybe he still cares for her..." They remained quiet for some time before Thorkild smiled at her.

"It's getting late. I'm sure you must be off to bed soon. I'm off soon, too."

"Yes..." Olava got up and smiled. "Sleep well and... thank you."

"Thank you, too, Olava. Goodnight and sleep well." Thorkild nodded back at her in a friendly way.

Olava had asked herself many times if there was something about her which made Gerda behave in the way she did, but something changed after that talk with Thorkild. Was Gerda sick? And what was the reason she behaved the way she did? Sometimes she almost felt sorry for her. How did she really feel about herself? Veronica had talked about the power of forgiveness. "You do it for yourself." Those were her words.

Olava began to see people, everyone had their own story. Her heart got bigger and she began to feel gratitude towards her own childhood. The light and love from her mother. That was her heritage. It was a gift. The light had almost gone out, but she could light it again herself. All the good memories from her childhood came back to her and filled her with joy.

One day Olava was standing in front of the mirror in her room looking at herself. All of a sudden she began to laugh. In that moment she saw something clearly. She looked at herself and laughed and laughed. It was so comical. She had thought that she was not worthy. How stupid was that. That she was not worthy. Deep inside herself she had believed that she was not worthy. For being exactly who she was. How could that happen? Olava laughed and laughed, she dried her eyes and laughed, a heartfelt laughter that came from deep within herself.

A dream began to grow in Olava. The first tentative thoughts began to take shape. A dream about her own bakery with a small café. That was what she wanted. To be a confectioner and have her own little pastry shop where people could come and have a cup of coffee and a piece of cake. But how? She began to do some research and visited Gunnhild and asked her for advice. Olava pictured which cakes she would have in the case and which furniture to choose. Curtains and table cloths. Lights on the tables and pictures on the walls. What if?

Olava got a letter from back home. Grandmother was dying and had asked for her. She knew right away that it was time for her to go home and the next day she explained the situation to the family and ordered train tickets. A couple of days later she was standing at the station. She had a long journey ahead of her.

18

Snow-capped peaks stretch towards the sky. Shining silvery in the sunlight. There is metal in the mountains. Melted out by will alone. Unshakable they stand. Knowing old wisdom. Rising up from deep fjords. Dark blue like the mirror of the soul. Lush green forests and wild waterfalls. Skimming milky-white from steep walls. Sharp peaks and deep gorges. A chain of mountains bound together forever. They sing with the same voice. A song in time and space.

Olava sat on the train and looked at the landscape that slowly changed from the flat, rolling hills to the tall, magnificent mountains. The further west she came, the steeper they got. "This is the land of your ancestors." She could almost hear Veronica's voice. Olava smiled at the thought. She was on her way home.

Runa and their father were rowing over the fjord to meet her. Olava was looking out over the water towards the little boat house and the boat that slowly came closer. It felt so unreal to stand here after all those years. She closed her eyes and felt the sorrow in her heart.

Runa got out of the boat first and pulled it closer to the shore. Her eyes looked almost questioning when they met Olava's and in that moment Olava realized what she had done to her little sister when she had left their home. Runa hadn't only lost her little brother, she had also lost her big sister, and she was the one who had stayed back with their parents and their heavy grief. Olava embraced her.

"I'm sorry, Runa..."

"But... for what?" Runa looked almost surprised and for a short moment they just looked at each other softly. Then they both smiled.

"It's so good to see you." Olava could hardly believe that her little sister had become almost a grown woman.

"It's good to see you, too." Runa smiled happily. Olava felt her heart sink when she saw her father. The disease had left its marks. His face and eyes were sad and weary and his movements slow and heavy.

"Hi, Dad."

"Hi, Olava. Welcome home." There was a glimpse of tenderness in his eyes.

"Thank you." She smiled and they gave each other a gentle hug.

"You must be tired after the long journey."

"Yes, a little, but it went well."

"That's good."

"How are you doing, Dad?"

"Well, it's so and so, I take one day at a time." Olava nodded and smiled carefully.

"And Grandmother...?" She was afraid that she might have come too late.

"It's not so good. She's very weak and sleeps most of the time. I don't think she's got much time left."

"I see." Olava nodded sadly.

"Mother and Gudrun are waiting at home. They are looking forward to seeing you so much. Maybe the two of you would like to row?"

"Yes." Runa and Olava looked at each other and nodded and when they were in the boat, they sat next to each other and took one oar each, just like they used to when they were younger.

On the way across the fjord they talked about this and that. Runa told her about the nursing education that she was going to start soon and their father told her what was going on in the community. Olava listened carefully but didn't say much. She had had many thoughts about what it would be like to see her father again and felt happy and relieved. Sometimes she looked at the circles in the water every time the oar hit the surface – how they grew and got bigger until they melted together.

Out in the courtyard, her mother and Gudrun came to meet her. They had been waiting by the window looking for her on the road and went outside as soon as they saw her coming. Her mother smiled, moved.

"Welcome home, Olava."

"Thank you, Mum."

"It's so good to see you." Gudrun dried her eyes with her apron.

"Hi, Gudrun. It's good to see you, too." They hugged.

"Come, let's go inside. Grandmother knows that you're coming. I think maybe she has waited until you came." Her mother smiled mildly at her and Olava nodded quietly.

As soon as she had taken off her jacket, she tiptoed in to Grandmother who was lying in the room next to the kitchen. Olava sat down quietly in the chair next to the bed.

"Hi Grandma, it's me, Olava." She whispered and took her hand carefully in hers. Grandmother opened her eyes. They lit up when she saw who it was and a little smile touched her lips. She tried to speak, but Olava couldn't hear the words.

"Would you like to say something?" asked Olava. Grandmother nodded almost imperceptibly and Olava bent forward and placed her ear close to her Grandmother's mouth. Olava was just able to hear the few words and they made her close her eyes for a moment. Then she looked at her old grandmother and nodded mildly.

"Yes, Grandma, I will do that." She dried her eyes with her palm and whispered something back into her grandmother's ear. Ragnhild blinked slowly. Then she went back to sleep.

Olava held her hand for a long time. With her head bent, she remembered the last time she sat in this room and now came the tears that hadn't come then.

Later that afternoon Olava walked up to the church. Her mother asked her if she should come with her, but Olava preferred to go by herself. She took all the time she needed to get there. It was a peaceful day and sometimes she stopped and let her eyes wander in every direction. Olava had almost forgotten how beautiful it was here. The mountains, the fjord, the woods and the fields. It was a masterpiece. She closed her eyes and felt the warming sun from the southeast and the wind's light caresses on her face.

Olava stopped at the wooden gate. At a distance she could see Eystein's grave. It was decorated with beautiful stones and flowers. Slowly she walked over to it. It took her a while before she sat down in the grass. Her eyes rested on the name in the stone. It struck her that his name almost began with the word "eye".

"Hi Eystein… It's me, Olava." She breathed in deeply and looked at the sky. "I haven't been here for a long time…" She shook her head quietly. "I have missed you so much and I have been so sad." She burst into tears. "But I'm okay now and I think about you every day." Olava took her necklace from under her sweater. "Do you remember the necklace that you gave me? You were just a little boy and you had made it together with Lukas. I wear it every day." Olava remembered how Eystein had stood in front of her with big, joyful eyes with his hands behind his back when he was giving it to her. She smiled through her tears.

"Grandmother will come soon. She's sick and sleeps most of the time, but I have talked to her... and she told me that she's very happy to be seeing you again soon..." A breath of wind made Olava close her eyes. She filled her lungs with fresh air and cried. "She has promised me that she will give you the biggest hug in the world... I'll come one day, too, but I'm going to stay here for some time before I do..." Olava dried her eyes. She took some of the soil from the flowerbed and let it slip gently through her fingers. "I will always miss you."

That afternoon Olava sat by Eystein's grave for hours and talked to him. The pain and the loss filled her with grief and love. She cried and she smiled and told him everything. The churchyard was surrounded by tall birch trees swaying softly in the mild breeze.

The next day Olava went on a discovery tour to relive old memories. To the stalls where she so often had talked to the horses. The barn where she and Runa used to play and where they had slept that night when Eystein was born. To the bedroom upstairs. The kitchen. The tree in the garden where the swing had hung. The path through the forest to Majbritt's farm. Everywhere she went, memories came flooding back and the voices from the past came to her like sweet breaths of wind.

"His name will be Odin, and he will be your horse, Olava." It was her father. "You have a baby brother now." It was Lukas that morning a long time ago. "Would you like to hold him?" Her mother from her bed the time when Olava saw Eystein for the first time. "You are very good at looking after your little brother." Gudrun's words in the kitchen. "Do you want to play?" It was Runa. "Did you plan all this by yourself?" Karin, the time when Eystein was so sick. "Little Oystein." Malou's loving smile when she held him in her arms. "My two girls... you are so brave..." Their mother in her bed. "I am not mad... I am proud of you." Grandmother that time in the kitchen. "Swing, swing, swing, swing." Eystein's happy singing when he sat in his swing.

Olava walked in the forest where she and Eystein had picked flowers for their mother. To the large willow where they used to sit. To the field where they used to lie on the grass and look at the clouds. To their secret strawberry place. Olava smiled to herself. In her memories she heard Eystein sing her name. "Lala, Lala." Two white butterflies danced lovingly over the meadow.

Grandmother died peacefully the next day and the funeral was prepared in silence. It was a mild and beautiful day. The swallows flew high in the sky and a soft southern wind danced farewell in the trees. Grandmother was with Eystein now. It was a comfort to them all.

A couple of days later it was time for Olava to leave. It was hard to say goodbye, but she promised she'd come home more often. Olava had begun to think about moving back west again, but she didn't say anything. It had to wait until the decision was final. Before she left she got an envelope from her mother. It was money from Grandmother, a nice sum, which she received with gratitude. It was an unexpected gift which opened up some possibilities. On her way back it struck Olava how things had begun to work out for her. The meeting with Malou, Veronica and the Roma-family. The friendship with Silje. The conversation with Thorkild. The journey back home and now the money from Grandmother.

A couple of weeks later Olava was ready to leave the hotel. Silje was the only one who knew about it and although she was sad that Olava was leaving, she understood her well.

Olava felt a touch of nervousness when she stood up at the dinner table, but she took a deep breath and told herself that everything was okay.

"I have decided to leave." For a short moment everyone was quiet. They looked at her in surprise, but then Gerda got up so fast that her chair tipped backwards.

"Is this how you thank us? After everything we've done for you?" Olava hadn't expected that Gerda would like the news, but her reaction was totally unexpected.

"Gerda, please..." Ole made a weak attempt to stop her. Steinar and Elin bent their heads. Silje looked almost stupefied.

"You... who never support me in anything." Gerda directed her anger at her husband, but then she stared at Olava again.

"I will make sure that wherever you go, they will know what kind of a person you are."

"Well, okay... just you do that, just tell the whole world what kind of person I am." Olava was completely calm.

"You will never get work again."

"If you say so." Olava shook her head and sighed.

"Just you wait and see." There was something threatening in Gerda's voice that Olava had never heard before and something told her to be careful.

Two days later Olava was standing on her chair in her room staring at the top shelf in her closet. The envelope with the money was gone, both what she had saved herself and the legacy from Grandmother. So was the little wooden chest with the letters from her mother and Karin and Lukas. A cold sensation crept along Olava's spine. Gerda. She had taken it. She had been in her room and looked through her things.

Would she really do anything to stop her? And how far would she go? Olava lay down on her bed. She tried to tell herself that everything was okay, but this time it was difficult. What would she do without money? She didn't even have enough for the ticket home. What about her plans? Now they all went awry.

Olava had just finished the thought when dust fell on her face. She sat up quickly and removed it. She looked up. The crack in the ceiling over her bed had become so big that plaster fell out. Olava was mystified.

The next days were strange and unpleasant. Olava felt almost paranoid and it didn't get any better when Gerda gave her a sharp kitchen knife and told her to be careful not to hurt herself. It had never happened before and Olava had a sneaking feeling. What was Gerda capable of? She tried to pretend that nothing was wrong but was instinctively on guard. Silje sent her worried looks but they both knew that it was best they didn't talk together. It had to wait.

Olava continued with her work as usual and tried to pretend that everything was normal. After a couple of days things calmed down a little. Maybe it was because a famous actor and his wife from Christiania came to visit the hotel. They had been there a few times before and had become good friends with Gerda and Ole.

As usual they were invited for dinner. Olava was going to help serve at the party and clean up afterwards. When the night came she was standing in the background observing the party, the magnificent table setting, the impressive food, the loud talking, the laughter and the glasses that were raised. Gerda was the center of attention and entertained everyone with good stories. When Olava went over to the table to take their plates, she realized that she was talking about her employees.

"Well, it's not always easy. You have to give them instructions. And to some, the truth might hurt." Olava noticed that Gerda sent her a look. She couldn't believe it, this was too absurd, and in that moment the devil took her.

"Yes, the truth might hurt. Like the truth about the money that you've stolen from my room. The money that I've saved from my salary and the money that I got from my grandmother. And the truth that you've stolen my letters."

Olava looked firmly at her and met Gerda's gaping look. The others at the table turned to Olava, obviously very confused, uncertain whether they had heard her correctly. A few seconds went by before Gerda began to speak. Frantically, she tried to pretend as if nothing had been said, but the rest of the party had become very quiet.

The next day Olava had a day off. It was a relief to get out of the choking atmosphere in the kitchen. She felt that she needed to set her mind straight. Early in the morning she packed her rucksack and left before anyone else was up. Olava walked further than she used to, past fields and lakes, through the woods and over to the other side of the mountain where she followed a small path that she had never walked before. The further she came the better she could feel her feet against the ground.

Olava was neither surprised nor angry anymore. It was as if every step she took was a step closer to a decision. She was going to leave the hotel no matter what, out into the unknown. The feeling grew inside her. She was going to leave if it was the last thing she did.

Olava was standing in the midst of the thickest woods and the path was almost invisible when she decided to turn around. It was late in the afternoon and grey clouds were closing in on the forest. It had begun to rain and blow a little and the fog came fast. Olava turned around but hadn't walked far before she was surrounded by thick fog. All of a sudden she felt insecure. Was she walking on the path? She stopped. It had been so overgrown with grass and straw that it had been difficult to see it in the end. She walked a few steps further but stopped again. This couldn't be right. She tried to concentrate. It was here a moment ago. She walked a few steps back. It couldn't be far away. She continued to look, but no matter where she walked, she couldn't find the path.

Finally she gave up and sat down by a tree trying to gather her thoughts. What was she going to do? If she continued to walk, she could risk getting further away from the path and in the wrong direction. She could stay where she was. She was after all only a few hours' walk from the town and the path had to be somewhere nearby. When the fog lifted, she was very likely to find it again. They would also find out that she was gone, maybe not before tomorrow morning, but then they would most likely start looking for her. Or maybe they would think that she had left? Her clothes and things were still in her room and they knew that she used to go out on her days off. Olava was almost certain that they would start looking for her when she didn't return.

She put on the extra sweater that she had in her rucksack and sat down by the tree. She was always well prepared when she was out walking and had brought a hat and mittens. She would be okay. It was still raining and blowing a little, but it wasn't much and her jacket and trousers would keep the rain and wind out. Underneath she was also wearing a thick knitted sweater, and although she didn't have any more food or drink, she was in good spirits.

Later in the afternoon the fog lifted and Olava got an idea. It was still clouded, but if she climbed up in a tree and were high enough, she might be able to see one of the lakes or the mountain she had crossed and find her way back. She could climb more trees as she got closer.

She placed her right foot on the bottom branch, grabbed a branch a little higher and hoisted herself up. She placed her left foot on a branch a little higher and slowly but surely she began to climb. She came higher and higher and was amazed at how smooth it went. Her legs and arms worked together and she felt light and agile. When she looked down, she felt excited. She was many meters above the ground and was so high up that the trunk was getting thinner. She looked in all directions, but the only thing she could see was spruce trees. It all looked the same, one tree after the other. Olava didn't know where she was. She was lost.

The afternoon turned to evening and darkness fell. The rain and the wind grew stronger and soon Olava began to freeze. She put on her hat and mittens and began to walk on the spot. It helped but then came night. Olava tried to seek shelter by the tree and curled up close to the trunk, but she had to move to stay warm. A feeling of despair overwhelmed her. This couldn't be true. She walked and walked on the spot but just got more and more tired. The wind grew in strength and the rain whipped against her face. Finally she tried to protect herself by wrapping her arms tightly around herself. The whole night continued in the same way.

When the morning came it was still grey and cloudy and the storm continued. Olava walked and walked on the spot but her legs could hardly carry her anymore. She was too tired to cry and in the end she was so overwhelmed from exhaustion and despair that she did the only thing she could do. She folded her hands and prayed to her Creator. She held her necklace with one hand and prayed for help and protection, again and again. A small opening in the sky gave her hope, but then it closed again. When the sun peeked out for a second in the afternoon, Olava cried from relief, but it wasn't long before the storm continued.

All of a sudden there was a deer standing in front of her. It was standing completely still on light feet without moving a muscle. It wasn't for long, but the beautiful, deep eyes looked at her. "Animals carry power that we humans can learn from." Those were Veronica's words. Olava looked at the elegant animal with all its senses awake. Then it ran away quickly and disappeared between the trees.

In the middle of the day Olava began to shout. If someone was out looking for her, there might be a chance that they could hear her. She shouted at the top of her lungs, but the only answer she got was the silence from the woods. During that day she continued to shout in the hope that someone would hear her, but in the end she had no voice left.

The afternoon turned to evening, evening turned to night, night turned to morning, morning turned to noon, noon turned to afternoon and then it was night again. Olava had not had anything to eat or drink in a long time, but it didn't matter much anymore now that she was so tired. She tried to drink some drops from the moist grass, but it wasn't much help.

Olava was lying on the ground with her arms wrapped around herself. She had broken off some of the branches on the tree and tried to seek shelter under them. It helped her keep warm a little and quietly she gave thanks to the trees. Veronica's words came to her. "Life is sacred, Olava. Everything around us is sacred. Every little living being is our brother or sister. We are all children of Mother Earth."

Surrounded by the dense, dark night, Olava lies on the ground. She curls up, wraps her arms around her legs. She folds her hands and sings quietly. The song from her childhood treasure. "I am little, but I will, child of Jesus always be. He can hear and see me, too, when I pray." She is not freezing anymore. She just closes her eyes and wants to sleep. Everything feels so calm and peaceful. Olava opens her eyes and is filled with a soft wonder. All around her beings of light are floating through the air. They surround her with a stunning white light. A light filled with peace, harmony and warmth. "You can come home now, Olava. The Creator never left you." The light fills her with love. She feels completely safe. Everything is the way it should be. Then Olava crosses over to the other side.

19

The leaves on the trees change colours. From all shades of green to a symphony of warm, red, orange and golden brown tones. The transformation continues until nature stands, beautiful in all her brightly coloured glory. Like a goddess she glows in the red evening sun and dances to the tiniest little movements of the late summer wind. The western sky is an ocean of flames.

The next morning everything was quiet. As if touched by magic, Olava woke up to a beautiful, warm and sunny day. The forest looked completely different in daylight and all the sounds from the storm were gone. She no longer knew what day it was or for how long she had been sleeping. She squinted at the sun. It was still morning.

Her body was battered after having lain on the ground and every muscle hurt when she tried to get up. She stretched her fingers carefully, closed her hands and opened them again. She moved her shoulders and lifted her arms. She put her face toward the ground and filled her lungs with the scent of the dark, wet soil, took some of it with her hands and let it slip through her fingers. "Mother Earth gives us food every day. She lives in us." Olava began to understand it now. She remained still for some time enjoying the warm rays of life from the sun. Her chest rose and fell, deeply and rhythmically. She could feel her own heartbeat, smooth and steady. It was the pulse of life.

With careful movements she managed to sit up. She rested her back against the tree. For a short while she sat completely still and listened to the sounds from the forest. Slowly she managed to get up by holding on to the tree. She felt dizzy and had to wait for a while before she took the first step. When she was certain that her legs could carry her, she began to walk around. As she moved her joints and muscles, it got better. After some time she took her rucksack and began to search for the path. She walked from the tree in bigger and bigger circles, and just as suddenly as the path had disappeared, it was there again. For a short moment Olava closed her eyes in relief. Thank you, thank you so much.

Olava walked back very slowly. Took one step at a time. Through the woods, along the path, over the mountain and further down towards the first lake. Stopped by a small creek. Sat down on her knees and ducked her head in the cold water. Sat on the grass and felt the warmth from the sun. Listened to the eternal song of the wind in the trees.

Late in the afternoon Olava was back at the hotel. She couldn't remember that she had ever been so tired before. In the reception Silje came out from the kitchen.

"Oh, Olava... you're back... where have you been?" She could see the relief in her friend's worried eyes.

"I couldn't find the path, I got lost in the fog."

"We have been so worried. Ole and Steinar have been out looking for you, but the fog was so thick and they came back."

"I walked very far..." Olava nodded carefully, she could hardly keep her eyes open.

"Thank goodness you're back safely. I thought

maybe you'd left." Silje's eyes were wet with tears.

"I'm leaving but don't tell anyone, I just need to get some sleep first."

"Yes... I'll bring you something to eat a little later. Gerda is in town and won't be back until later tonight." Olava nodded and smiled to her friend. Then she went down to her room and went straight to bed. She fell asleep right away.

Olava didn't know for how long she had been sleeping when someone knocked on the door. Silje peeked in to see if she was awake.

"Come in." Olava smiled at her friend.

"Are you okay?" Silje still looked worried.

"Yes... I'm fine."

"I brought you something to eat."

"Thank you so much." Olava sat up slowly in her bed and placed the tray with dinner on the quilt in front of her. It was salmon with small potatoes, fresh vegetables and butter sauce. Silje sat down on her knees next to the bed.

"What are you going to do now?"

"I'm leaving tomorrow morning."

"I see... I brought you some money, it's not much, but some for the ticket." Silje gave her an envelope.

"But... won't you be needing it yourself?"

"No no..."

"Thank you..." Olava didn't quite know what to say.

"Thank you, too, Olava."

"You'll get it back as soon as possible."

"Don't think about that." Silje smiled and Olava nodded gratefully. They were quiet for a moment before Silje got up from the floor.

"It's dinner soon. I'll have to get back to the kitchen."

"Yes, of course…" Olava nodded. "Goodbye for now. I'll miss you."

"I'll miss you, too, but we'll meet again."

"Yes, we will. Take good care of yourself, will you?"

"Yes, I will and you, too." They gave each other a warm hug before Silje left. Olava sat still for some time with tears in her eyes. Then she began to eat.

It was in the middle of the night and completely dark outside when there was another knock on Olava's door. She opened her eyes and listened. There it was again, very weak. Who could it be this late? Olava got up and walked over to her door and placed her ear against it.

"Who is it?" She whispered.

"It's me, Ole. May I come in?" He spoke so low that she could hardly hear him.

"What do you want?"

"I have something for you." Still the low voice. Olava opened the door carefully and let him in.

"I found this." He looked embarrassed. Olava stared at the wooden chest with the letters. It was still locked and she could feel the relief.

"Thank you… you found it?"

"Yes, I'm sorry…" Ole shook his head unhappily. "I couldn't find the money, but I have some for you here." He gave her a stack of money.

"Oh but… thank you…"

"I'm very sorry about all this, Olava." Ole lowered his head. He didn't seem to know what to say.

"It's okay, it's got nothing to do with you." Olava looked at the friendly man with the kind eyes and the warm smile.

"Well, I believe it has, somehow, anyway…" He

looked at her and smiled sadly. "Good luck, Olava."

"Thank you. Will you give my love to Elin and Steinar and Gunnhild when you see her?"

"Yes, I will." Ole took her hand and Olava gave him a gentle hug. He turned around to leave.

"Ole?"

"Yes?" Olava was a bit uncertain, but there was something she wanted to say.

"Will you give my regards to Gerda, too... and give her my thanks." Ole looked surprised at first but then he nodded understandingly. Then he left her room and Olava remained sitting on her bed, moved to tears.

The next day Olava was sitting on the train looking at the rolling hills. She enjoyed the gentle dance of the leaves in the trees and felt the small quivering movements like caresses in her body. From the hillside two eyes in a boulder blinked at her. The conductor came to see her ticket and Olava was struck by how good he looked. She smiled at him and showed him her ticket. She rested her head against the seat and closed her eyes. "I love you." It was a tiny voice. Olava was filled with a mild wonder. "I love you." There it was again, soft and loving. It came from inside herself. Olava could sense how good it felt. As if someone looked after her. "I love you." She smiled touched. The words came from a big power, bigger than herself. It was the power of love. "I love you." Olava could feel how she was filled with a warm and nurturing love for herself. It was also her own words. Olava's own heart had spoken.

THE BEGINNING

20

The evening sun hangs low in the sky. An orange-red ball of fire. Golden rays flicker gently in the ocean. Twinkle a beautiful farewell. Olava is lying in her bed. She is old and tired now, but her face is smooth and fine and she looks like a little girl. The last couple of days she's been floating in and out of sleep. Her children are by her side. They stand by the bed, take her hand and smile carefully. Olava wants to say something but is too weak. She closes her eyes. Her consciousness travels through time and space.

Olava walks in the spring forest. She delights in the powerful transformation. Watches as new life grows with mild and lush determination. She's young and strong, feels the strength in her body. Olava observes and listens. Uses her senses. Learns how to trust the signs. She stops by the big rock. Sits down and ponders. Gives thanks to this day and to her life, to her home and to her family. Gives thanks to all her relations and to be part of the circle of life. At home she lights a candle and reads about Jesus in the Bible. She reads about the healing power of light and love.

Olava is back again in the room and in her bed. She remembers how she worked her way back to her own power. How she made that conscious decision in her life. The door opens carefully and someone comes in. It's the nurse. Olava can hear low voices.

Then the room flickers before her eyes and she's again young and strong. The late summer is beautiful, bursting with fruit and berries. Olava enjoys this time of year. She walks in the forest and on the meadows. Gives a little to Mother Earth and takes what she needs. In the kitchen to her pastry shop she looks at the big, fresh raspberries and blueberries. On the table she's got strawberries, apples, eggs, flour, sugar, butter, milk, nuts, almonds and raisins. They're all gifts from Mother Earth. She blesses the food. Then she begins to mix and bake and decorate. She loves this kind of work. Creates new recipes and gets new ideas. The door to the little café opens and Olava goes out of the kitchen. It's two new customers. The rumour of her little place is spreading in town. In time it becomes more than a café. It becomes a meeting place and some of those who come become her friends.

Olava's eyes flutter and shut. She had made her dream real. She found a way through all the challenges and opened a café. It was her natural place in life. Olava's oldest son comes over to her bed. He looks so much like his father. The calm, smiling eyes. The natural caring. A smile touches her lips. Then she travels once again to the land of memories. Olava is standing by the beautiful forest lake. An oasis among the trees. She watches the full moon on the quiet water. Senses the mild evening breeze. Takes off her clothes. Slowly with her eyes resting on the calm surface. Stands naked by the shore. Dips one foot in the water. Makes little circles. Then she walks out into the water. Takes a few steps further out. The water is up to her knees. She caresses the surface with her fingertips. Walks a little further out. The water is up to her thighs. She wets her arms.

Places her hands gently on her round belly. A little kick is a greeting from the stars. A little further out a small fish jumps. She begins to swim. The fresh summer warm water embraces her. She turns around and waves. Her husband smiles at her and walks out to her. Together they swim under the starry sky.

Olava returns from the past. Remembers her husband with a quiet joy. They were each other's support through life. In good times and bad. It was through the love for herself that she found it in him. Olava tries to turn around in her bed but hasn't got the strength. The nurse comes over and tucks her in. Grateful, Olava closes her eyes. Two women are standing by her side. It's a beautiful autumn night. The first stars light up the sky. Olava is giving birth to her first child. For one exhausting day the contractions have grown stronger and now they overwhelm her with a tremendous force. Only the short time between the pains is blessed moments. Then she folds her hands and sings quietly. "I am little, but I will, child of Jesus always be. He can hear and see me, too, when I pray." She connects to her universal primal force and pushes. With raw strength, willpower and a boundless force she lets go of her resistance and pushes. The sound of the first faint cry. The midwife gives her the baby. Olava takes him gently to her chest. It's the miracle of life.

Olava's breathing is deep and calm. Her heart is full of love for her children. She remembers how she took back her power of womanhood. The power that she had always had inside herself and that awakened when she was 13 years old and saw her little brother for the first time. A soft hand caresses her cheek. It's her youngest son. That wild thing.

Such a good heart and light mind. A smile spreads across her face. She remembers that night a long time ago. They are lying under the large willow in the garden. She and her husband. In hiding under the big branches. The tree shivers from the fervent caresses of the eastern wind. Trembling in rhythmical waves. It was those years. They couldn't keep their hands off each other. She just knows. It was that night their youngest son was conceived.

Olava smiles between the world of the past and the present. Even an old dying woman must be allowed to remember. She coughs weakly a couple of times. Her daughter takes her hand gently in hers. Olava can dimly see her careful smile and her tearful eyes. Her daughter. So beautiful and strong. Then she drifts back to her memories again. From the church they can see the sea. The most beautiful gold treasure is where the sun touches the sea. Olava is with her two little boys. She's expecting her third child. They sit down by little brother's grave. The boys crawl into her lap. Olava tells them about Eystein. Her heart sings with love and longing. What is it like in heaven, Mummy? The little ones ask and Olava answers. It's a lovely place. Then they go down the hill to Grandmother and Grandfather. They are having waffles. The boys are running and jumping and laughing and talking. Above them the clouds are floating happily in the sky.

Olava smiles, moved and grateful. It was through the pain and the grief that she took back her power and she learnt the art of forgiveness. Olava can hear voices in the room. Someone is whispering, but she cannot hear what they say. It doesn't matter. She's so tired. Only wants to sleep. She runs into her kitchen. There are flames in the oven in her bakery. She shouts in surprise. Gets a bucket of water and throws it on the fire. The smoke fills up the room. She opens the door. The cool winter air flows into the kitchen. Olava knows herself well enough now. Knows that she's too busy, is out of balance and loses power. Time for change. She hires extra help in the pastry shop. A wonderful girl. Eager and skillful.

Olava can feel the warm quilt wrapped around her body and sends a thought of gratitude to the caring hands that look after her. She learnt the power of change and the power of her own thoughts. A wave of love rushes through her and sends her back in time. The summer is mild and soft. Olava is contemplating the way she's learnt from Veronica. She travels through time and space. To the large willow which stretches to the sky. The long branches that bend toward the ground. The roots that go deep. By the foot of the tree the earth opens beneath her. She sinks deeper and deeper into the ground. Finally she flies through the air and lands in a cave. There is a small pond and by the edge there is a boat. She goes on board and begins to row. A creek leads out of the cave. Outside the sun is shining brightly. She rows over the lake to the shore. Goes ashore. Before her is a green meadow. The grass is stretching towards the sun. She looks around. Then she asks her helpers for advice.

With much effort, Olava tries to touch her heart-shaped necklace. A tear runs down her cheek. She met many helpers in her life. Olava remembers with tenderness but also with sorrow. She's standing by her window in her living room looking out. The world is bleak and quiet. The autumn fog is thick and heavy. She hears rumours in town. The Roma people's horses are being shot. Their children taken away and sent to orphanages. A cold shiver runs down her spine. It cannot be true. It must not be true. But it is true. The sneaking fear and uncertainty has spread everywhere. The anger and ignorance is directed towards the Roma-people, their way of life and their belief in the free spirit in everyone. Olava cannot believe it. These people that helped her so much. She sits alone by her altar. Lights a candle, cries and prays. Recalls Veronica's words: "Every step that we take in our lives is a little prayer."

Someone wipes Olava's wet cheek. She looks up. It's her daughter. Olava remembers the Roma-family with love and admiration. They taught her to recognize the power of her emotions. She tries to lift her hands. Her daughter helps her and gently she folds her hands over the necklace. She's back in her house. Peeks through a small crack in the curtains in her bedroom. The night is pitch-dark. Black clouds roll across the sky. Olava goes to bed but cannot sleep. She prays sincerely and silently. She prays for her husband and two sons that have joined the resistance movement. She prays for the family that are hiding in the basement in her café. The mother, father and two children running away from evil. She prays for the two fishermen that are on their way in with their boat, sheltered by the dark night, to help the persecuted people out of the country. She prays for the ones who carry the burden of evil.

Olava wakes again. She knows deep within herself what a gift it has been for her through life to get help and strength from the power of prayer. She can hear soft crying. It comes from outside the room. The door opens slowly and her youngest grandchild comes in and over to her bed. She's a beautiful young woman. Olava smiles weakly. They chuckle and laugh together with the spring creek. Olava and her grandchild. The girl dances happily next to her grandmother. The little child's hand rests safely in Olava's. Together they listen to the sound of their feet against the twigs on the forest floor. They notice the position of the sun in the sky and feel its warming rays. Olava talks about the power of the four directions, about the power in thoughts and feelings, body and spirit. She talks about Mother Earth, Grandfather Sun and Grandmother Moon. Together they look at the flowers, the bushes, the trees, the rocks, the mountains and the waters and Olava talks about how they are connected to everything around them. The little girl listens and smiles. "When I grow up, I want to be exactly like you, Grandma, only not old." Olava laughs heartily together with her little grandchild.

Olava feels calm and peaceful as she is lying there in her bed. She once got a gift that she passed on to the next generations. She dozes off. The last sunbeams disappear behind the hills, colour the sky red and golden. The voice of the soul whispers in the trees. Olava opens her eyes. All of a sudden she feels wide awake. Her children are by her side. She looks at them in love and whispers. "I love you." Their teary eyes look at her. "We love you, too, Mummy." Olava holds her necklace. Close to her chest. Everything around her is so beautiful and light. Then she hears a voice. "Olava. Olava." It's Eystein. He's calling her home. Home to the Creator. Olava. Her name. The name she got at birth. The name she has carried all her life. Deep in her memory she remembers the meaning of her name – ancestor and inheritor. She understands it now. Feels it deep within herself. She was the carrier of an old pain and it was through healing and releasing that she took her power back. A warm and peaceful smile spreads across her face. Olava's eyes are clear with no fear. She is ready to meet her Eystein. Then Olava lets go and leaves this world.

Made in the USA
Las Vegas, NV
27 February 2021